"We have to operate on the assumption that Conner is hunting down his witness—you—and that he is pretty much ruthless," Frank said. "That means you have to stay in hiding."

"Great idea," I agreed.

"That doesn't sound like you. You must be really scared."

"Sure, I'm scared, but the best place to hide is in plain sight," I reminded him. His mouth tightened, but he didn't interrupt me. "So first I'll register for the tournament—"

"Too late, entries are closed," Frank said.

"In Ben's place," I finished.

Frank shook his head. "They won't allow substitutions."

"I won't have to be one. He registered as B. Cooley. I am B. Cooley. I'll just adopt his address and phone number."

"And you'll sure make it easy for Conner to find you." Frank gave me a wry grin. "Bee, understand that I'm agreeing to it, but I don't like it. And there's one part of the plan you haven't covered: How are you going to learn Texas Hold 'Em by tomorrow night?"

I smiled. "You're going to teach me."

Death on the Flop

JACKIE CHANCE

BERKLEY PRIME CRIME, NEW YORK

THE BERKLEY PUBLISHING GROUP
Published by the Penguin Group
Penguin Group (USA) Inc.
375 Hudson Street, New York, New York 10014, USA

Penguin Group (Canada), 90 Eglinton Avenue East, Suite 700, Toronto, Ontario M4P 2Y3, Canada
(a division of Pearson Penguin Canada Inc.)
Penguin Books Ltd., 80 Strand, London WC2R 0RL, England
Penguin Group Ireland, 25 St. Stephen's Green, Dublin 2, Ireland (a division of Penguin Books Ltd.)
Penguin Group (Australia), 250 Camberwell Road, Camberwell, Victoria 3124, Australia
(a division of Pearson Australia Group Pty. Ltd.)
Penguin Books India Pvt. Ltd., 11 Community Centre, Panchsheel Park, New Delhi—110 017, India
Penguin Group (NZ), Cnr. Airborne and Rosedale Roads, Albany, Auckland 1310, New Zealand
(a division of Pearson New Zealand Ltd.)
Penguin Books (South Africa) (Pty.) Ltd., 24 Sturdee Avenue, Rosebank, Johannesburg 2196,
South Africa

Penguin Books Ltd., Registered Offices: 80 Strand, London WC2R 0RL, England

This is a work of fiction. Names, characters, places, and incidents either are the product of the author's imagination or are used fictitiously, and any resemblance to actual persons, living or dead, business establishments, events, or locales is entirely coincidental. The publisher does not have any control over and does not assume any responsibility for author or third-party websites or their content.

DEATH ON THE FLOP

A Berkley Prime Crime Book / published by arrangement with the author

PRINTING HISTORY
Berkley Prime Crime mass-market edition / January 2007

ISBN: 978-0-425-21348-3

As always, thanks to my daughters
who are the first readers of all I write
and make all my books better.
I love you.

This book is for the members of my family
who always had cards in their hands,
especially my grandfather,
Orlin Copeland,
who would have loved that
I wrote a book about his favorite game.
There is a reason my first word was "pass,"
after all those bridge games I had
to watch from my high chair!

I must acknowledge the help I received in researching this book. I couldn't have done it without the assistance of so many. My eternal gratitude to all those in law enforcement, wishing to remain anonymous, who've shared their knowledge and to my brother-in-law, cop-in-the-family, who prefers not to remain anonymous. Thanks Mike Zimmerhanzel with the Sugarland Police Department for all the cop stories over the years. The gambling expertise came to me especially from two people: Donna Drayton, who introduced me to Las Vegas for the first time and showed me her cards (even when she didn't have to), and Dr. Jake R. Wells, Jr., who not only gave me time off work to write but invited a neophyte to his Texas Hold 'Em table to teach me secrets behind the chips. Any errors on the felt are mine and not theirs.

Cards are war, in disguise of a sport.

—*Charles Lamb,*
Essays of Elia *(1832)*

One

"Ugh. Why are you half-naked? It's disgusting."

Without answering, I turned my back on my grinning visitor, leaving the front door standing wide open. Not my first mistake of the day, not by a long shot, and I could tell it was about to get worse. He caught me before I could even get out of the tiny foyer of my condo, grabbing me by the hand and the waist, spinning me around to bump and grind to AC/DC blaring out of the stereo. Trust me, *Back In Black* doesn't lend itself well to dancing. That only one of my stilettos had a heel didn't help me keep time either.

"Ben, I'm really not in the mood," I groused as I pushed my brother away and resumed limping my way back to the kitchen table, where I'd sat since my day went to hell.

He danced up next to me. "Is your mood the reason you look like you're fresh out of a bar fight? You know you have two black eyes, don't you?" Ben observed, cheerfully, putting his hands on my shoulders and pivoting me so I could see my reflection in the hall mirror.

Ugh. Soggy mascara ringed my eyes, left tracks on my cheeks and stained my satin camisole (thank goodness I hadn't put on my favorite silk blouse). Who knew mascara could spread so far? So much for opting for the waterproof variety.

My pity party was going into its eighth hour. It all started when the heel of my left shoe gave way with a crack as I tried to zip up a skirt that was perhaps a bit too snug. I lost my balance, flailed about until I heard the aforementioned skirt rip straight up the seam in back, all the way to the waistband, which induced the bottomless supply of tears, snorts and hiccups. Needless to say, I never made it to where I was supposed to go—an interview for a much-needed job.

Ben now spun me around so I could see my backside in the mirror. And I thought I couldn't get more depressed. He raised his eyebrows at my Hanes Her Ways. "And the reason you have a hard time keeping a man is you wear old lady undies. The thong is the thing, you know."

"I don't remember inviting you over." I pointed out as I resumed my pilgrimage to the kitchen table where I'd sat staring out the window all day. "Especially not for an underwear appraisal."

"Hey, you're the one with your ass hanging out for God and everybody to see. You're just lucky it was me and not Ma at the door."

I grunted and reached for the remote on the side table to turn the music up. Ben beat me to it and silenced it. I felt bereft without the CD that had accompanied my sobs. I think AC/DC and I had become codependent. Ben cleared his throat and sounded about ten years old as he said softly, "Hey, I heard about Toby."

I narrowed my eyes. "*Obviously*, considering your ultra-sensitive 'unable to keep a man' comment."

"Hey, Bee Bee, I'm sorry." Ben snatched me in a quick hug and kissed me on the top of my head. "I'm a jerk, which is the reason I can't keep a woman."

If I were feeling like myself, I would've jumped on that open invitation to dispense some love life advice, which incidentally, he sorely needed. Instead, I wiggled out of his grasp, plopped into the chair, pressed my face to the tabletop and peered down through the glass and wrought iron design at the chipped Tangerine Trouble nail polish on my big toe peeking out of the wounded footwear. I had a brief automatic urge to grab the polish remover and repaint it before Toby could see it—he hated when my polish chipped. He'd even given me a gift to celebrate our recent engagement; a year's worth of weekly visits to his pedicurist. But then I remembered Toby McKnight wouldn't be seeing my big toe, or any part of me, ever again.

Grrr. Sniff.

"Wow, you must really be depressed, I just declared open season on Bad Boy Ben and you didn't even fire a single shot," Ben said, ruffling my hair.

When I still didn't respond, Ben leaned over to open the refrigerator. I heard him slide open the hydrator. A cellophane bag full of carrots slapped down next to my face on the table. Ben eased into the seat across from me. I stared at his denim knees. "You could've called me, you know," he said reproachfully, now sounding about eight years old.

"Why?" I raised my head. "So you could say I told you so?"

Ben raised his eyebrows over devilish green eyes, ran his hand through his longish silken black hair, blew a breath out of lips surrounded by a carefully crafted day old dark stubble and gave me every reason to start crying all over again. After all, it wasn't fair. He was older by ten minutes and looked ten years younger and ten times sexier than I did. Ben could be Colin Farrell's twin and instead he was mine. Go figure fate on this one. Somehow I ended up with pale freckled skin to his suave olive complexion. Somehow I ended up with soft curves that resisted every fitness machine known to man while he got six-pack abs simply from breathing. Somehow he had an endless supply of lovers when I couldn't even hang on to the only one I'd had for the last five years. Somehow, I thought, as I watched him gnawing on his third carrot, he ended up with a maniacal drive and I was so laid back I could barely get up and get dressed in time to make it to work.

When I had a career, that is.

"Belinda Cooley, you don't need me to tell you." Ben pointed at me with his half of a carrot. "You know very well that having a fling with your boss was a mistake."

"It was more than a fling; we were engaged." I corrected.

"Worse mistake." The carrot waggled. "Although the biggest one of all was quitting your job. Why the hell did you do that, Bee? You know that if you had kept your famous cool, the prick wouldn't have been able to stomach seeing you day in day out. Guilt would've driven him to leave before you'd have to."

"It wouldn't have been guilt, the chipped nail polish would've done it," I quipped.

"Huh?" Ben paused in midchew and cocked his head.

Sometimes guys just don't get it, even twin brothers, so I didn't try to explain. "Inside joke. Listen, Ben, I had to quit to maintain one iota of pride. You didn't expect me to keep taking orders from Toby over the intercom while he was boinking his new twenty-two-year-old assistant in his office?"

"She's just twenty-two?" Ben asked, wiggling his eyebrows up and down. "Ooolala."

"Ben . . ." I warned.

Winking, he tapped the carrot to his temple thoughtfully. "You're right, Bee. I guess you had to leave. Still, it's all for the best. You'll end up at another advertising firm where you can kick ass. Stick-up-his-butt Toby was always so worried you'd show him up he never gave you free rein anyway. Now, before you go pounding the pavement, you're due a getaway. Also, I owe you a birthday present and I had a great idea . . ."

Uh-oh. The last time Ben had a great idea I was thirty, and we ended up in jail in Bermuda.

"Hey, Miz Cooley." Ben deepened his voice to a fakey broadcaster level. "You've just *won* your life back. And, *where are you going?*" Ben swung the carrot around to hover in front of my mouth. I stared stonily at him. He shoved it closer. I didn't move a muscle, just threw a little more acid in my stare, hoping it was approaching a glare. But as usual my brother was impervious. He wiggled his eyebrows once more in invitation, then slid his head next to mine and shouted into the carrot microphone with his voice now two octaves higher than usual, in a lame attempt to sound like my soprano. "I won, Mr. TV Announcer Man, and I'm going to Vegas!"

"Isn't it supposed to be Disneyland?" I deadpanned.

"Disneyland?" Ben bit off the top of the carrot and chewed as he slid back onto his chair across from me. "Why would you want to waste that terrific poker face of yours on some kiddy park when you can use your rare talent to take suckers' money left and right in the city that never sleeps?"

"Uh, maybe because I don't know *how* to play poker?" I rolled my eyes and tried to resist the tears that suddenly threatened again.

"That, my dear sister, is easily remedied." Ben jumped up, grabbed my shoulders, pulled me to my feet and guided me to the computer that sat in the small office adjacent to the kitchen. He shoved me down in the chair and signed onto the internet over my shoulder. "Bee, someone with your God given gifts for the game shouldn't waste any more time in not playing."

"What, pray tell, are 'God given gifts' for the game of poker—the ability to sit stock still for hours, inhale cigar smoke without choking and mainline martinis without passing out? Look, Ben, I'm a forty-year-old spinster now, I can't afford any more butt spread."

"Bee, Bee, Bee . . ." Ben took a moment to tsk-tsk over-dramatically. "You are imagining old-fashioned poker. The new game is so different. Texas Hold 'Em is edge-of-your-seat hip."

"One has to be on the 'edge of your seat' when one's hips are the size of the Lone Star State from sitting too much."

Ben's eyes were unnaturally bright. It was beginning to make me nervous. "Bee, really, this game will leave you breathless."

"What? You poker players do spin aerobics while you're dealing and Pilates in between bets?"

"Better than that."

"Better than Pilates? So you have . . ." I paused weightily before saying, "*sex* when you play then?"

Ignoring my attempt at sarcasm and not running with my invitation to tease, Ben shifted into what the family called "focus mode." Uh-oh. He leaned over my shoulder and began to manipulate the mouse. In a few moments, he was signed onto an online poker game, one of eight players in a game of Texas Hold 'Em. I didn't know there was such a thing as online poker, but I was so wary of interacting with strangers from the internet that even lurking in chatrooms scared me, much less participating in one. Gambling online seemed akin to kamikaze behavior. I knew he played in a Friday night face-to-face game with his buddies every week but apparently he was brushing up his poker skills online too. I felt Ben's body electrify with tension. He began muttering at the computer screen, oblivious to me. It reminded me of the time he'd gotten addicted to Pac-Man and flunked out of engineering school. "Horse Doc, you'd better watch it. Sara90210 is going to take you out."

"Ben?"

He looked at me, blinking blankly. "How can Judge and Jury be so stupid? He's gotta know what she's got in her hand. Look at that bet, would you?"

I followed his index finger to the screen. What did "raising" mean? I'd barely mastered Old Maid, how was I supposed to learn a game where the stakes had dollar signs attached?

Ben must have forgotten he was supposed to be teaching me what was going on. He whistled under his breath at the cartoon icons sitting around the simulated table on my seventeen-inch screen. A new bet popped up. Horse Doc was "all in." Someone named Take a Chance Chuck folded before the last card was dealt, which I thought ironic just based on the nomenclature.

The dealer, an intimidating looking dude that reminded

me of Samuel L. Jackson as a bad guy, turned over the first three community cards the screen was calling "The Flop." Suddenly there was a Queen of hearts, three of diamonds and King of clubs face up on the table. Everyone had two cards down, but it seemed they shared the three cards up.

The next round of betting began. Everyone else at the table folded except a player named Lucky Lula who pushed all her chips into the "pot."

"Lula, you are going to lose it all, girlfriend!" Ben whispered tensely.

"Ben," I tugged on the sleeve of his golf shirt as the hand ended, and she did indeed lose it all when the dealer flipped a Queen of spades that made the Doc's other two Queens unbeatable. Lucky Lula wasn't so lucky after all. Being a natural tightwad myself, I felt her pain.

Ben began typing rapidly on the keyboard and it took me a minute to realize he was in the game of now six players as Rotten Irish Rogue. As I watched him play a half dozen hands, I was surprised to find out I understood the mechanics of the game already. It was *that* easy? Not quite. I played a hand in my head and found mechanics wouldn't get you far with Hold 'Em. It was a game of strategy. It was a game of luck. It was really scary. I wondered how many people a day were suckered in by thinking they knew how to play, thinking the next hand would be a winner. I guess plenty since Ben thought I could take their money without knowing the game.

Ben was now alternately pounding on the keyboard and muttering invectives at his virtual players. Or were they real people? That was even scarier. I concentrated on following the game not because I was interested, I told myself, but because Ben's obsession was worrying me. They played hand after hand in which I learned zero strategy. Yikes.

"The strategy escapes me," I said out loud.

Ben talked to me with an eye on the game. "Some of it's instinct, some is education, but it could be you are a pure body language player. Lots of women are. You need to play in person, not on the net. Plus, your natural talents would be wasted online."

Finally, the game ended. Ben had won. I noticed for the first time the sweat that pebbled his forehead. Horse Doc congratulated him, typing, "Good luck at the Big Kahuna in Vegas, Rogue. We all hope you're the one who can bring Steely Stan down." The one called Bimbo Bombshell, whose identifying icon looked like Jessica Rabbit on speed and who'd gotten knocked out of the game earlier, echoed the sentiment. "Do it for us, Rogue. We're rooting for you."

Ben thanked them both and told them, "Good game." As heated as the Hold 'Em had been, even playing distanced by keyboards, screens, icons and mice, I was surprised and frankly, gratified, to see this good sportsmanship. I was also relieved to see Ben had only won forty-nine dollars. Even though he might be a candidate for Gamblers Anonymous at least he wasn't going broke online. The local game was another story. I was going to have to check into that. And Vegas, well, I shuddered to think how much he might lose there.

Suddenly, Ben let loose with an explosive sigh and slumped in my office chair, which I'd given up to him after, in the heat of a hand, he'd nearly squashed me to death. After about half a minute, in which I wondered if he hadn't suffered a stroke, he attacked the keyboard again, typing his way onto another online table, swearing mightily when there was a waiting list, and going in search of an empty table.

That was it. I'd had enough. I jammed my hands on my hips and yelled: "Hello? Earth to Ben!"

He ignored me, signing onto a new game. Finally, I yanked the chair back so the keyboard was out of reach.

"Hey, Bee! They're waiting on my bet."

I stomped a foot, the impact diluted a bit because it was the foot without the heel and I wobbled. "They'll just have to wait."

"What is your problem?" Ben asked, still letting his gaze stray to the computer screen. I moved in front of it. He frowned.

"Look, I've had the week from hell—I turned forty, lost my fiancé and my job in that order. Now my darling brother is in my house ignoring me and my miseries in favor of some stupid card game on the computer. I know life up to now has been all about Ben, but guess what? Newsflash: the next forty years are going to be all about Belinda!"

Ben blinked, the only time in our lifetime I'd seen him struck dumb with amazement. "Wow. I didn't know you minded me being selfish."

I almost smiled because the comment was so like my brother. He didn't apologize for his flaw, just how it affected me. He might be a lot of things but hypocritical wasn't one of them. Considering the king of hypocrisy I had been about to marry, I had to appreciate Ben's honesty. "Well, I do mind your self-absorption sometimes. Now, speaking of which, tell me about The Big Kahuna," I demanded, realizing I had to keep an eye on his growing addiction. "Would it happen to be in Vegas at the time you wanted to take me for *my* birthday present?"

Ben had the grace to look a little sheepish. "Yes, but I want to take you because I want you to have as much fun as I'm having playing. It's a brain game and at the same time a total adrenaline rush. Better than chess and more exciting than bungee jumping. You just need to win once, Bee and you'll be hooked. It's not about the money. And you can see how supportive everyone is, even in the heat of competition. It's not all that bad as far as hobbies go, sis. Besides there are other things to do in Vegas, considering your new, ah, liberated taste in dress, you might find a new job in no time . . ."

"Very funny," I told him, cracking a smile, relieved to see my brother did still exist within this poker obsessed man.

"Really, Bee, Vegas is a cool town. It's the best place to forget your troubles, cuz there's just too much to see and do. You have more world class performers within one city's limits than probably anywhere in the world. You can hear Celine Dion, walk across the street and watch David Copperfield and then go next door and enjoy Cirque du Soleil.

If you're tired of just watching, get pampered at a spa, dance beyond dawn, shop for the best of everything under the sun. You deserve it all. Nothing is too good for my favorite sister."

"Only sister," I corrected. "Only, penniless, unemployed sister . . ."

"Come on, Bee, at best, it will be a great vacation—maybe you'll fall in love and win a million dollars. At worst, it will be a change of scene and you'll learn a little something about your bro's favorite hobby."

"As long as it stays a hobby," I warned carefully, not wanting to admit out loud that it had advanced to the next level already. He just grinned and tried to get a look around my heinie at the screen when the computer dinged.

"Who's this Steely Stan guy?"

Ben wrinkled his brow. "He's a pro on the World Poker Tour. This guy gives poker a bad rep because he's such a poor sport and a big head. He thinks he's so cool, running around everywhere in his shades with at least two different women on his arm at a time, squashing amateurs in his wake. He thinks he's untouchable and that makes him dangerous."

I raised my eyebrows. Hmm. Ben was taking this a little too personally. "Isn't that the point of the sport: to win?"

"Yeah, but you see how supportive all the players are, and he isn't like that." Ben ground his molars together so hard his jaw popped out on the right side. He only did that when he was really upset. Or maniacally driven. Focus mode. Hmm. "It's time for someone to take him down and I want to see it happen or, better yet, make it happen. Steely Stan is the celebrity pro who'll play the four amateurs to make it to the final round of this Hold 'Em tournament. Please say you'll go with me, Bee."

I could see clearly that this Vegas vacation was about Ben and some weird vendetta against a larger-than-life stranger and not about me, no matter what he said. But, the truth was, I was too afraid that his poker obsession was out of control to let him go alone. His focus mode was usually properly directed, like on succeeding in business, but the Pac-Man obsession nearly got him kicked out of college. It was only when I stepped in that I got him to switch majors and actually graduate. I shivered when I thought how he might have ended up, bartending in some dark dive living on those little martini onions, one hand on the Pac-Man control.

"What about work? I thought you weren't due time off until later in the year?" Ben was a pharmaceutical salesman. He'd been lucky to get the job when the medical supply company he had started four years ago went belly-up.

"I already met my quota. The deal is when I do that, I get an extra week off every six months."

Whoa. Was it because he needed to impress his bosses or get that time off?

"You won't be sorry, Bee. This will definitely make you forget your troubles."

That was what I was afraid of. I would be trading worry over my troubles for worry over his. Swell. Sounded like a blast.

Ben scooted me out of the way long enough to sign out of the game. He was nearly vibrating with excitement as he made for the front door.

"So, you never finished explaining." I pointed out, delaying making a decision. "What other talents do I have for this game besides my—disputable—poker face?"

In the hallway, Ben paused with a grin. "Innocent eyes, long legs, and . . . how do I put this delicately . . . size D's."

Who knew I was so talented? "Great, so as long as I wear mascara, a push up bra and a miniskirt, I've got it made at the Hold 'Em table, huh?"

I opened the front door and he winked as he walked out. "No, those are just to distract the other players and hide how smart you are. You've got to learn the game in order to act like you don't know it."

"Sounds dishonest."

"It's called bluffing, sis. A fun way to lie. And in Vegas it's expected." Ben reached in his back pocket and handed me a thick envelope with a travel agency logo on it.

Uh-oh. "You certainly were sure of yourself. You already bought the tickets?"

Ben flashed a dimpled grin and shrugged apologetically. Damn. After what he still owed business creditors, he couldn't afford to go squandering airfare. I groaned. "I guess I *have* to go, don't I?"

"Cool!" He kissed the top of my head again, then jogged down the walk to his parked car. "I'll pick you up in two hours. You won't be sorry."

Too late, I already was. As he zipped off with a wave in his red Spyder, I opened the envelope and saw it held no plane tickets, just folded pieces of magazine paper. I pulled out the top one. Ben's sprawling script read: *It worked, huh? We'll get tickets at the airport. This is your first poker lesson, Sis. You've been bluffed.*

Two

Considering I was allergic to spontaneity, packing in an hour to go to the sin capital of the world was akin to an out-of-body experience. I was so accustomed to dressing as an advertising exec during the week and, on weekends, as fiancée of an advertising head honcho with a strict girl-friend dress code that I had no clue what I should wear when I no longer had either of those roles to fill. Well, I reminded myself, I was going on this trip as my brother's protector. What fashion challenges would that role require?

Immediately an image of a silvering haired spinster in sensible black shoes and loose, calf-length navy dress with a Peter Pan collar, possibly carrying a bag of knitting popped into my mind's eye. I glanced at my row of short-skirted suits, lacy silk camisoles, low rise Calvins and the three-inch Steve Madden heels on the floor below them and decided I wasn't fit for this job. My glance in the mirror at my chestnut hair, with some random gray strands at the roots, and chipped nail polish confirmed the suspicion. Tears threatened again. Was I good for nothing anymore?

The doorbell dinged. I stared at my neon Swatch. Way

too early for Ben. On time was too early for Ben and he had another hour to be that. Perhaps it was Toby, here to beg me to come back to him and to work, thus saving me from this torture.

Banging began on my front door. Not knocking, banging. That's when I knew it had to be either the cops on a raid or my best friend, Shana.

She pushed through the door before I even had it half-open. "Bee Cooley, what the hell do you think you are doing?"

Good question. I wasn't sure how to answer it. "Um," I began.

"You aren't answering either one of your phones. I was worried. Don't tell me you are going to become a recluse, just because you're forty and your best years are behind you, you got dumped by the hottest man you'll ever hope to marry and got canned from the best job you ever had?"

Leave it to Shana to tell it like it was. That was why I liked her so much, no artifice. What you saw with her was what you got. She'd never stab you in the back. She would prefer a frontal attack so you could watch.

"Well?" she demanded, looking around at the stack of plates, bowls and utensils in the sink.

"No, I'm not becoming a recluse," I retorted definitively, although AC/DC might argue.

Shana jammed her hands on her hips. "Prove it."

Ha. I'd show her. "I'm going to Las Vegas."

Her big brown eyes widened so far I thought they'd pop out and roll across the floor. Her mouth moved but no sound came out for at least thirty seconds. I was slightly insulted. I mean, I wasn't *that* boring, was I?

"Vegas? You? No way!" she finally sputtered.

Humph. "Why not Vegas? Why not me?"

"Because." Shana pursed her lips and drew her eyebrows together. She jerked her hands off her hips and gestured something indecipherable before she clasped them together. "Because you like everything in its place and nothing is in its place in Vegas. Or, better said, everything is so 'far out' there, that there is no 'proper place' for anything. It'll blow your mind."

"Huh?"

Shana rolled her eyes to the ceiling then said on her exhale, "I mean, you give new meaning to the word anal-retentive and Vegas is the exact opposite. Vegas is wild, loose, unexpected." She drew in a breath, held it a moment, then blew it out in a rush. "You'll hate it."

"Maybe not. Maybe since my 'best years are behind me' I want to turn over a new leaf. Maybe I want to be wild, loose and unexpected."

"Sure you do." Shana wasn't buying it. "You've never even had sex anywhere but in a bed. Have you?"

I frowned and looked away. Ugh. I guess I *was* that big a stick in the mud. Where did most people have sex anyway?

Shana was still chortling. "Wild, loose, unexpected, yada yada."

"Okay, maybe my brother is making me go to Vegas with him to some poker tournament."

Shana burst out laughing. No it was more like guffawing. Belly busting. Finally, she choked out: "You? Ben? Vegas? Poker? The tightest tight ass I know is going to Sin City to gamble with a lunatic." She snorted once more, then sobered and bored me with a look. "You aren't on antidepressants are you?"

"No!"

"Are you sure, because they can cause, you know, hallucinations."

I turned away and marched back to my bedroom. Shana followed, still chuckling. I began yanking clothes out of my closet and throwing them into the suitcase with angry abandon—silver lace camisole, black leather mini skirt, fire red silk jacket, a bunch of suede this and satin that.

Shana gasped, pointing. "You are separating suits, mixing labels. I've never seen you do that before."

"You're going to be seeing me do a lot that I've never

done before. Just wait," I promised with a bravado fed by fury. "I'm going to start French-kissing life, beginning today!"

Lips curling in a skeptical smile, Shana asked: "Goody. Can I come watch you do all this French-kissing of life?"

"No." Normally, I'd welcome Shana. She had a wild streak that I probably needed to follow through with this promise in Vegas. But Ben was going, so she couldn't. I'd been trying to keep Ben and Shana away from each other for years. Shana had a huge crush on my brother and he, unbeknownst to her, had the hots for her. Of course, Ben had the hots for any semiattractive woman between the ages of sixteen and sixty. No kidding, he just got through dating Ruby, a fifty-nine-year-old bartender who Ben claimed was the most fun he'd ever had. Anyway, I didn't want Ben using and abusing my best friend only to discard her the moment he got bored. I thought it might strain our friendship. And a quickie for either of them wasn't worth that, I decided.

Shana shoved her lower lip out, crossed her arms over her chest and watched as I flipped more mix-matched separates onto the pile. "What accessories are you going to wear with those?"

I tried to hide my panic. I never wore anything but the same accessories with the same outfits. I just didn't have a knack for throwing earrings and bracelets and necklaces and scarves and belts together without a diagram. I was famous for buying what the mannequins or models in catalogs wore from head to toe and wearing that ensemble without changing a piece several times. I had been given complete ensembles as thank-yous for my ad campaigns and never wore them except exactly as the models had. But now I narrowed my eyes at Shana, marched to my dresser, reached for my jewelry box and overturned it into the pocket of the suitcase, shrugging for effect. "I'll just figure out what to wear when I get there."

Shana's eyebrows went skyward. "You *must* be on something."

We heard the front door swing open. I guess I didn't shut it properly in the wake of Shana's onslaught. A familiar male voice rang out. "Knock. Knock. Ding. Dong. Your prince has come!"

Reflexively, Shana's gaze flew to the mirror. She ran a fingertip along the edge of her lip gloss, shook her thick straight black hair artfully around her heart-shaped face and grinned at herself coquettishly. Ugh. "We're back here, Ben," she called in a frilly voice that made me nauseous.

Ben walked in with a paper sack full of clothes and gave Shana an appreciative once-over. She blushed. Double ugh. He gave my overflowing suitcase an even more appreciative once-over. He dumped his clothes on top and smashed the pile down. It was going to be so much fun to travel with my brother. I just hoped the hotel had an iron.

"I'm impressed," Ben said, pulling my Burberry case upright. "I thought I'd have to pack for you, sis."

"Bee's decided to French-kiss life." Shana put in.

Ben whistled. "Sounds like fun." He winked at Shana. "The French-kissing part." She blushed a deeper crimson. Triple ugh.

"The poker part sounds fun to me," Shana said coyly.

"*You* play poker?" Ben and I responded in unison, but with completely different inflections. My "you" made her sound like a leper, his "you" made her sound like she'd revealed her secret occupation as a stripper.

"I play some Hold 'Em on the Net," she admitted.

"Limit, No Limit or Pot Limit?" he asked.

"I like No Limit."

Ben whistled. "That's my game. I bet you are a bit of a Maniac at the table."

I thought she'd be offended, but instead, Shana giggled. "I'd like to learn to play like a Rock but I just can't help going for it sometimes." *Huh?*

They were speaking a foreign language. "My brother and best friend are strangers to me," I muttered to myself.

"You ought to go to Vegas with us sometime to play in a live tourney," Ben offered.

My turn to bluff. "Shana can go in my place," I suggested with a bright smile.

She bit down on her lower lip, doe eyes hopeful. With a glance at Shana, he looked like he might be tempted but, after a beat, Ben shook his head at me. "Not this time. This is brother-sister bonding time. I'm going to teach you how to check and raise, how to pray for a boat on the river and for quads on the flop, Bee Bee."

Okay. Sounded like we were going sailing or to the gym.

"And," Ben continued, "I'm going to teach you how to bluff better than your sad attempt just now."

"You do have to be careful with that, Bee, especially playing in person," Shana nodded. "I love bluffing and lost my pants in a tournament."

Ben's eyebrows waggled. I wanted to gag. I shook my head instead. "When have you been doing all this poker playing? And why didn't you tell me about it? It's not like it's a closet drug habit or something."

Shana and Ben both looked at me with the same expression. It said "duh." Finally, Shana answered, "You have to admit, Bee, this wouldn't be your first choice of hobby for either of us."

I cocked my head in question.

Ben snorted. "Come on, admit it, you'd prefer we were skydiving or bull riding rather than poker playing."

I stretched the beaded bracelets on my wrist, snapping one a little too hard. Ouch. "I'm just not a fan of gambling. I think it can be dangerous."

They looked at each other with smug little grins.

"Medical bills from being gored by a bull couldn't add up to as much as you could lose one night at the poker table, right?"

Their grins just got wider.

"Okay, okay," I interjected loudly. "Maybe I'm fatalistic about poker because I don't know enough about it. Fear of the unknown and all that."

"How open-minded of you," Shana offered, her gaze

following Ben as he enveloped me in a bear hug. I stuck my tongue out at her over his shoulder and she winked at me.

"That's the perfect attitude to have, Bee. I am so proud of you," Ben said. "Let's zip up your suitcase and we're out of here."

He released me, leaned down and flipped the lid closed. Uh-oh. I put my hand on his shoulder. "Wait, let me double check what I've got in there."

"No can do." Ben yanked the zipper and snatched up the suitcase by its handle all in one swift motion.

"What if I forgot something?" I tried to keep the panic out of my voice. Why did I just throw things willy-nilly in there? What was I trying to prove? Why didn't I play it safe and grab my tried and true combinations instead of risking being sorry that I let my temper take control?

Ben strode out of the bedroom, calling over his shoulder, "Anything you need, I'll win enough in this tournament to buy you. Anything you have, I'll win enough to replace with something first-class. Got rhinestone earrings? I'll get you diamonds. Got a mere Coach knock-off bag? I'll buy you Prada."

Shana sighed audibly from behind us. Geez. And I'd always thought of Shana as having good sense. She was buying this load of BS?

"Where did you learn so much about women's fashion? I thought only gay guys knew this much," I said hoping to slow him down.

"I pay attention to women," he informed us.

"Yeah, when you think you might get them into bed." I muttered under my breath.

"Bee! You are offending Shana."

Shana didn't look offended. Shana looked excited. Enough of that line of conversation. I turned the lights off as we passed through the living room and into the kitchen. "I can't go," I stated flatly.

Ben stopped in his tracks. Shana opened her mouth, ready, no doubt to take my seat on the plane.

"What's your excuse now?" Ben asked.

"Grog." I waved at the aquarium on the counter. A forked tongue flicked out from behind a pile of rocks. The python was the only pet I'd ever had. Friends always recommended I get a cat but that always seemed like such a big commitment. After one too many margaritas at Grog's Bar a year ago, Shana and the bartender dared me to get a pet and I'd ended up taking the bar's namesake home. I tried to take it back when I'd sobered up but Grog's was boarded up, repoed by the bank, which is no doubt why the bartender had been so eager to get rid of the damned thing. I'd been hunting down food alternatives to live mice for him ever since.

That incident described my life in a nutshell. I never did anything spontaneous without paying dearly for it.

How would I look back on the grand Las Vegas Texas Hold 'Em adventure? Probably not a whole lot more fondly.

"Affie will take care of Grog. She's looking for a little extra money. She wants to get her hand pierced."

Ben drew his eyebrows together. "Is she doing a Jesus on the cross play at school or something?"

Shana shook her head. "No. She really is going to pierce it right here." She pointed to the muscle between the thumb and forefinger. Ben and I both shivered.

"Why?" I asked when the nausea had passed.

"Because I won't let her pierce her belly button or her tongue," Shana answered matter-of-factly, as if that were the obvious answer. I guess I couldn't argue—when it came to teenage girls, I was in the dark. Shana had given birth to Aphrodite without benefit of marriage and named her for the goddess of love even though I'd argued at the time that a name predestines us to a certain kind of life. I certainly was a boring Belinda. Shana was a wild Indian flame. And Affie had spent most of her life with her head in the clouds, doing unrealistic things.

Still, she was my goddaughter and I loved her. "Okay, I'll pay her ten bucks a day to bring in my mail, water the plants and feed Grog. But tell her if she pierces her hand I *will* cut her out of the will." .

"Whoo-whoo." Shana rolled her eyes. "If you were still about to become Mrs. McKnight, that threat might carry a little more weight."

I got no respect. That was going to be goal numero uno when I got to Vegas, to earn some respect. From a bunch of gambling addicts. Great start.

Ben threw Shana his spare key and hustled me out the front door. And then grabbed my arm. "Last thing, leave your cell phone here. I left mine at home. This is going to be a true vacation. No outside interruptions."

"What if there is an emergency?" I asked, handing my phone to Shana with trepidation.

"With your snake?"

"I was thinking more about Mom or Dad." I tried not to roll my eyes. After forty years of self-absorption, Ben wasn't going to change now.

"We'll call with our room number when we get there," Ben offered generously as he shoved me toward the stair-well, dragging the suitcase along.

"When are y'all going to be back?" Shana called from the door.

"When we can afford to," Ben called as he went around me, jogging down the stairs and out of sight.

Three

◆ ♣ ♥ ♠

Slot machines greeting us as we exited the concourse was a little disconcerting for a girl born and raised in Texas, where dancing is illegal in some counties. The person in the airport women's room who had a five o'clock shadow and was duct taping something under her hot pink miniskirt was another clue that this Dorothy wasn't in Kansas anymore.

The Twilight Zoneness of it all made those incidents easier to deal with than ordinary people doing bizarre things. After we shared a cab with a married sixty-something couple from Anchorage, I nearly begged Ben to go back to the airport and home. The cabbie was told to drop the wife to meet friends at the David Copperfield show; then after telling her he was going to rest at their hotel room, the husband proceeded to pull out a wad of cash, count out fifty thousand dollars and ask to be dropped off at "the biggest stakes craps table in town." Nothing like gambling the farm away while Mama watched magic tricks.

"Aw, Bee," Ben assured me, patting my hand, "anything goes in Vegas."

"That's what scares me."

"Think of it as liberating. What you do here, stays here."

"Life is never that easy, Ben."

"Oh okay, it is that. Free and easy." The heavily-accented taxi driver agreed with Ben, nodding and smiling as Ben handed him a sizeable tip along with the fare.

"See." Ben gestured to the retreating cabbie. "Vegas is as easy as that."

"'Free and easy' philosophy by a foreign taxi driver from a country that hasn't had the same government for more than thirty minutes at a time," I grumbled as I looked with amazement at the opulence surrounding us. It was a good thing that the airplane magazine had a feature article on what was in store for me or I might have been in shock. Still, the sight was more than I'd expected. The Strip was a five-and-a-half-mile stretch of Las Vegas Boulevard lined with thirty-two casinos. Really, calling them mere casinos did them an injustice, for they were rambling neon, golden, glittering, overdone fantasies, each competing for attention with its equally otherworldly neighbor. Flanked by Luxor's life-size pyramid, complete with Pharaoh head on the south end and the world's tallest observation tower of the 113-floor Stratosphere on the north end and everything from palaces to treasure islands to genie's lairs to medieval monstrosities in between, The Vegas Strip was truly an awesome grown-up playground, even for someone like me, for whom playing is uncomfortable at best.

"You can say it, sis." Ben jostled me with his shoulder. "I can see the 'wow' in your eyes."

"'Wow' doesn't cover it." I admitted with a slight head-shake.

Ben danced around me for a minute, then started to explain the three day poker tournament he'd be playing in at the newest hotel on The Strip, the Lanai. It involved about two thousand people, starting with two hundred tables of eight amateurs and one pro on each table. It was an elimination tournament and the final round would be televised live by ESPN. Steely Stan, Ben's apparent self-proclaimed nemesis, would play in the final two rounds. The first round was two days away, starting at seven in the evening so even after it began, we had all the daytime hours for more fun and games.

"Yippee," I said with zero enthusiasm.

"Mark my words, Bee Bee, you are going to have the time of your life here." Ben flashed a grin that stopped foot traffic on the sidewalk. A roly-poly man poked his wife in the back when she paused to give Ben a second glance. A pair of coeds in ragged denim miniskirts and fur-topped Uggs giggled and whispered to each other. Ben winked.

"We're going to play blackjack at Caesars," they called out before sashaying off with as much sway as their size zero hips would give them.

"See you there," Ben called back, adding pointedly, "After *my sister* and I check in at the Lanai, where I am playing in a Hold 'Em tournament. Look me up."

They giggled again and fluttered their fingers in a wave. The redhead bent her knee, flipping her furry suede boot up coquettishly. Sexy.

"Think they come as a pair?" I asked, feeling like the sour old maid that I was.

"Maybe, but I like to hold out for three of a kind," Ben said, waggling his eyebrows.

I shook my head. "Don't tell me you are going to make sad poker-themed sex jokes this whole trip."

"You caught the poker reference!" He yanked my hair out of its bun.

I shoved Ben out of reach, shaking the hair out of my eyes. "I'm not a total idiot."

"Says who?" Ben threw back.

I felt a hand close on my right elbow, drawing me off the sidewalk and behind one of the manicured bushes on the grounds of the Bellagio. A hand that dragged conveniently across my rear end. A smooth voice sounded behind me. "You know, you don't have to stand for that kind of abuse, you are too beautiful a woman."

I swung out of the stranger's grasp and faced a staid silver-haired man. "Huh?"

"I couldn't stand by and watch this gentleman treat you so despicably," he gave a half bow. I could see Ben out of the corner of my eye. He'd retrieved my suitcase, and was now rocking back on the heels of his black snakeskin Luccheses, grinning. Big help he was.

"Uh, this is no gentleman," I began.

"Indeed!" the stranger interjected with a glare at Ben, who just grinned wider.

"I mean, he's my brother."

"Really?" The man raised his plucked eyebrows slowly, his contact enhanced blue eyes taking on a shiny cast. He was well dressed, in Bruno Magli loafers, an Armani sweater and a Loro Piana cashmere coat I knew cost several thousand dollars because we'd featured one like it in an ad for an exclusive men's wear store back home. Ack. He was walking around wearing more than my bank account. "So he is your brother," he said smoothly in his accentless voice.

I looked for a hearing aid behind his well cut if longish hair. I spoke slowly, articulating clearly, "Yes, he is my brother. Same mother, father, you know."

"Yes." His shiny eyes became sharp. "So you aren't attached?"

"Like conjoined twins? Heaven forbid," I laughed.

"No, I should say, you are in Vegas with your brother, so I can only ascertain that you are without a husband or boyfriend."

Hey, did I have a scarlet L for "Loser in Love" on my forehead or what? How could this yahoo know I was hard up?

Ben, recognizing my anger, chuckled. That just fueled my fury. "Listen, mister, I don't think it's any of your business."

"Actually, it is my business. I am searching for a girl just like you." His hand dipped into the pocket and I braced, for what I didn't know . . . maybe a microphone to interview me for a show about single women with aging eggs. Instead, he extracted a business card. A psychologist? I knew it. He was some kind of love doctor and he thought I needed therapy. I probably did.

"I just wanted to make sure you could make your own decisions, without having to consult a mate," he was saying while I read his card. Black suedey paper with gold lettering. Just the name Cyrano and a telephone number with a New York City area code. Okay, so he wasn't a sleazy reporter. The pricey clothes should have tipped me off. He wasn't a shrink either, since they rarely paid their clients. Who paid for types of people? Someone fitting a script. "You're some kind of talent scout?" I asked, suddenly feeling in my element again.

His mouth curved slowly into a smile. Ben had moved up next to me.

"Exactly," Cyrano said, reaching over to put my hand in his. He had one of those cold fish handshakes. Ick. "Miss . . . ?"

I wasn't sure I trusted Cyrano even though I'd pinpointed his line of work. Hadn't Ben said I could be anyone I wanted in Vegas? Glancing over Cyrano's shoulder past Bellagio's expanse of fountains and gardens, I caught just half of a sign from a hotel down the strip. "Carlo. Paris Carlo."

"Lovely name. Perfect in fact. And you, sir?' he asked Ben.

"Monty," Ben answered. Smart ass. But, good ole Cyrano was too busy giving me the heebie-jeebies with his X-ray eyes to catch on.

"So, are you available for a session?" It looked like Cyrano was sizing me for the costume.

"Not right now, dude," Ben said, trying to edge me back out onto the sidewalk. "We need to check into our hotel room."

"Of course." He nodded. "And where would that be?"

Ben put a hand on my back and began to propel me away. "Off The Strip," he answered over his shoulder.

Cyrano nodded. "When you get settled in, call me. I pay two thousand dollars an hour. Triple if you allow a CD."

I stumbled. Ben caught my forearm, locking my wide-eyed gaze with one of his own. Whoa. What kind of talent was this guy looking for anyway? Six thousand dollars was a lot of money for an out of work ad exec. I turned around. "That much even though I don't have any experience acting?"

"Hmm. I prefer that, actually."

Ben was pulling me by the hem of my baby tee. Cyrano didn't seem to mind. He was looking at my exposed midriff.

Ben yanked me down the sidewalk. "Thanks, she's not interested."

"Hey," I said, spinning around. "Maybe I am. Not all of us get a regular paycheck anymore." Not that I'd be any good at acting but once would be enough to pay my rent for a while. Ben glowered at me.

"Miss Carlo, feel free to contact me after you check in," Cyrano called out, pulling up his sleeve to consult a diamond encrusted Rolex in case I'd missed the price tag on the clothes.

"Get real, dude," Ben said, under his breath, hustling me across the street and then doubling back across and into the entrance to Caesars Palace.

Once we were inside the doors, the dings of the slot machines and the yells from the players at the roulette tables made me pause. After I took in the charged atmosphere for a moment, I turned to my brother. "I know that guy was creepy, but why were you in such a hurry?"

"Bee, don't tell me you are that naïve?"

"Listen, I worked on that side of the ad business for a long time. All those talent agents are creeps. You learn to live with it. I know I'm not young anymore, Ben, but they even have senior citizens do work in commercials for goodness sake! Some types are hard to find for certain shoots." I jammed my hands on my hips.

"What is your *type* then, Bee?" Ben asked, raising his eyebrows.

"Um . . ." I felt my righteous indignation waver. "Mature single woman with semidecent legs and good hair."

"Don't forget a big rack."

"Well," I said, "I don't think that matters unless you are doing a bra commercial."

"Huh, I don't think he wants you wearing a bra," Ben snorted. "And I'm sure you are exactly the type this guy is looking for."

"See." I jammed my hands on my hips. "I could have found a job and you ruined it for me."

"Bee." Ben shook his head. "Have you done anything kinky with your boyfriends?"

Why was the world suddenly obsessed with my sex life now that I didn't have one? "Ben, this is none of your business!"

"I take that as a no. So I can also assume you never watched a naughty video either?"

Fighting the heat rising up my neck, I looked around to see who was listening. A May-December couple passed us but didn't seem to take offense at our conversational topic. In fact, she had her hand a little too far down the front of his slacks to be quite polite. I nudged Ben and nodded in their direction.

"You are avoiding my question, but if that sight makes you blush then I know the answer. You've never seen a skin flick."

The temperature of my face would register at about three hundred degrees. "Ben!"

"If that's the case, maybe calling good ole Cyrano might do you some good then!"

"What are you talking about?"

"Cyrano was a pervert, albeit a rich one. Porn was his business. He wanted to see you 'in action,' either alone or with someone else and put it on CD to see over and over and over."

"Gross!" I shivered. "You have a sick, demented mind, Ben. There's no way anyone would want to see *that*."

Ben just sighed and shook his head. "Welcome to Vegas, where the underbelly of the world is the norm. Tell you what, let's go play poker and maybe you'll meet some semi-normal folks."

"I thought we were going to check into our hotel?" I rubbed on my bare arms. "I feel dirty suddenly. I need a shower."

"We've got plenty of time for that. Let's play a hand or two at a table here." Ben took off toward the mass of tables crowded with players. What were they thinking? It was midnight. It was past my bedtime.

I felt my heart leap in my chest as I chased him. "But I don't know how to play."

Just one look at Ben's eyes told me he was already in focus mode. I nudged him to make sure he heard me. He barely spared me a look. This was the Ben I saw playing poker on the Net. Swell.

"I need to teach you first, before you sit down at a table," he said more to himself than to me. He grabbed my arm and steered me to a seat at the bar. He parked the suitcase next to me. "Have a drink and unwind." He motioned to the bartender. "Get the lady anything she wants and run a tab for me." The world-weary looking brunette nodded. Ben patted me on the head. "I'll be back in a few minutes."

I watched his long strides carry him across the room and around the corner. Great, abandoned in Vegas where I knew no one but a porn purveyor named Cyrano. I'd even forgotten the name of our hotel so I couldn't scoot off and check in. "Damn." I swore under my breath.

"Was he going to play Hold 'Em?"

I looked at the man sitting one seat over from me. I hadn't noticed him there earlier, but then again, I'd been distracted. In his forties, he was attractive in an unkempt way—wavy dark blond hair just overdue for a cut, tan face hours out of a five o'clock shadow and clothes just rumpled enough to look like they might have been worn days before being washed. He struck me as a man who might clean up well if he ever cared to try. The waitress brought him a drink in a highball glass. He took a sip and withstood my appraisal without comment.

"Hold 'Em?" I answered finally. It sounded familiar but I was so unsure of anything in this new world, I didn't want to go out on a limb and respond in the affirmative. It might have been Beat 'Em or Deal 'Em for all I remembered.

"Poker," he reiterated patiently. "Texas Hold 'Em is a kind of poker. Sounds from your accent like you might know a little about Texas, if not poker."

I narrowed my eyes at him. He looked sort of normal, but then the couple from Omaha had too. "Tell me you aren't a 'talent agent.' You don't have a card, do you?"

"No. This isn't a convention, you know."

"Sure it is. Vegas is a convention of freaks, as far as I can tell," I blurted.

His crow's feet crinkled, warming his dark eyes. He had a rich, ironic laugh that made me shift on my stool a bit. "You're very articulate. Well put."

"Where are you from?"

"I grew up in Vegas," he answered.

My blush crept back with a vengeance. "Oh, I'm sorry."

"Don't be. Frank Gilbert." He offered his hand over the seat between us. With only a slight pause, I shook it. He had big hands that had known outdoor work and a firm, strong shake. Very nice.

I remembered my last introduction and couldn't help smiling. He tilted his head quizzically.

"I introduced myself earlier as Paris Carlo," I chuckled and shook my head, disbelieving the whole crazy episode all over again.

He hitched his right eyebrow. "Aha, with an Italian/ French accent, no doubt. I guess I should be asking you if *you* don't have a card?"

I knew I should have been affronted, but the way he said it, just struck me as funny. I laughed, and he did too. Finally,

I shook my head. "I don't have a card, although maybe now I wish I did."

I clapped my hand over my mouth. "I can't believe I said that."

Crow's feet crinkled. He reminded me of Brad Pitt in *Mr. and Mrs. Smith*, a little dangerous, a little sexy, a little funny. A man with some secrets. "I'm glad you did. So, who are you now? With your twang, maybe Christie Houston, or perhaps Debbie Dallas?"

Shaking my head, I was surprised that his nomenclature didn't make me blush. I might have never seen an adult video but I had heard of the most infamous one. "Is everything about sex here in Vegas?"

"Not everything." Frank took another sip of his drink and looked off into the crowd around one of the green felt covered tables on the floor. "Some things are about money. Some things are about both."

Some of those secrets were simmering under the surface. For some irresistible reason, I wanted to pry, but I had to remind myself that Frank was a stranger in a strange place and prying could only lead to trouble. Plus, his secrets were none of my business. In five minutes, he'd be a memory like good ole Cyrano.

Frank drew out of his reverie and motioned at me with his glass. "What are you drinking? Your husband told you to have the house."

"Oh, no," I corrected quickly, "Ben isn't my husband." I wiggled my left hand fingers at him to show the absence of a ring.

Frank chuckled. "Don't rely on rings in Vegas to tell you who's attached. Half the rings in town disappear into pockets once the cabs turn onto The Strip."

"I noticed," I said dryly.

"There's a story there." Frank observed.

"One that wouldn't shock you, I'm sure."

"I'd advise you to order a drink so your boyfriend won't feel so bad when he's three hours at the table."

"He's not my boyfriend, he's my brother. And I'm sure

he won't be three hours—we still have to check into our hotel."

With a wry smile, Frank shook his head. "Sorry, honey, but he had The Look. I'd venture to say he's a candidate for Gamblers Anonymous. Don't get me wrong, I'm not saying he's in the poorhouse or anything. Yet. Just, he can't resist the call of the chips when he gets in a situation where they're offered. Like he'd be okay outside walking The Strip, but once inside, with the noise, he gravitates to the tables. I bet when he's at home when the computer is on, he's just got to go check out what's up on Poker Stars. Right?"

My face answered, I guess, because Frank nodded and finished his highball and signaled the bartender for another. "Give her a chardonnay."

Toby had ordered for me always and I never argued, but for some reason it bothered me that this Frank guy would try it. "No, thanks. I'll take a pinot grigio."

Frank laughed. "An independent woman. Almost as rare a species here as an honest one."

"It sounds like you have a bad history with the opposite sex," I offered taking a sip of my white wine.

Frank threw me a dark look and took a slug. The bartender appeared with a bottle of Chivas Regal and refilled his glass.

"Then we have something in common, because I do too," I said, surprising myself. The Caught Banging the Young Secretary Incident still smarted. Why would I tell a total stranger that I was a loser? I decided it was the white knuckle grip he put on his glass at the mention of women. His must have been bad. If misery really does love company I was trying to make him seem not so alone.

Frank lapsed into silence. I took the opportunity to soak up the surroundings inside Caesars. The variety of people in various types of dress surprised me, from couples in matching aloha wear to sequined dresses and tuxedos. After a few minutes I did notice that there were an inordinate amount of May-December couples like the one we saw when we first entered. Older men, much younger women. Hmm.

"I hope you're not planning on playing poker with your brother," Frank offered.

"Why not?" Did I look like a loser in cards as much as I did a loser in love?

"Because your face is an open book. They'll see the cards in your eyes."

"Okay, what was I thinking?"

"You were wondering why so many rich old coots are walking around with gorgeous jailbait on their arms."

I deflated. And Ben had claimed I had a poker face. "Bingo," I muttered.

Frank continued. "And the answer is, each casino has a certain type that gravitates to it—either by the casino's design or the natural order of things. Most of these are call girls, pro or amateur."

"Amateur call girl?"

"Any woman who'll use sex to get money is a call girl."

Hmm. To call his tone bitter would have been generous. At least one of Frank's secrets definitely involved a woman.

Frank drained his glass again. The bartender shook her head when he asked for another. "Frank, don't do this," she said as she walked by. He tapped her arm and she nodded slightly, pouring him another. He didn't act drunk to me, but he was a muscular guy, so he could probably withstand a few extra drinks without showing it. I, on the other hand, was already feeling a little looser just halfway through my first glass of vino. I'd better watch it.

"So what are you going to do in Vegas while your brother loses his shirt?"

"Stand by his chair at the tournament I guess and make sure he keeps it."

Frank shook his head. "They won't let you stand by any chair, honey."

"Why not?"

"You might give other players signals. You might give your brother a signal."

"But I don't know poker!"

"They don't know that. Besides, that's just what you say and all poker players are liars."

"Then what am I going to do while Ben's at the tournament?" I asked myself more than Frank.

"What tournament?"

"Some big one," I mused. "Let me see if I can remember, it's some Hawaiian island."

"The Lanai Pro-Am?"

"Yes, that's it."

"He must be good, then, your brother. Or rich."

"What do you mean?"

"The only way you get into this particular tournament is by being invited as a pro or paying your way in as an amateur."

Uh-oh. Ben hadn't been traveling around the nation playing professional poker, I knew that much. "How much does it cost to get a seat?"

"Five thousand dollars."

Four

"**F**ive thousand dollars!" I gasped. Several people at the bar lifted their glasses in a toast, no doubt assuming I was talking to Frank about some sort of gaming win. I lowered my voice and mused, "What is Ben thinking? Surely he can't hope to win that back."

"He could win that and more. Last year's World Poker Tour Main Event gave out fifty-two million dollars in prize money. I know the Lanai has put up a bunch of prize money on top of the pool, so the winnings would be up there. But with a couple thousand playing in the tournament, odds are low that he will bring in any big money unless he's a pro."

Frank had drained another glass. I was beginning to wonder when he was going to fall off the stool, although he didn't seem drunk. He was getting that faraway look more often, however, which made me wonder why he'd drink to avoid his ghosts if it just seemed to bring them back to him. Ah, perhaps I was being too psychoanalytic. Maybe he was just drinking at the bar to pick up women, biding his time while his wife was feeding slots or drinking up the courage to hit his own gaming table.

"You seem to know a lot about it, do you play Texas Hold 'Em, Frank?"

Faraway look accompanied by a headshake. More secrets. "I used to play Hold 'Em," he murmured. "Now, when I play at all, I stick to blackjack."

"Why is that?"

"Poker is a game of thirty percent luck and seventy percent skill. I went through a time where Lady Luck wasn't shining on me in any part in my life, so I decided to go with a game where I could have more control over my wins. You play it right, and blackjack is just about ninety percent skill."

The waitress, who obviously knew Frank, walked past and raised her eyebrows. Hmm. I had a feeling Frank was telling me more than he probably would have if he'd stopped a few whiskeys ago. I was intrigued. There was something vulnerable behind this guy's rather hard exterior, something that made me want to draw it out, but it was obvious there would be thorns to go through along the way. He definitely had more dimension than Toby, which might not necessarily be a good thing. Toby was a simple creature for the most part, predictable and easy to have a relationship with. Of course he was also simply a cheating scum. Perhaps I should look for complicated in a relationship partner this time. I looked at Frank again. Hmm. He was damned sexy, even if he was a little morose. Unaware of my musings, he stared into the bottom of his glass.

I sighed. Another time I might want to take up the Frank challenge. Not tonight. Not this trip. Keeping Ben out of hock was challenge enough for me right now. There'd be another Frank in my future. Of course, I might be using a walker and Depends by then.

"Thanks so much for the education," I said, sliding off the seat as I felt in my purse for cash to pay for my glass of wine. Frank signaled the waitress with some obscure finger wiggle; she nodded and called out, "Frank's taken care of your tab, miss."

"Oh, that's not necessary," I argued, turning to Frank.

"It's been my pleasure," he said, flashing a warm grin.

For an instant that too often used platitude seemed completely sincere. It was a good thing I was taking off, because the Pinot Grigio had loosened my inhibitions enough to get me in trouble with Frank Gilbert. "Wish your brother good luck, sharp skill and an extra dose of sportsmanship for the tournament."

"Thank you, as long as he doesn't go into debt or lose his mind over this, I'll be happy, and as long as he can get close to beating some guy named Steely Stan, he'll be happy."

Frank frowned and snapped, "What do you know about Steely Stan?"

His tone was so ominous, I took a step back into my stool. "I don't know anything about him, except that my brother seems to dislike him. Ben thinks he's a bad sport, bad ambassador for the game. I guess he's the best player and the guy to beat. It sounds like overblown competitive male egos if you ask me."

"I hope it's just that," Frank said seriously, laying a hand on my forearm. "Just tell your brother to be careful. Stan Trident is a powerful guy."

"Oh." I leaned in, whispering, "Like Ben shouldn't rock the boat because these tournaments are fixed?"

"No." Frank shook his head decisively. "This one isn't fixed, I can guarantee that. Just tell Ben to play his game, but not to get on the wrong side of Stan *outside* the tables."

I folded my arms over my chest. "Sounds a little overdramatic to me."

Frank glowered. "This is serious stuff. Where are you two staying?"

I shrugged. "Ben failed to tell me before he ran off to lose money."

Standing, Frank reached into the back pocket of his well worn Levi's, stretching the old denim impressively over his hips. I forced my gaze back up. Bad girl. He grabbed my right hand and put a business card in it. Uh-oh. Not another Cyrano.

He met my gaze with his dark-eyed one that bored into

my core. Frank was nothing if not intense. I resisted the shiver that tickled at the base of my spine. "Listen, if you need anything while you are here, call me," he whispered quietly but not softly. "That has my cell phone on the front and my room number at the Lanai is on the back. Call me if you have any questions or need any help. Okay?"

Great, I hadn't been in Vegas an hour and I already had two men force their phone numbers on me. I guess I wasn't totally over the hill yet. Of course, I don't think either one wanted to sleep with me. One wanted to watch me sleep with someone else and the other just wanted to protect my brother. Here we go again. Life was all about other people. I sighed. "Thanks, Frank."

Turning his back to me, he reached into his pocket again and I resisted the urge to be jealous of his hand. He threw a wad of bills on the bar, knocked on it and pointed at the waitress, another secret signal, no doubt. She waved him off with concern in her eyes. Frank spared me one more deep glance carrying a meaning I couldn't interpret and strode off toward the front door of the casino. He was taller than he'd seemed slumped on the bar stool, about six-one, and his long strides consumed the floor so confidently I wouldn't have believed he'd had as much to drink as I'd seen. Maybe his whisky had been watered down. I picked up his empty glass and sniffed. Nope.

When he was out of sight, I opened my fingers to read the card in my hand.

FRANK GILBERT
Security

Security? A Bruce Willis commando type or polyester uniform security guard type? What or who was he securing anyway? I turned the card over. In a bold, heavy script he'd written *Rm 2521*. Did he have this handy to pass out to every available woman he encountered?

And if he was a Las Vegas local, why was he staying in a casino hotel?

"Don't hurt yourself," the bartender, whose name tag read "Spring," warned as she collected Frank's glass.

"What?"

She laughed, deep and throaty. "Smoke's coming out your ears, girl." She shook her head at me. "Let me give you a piece of advice. Don't try to make things make sense in Vegas, just take things as they come. And don't try to figure out Frank Gilbert. There's a reason he lives in Vegas, and the reason is he wants to keep his secrets. Here, we let him."

"So, Frank's your friend?" I asked.

"I know Frank. I see him around here a couple of times a week. I wouldn't call him my friend. Friends are few and far between here. Too many of us just pass through. It's best to keep things friendly but not make friends."

I thought about Shana and how much mileage in life we'd shared and how much that helped when I just needed an ear to listen or a word of advice. Sometimes knowing that she was there was enough. "That seems lonely," I finally told Spring.

She shrugged and turned away to help a man hailing her from the other end of the bar.

I sighed and grabbed the handle of the suitcase, rolling it behind me out of the bar. Of course, I had no idea where I was going. I needed to find the poker tables. At the slot machines, I passed a seventy-something blue-haired woman in a caftan who wore a heavy looking baby sling over her chest. I assumed her grandchildren had left her with babysitting duty. "Sumbitch," she hissed when the rollers came to rest. Quaint. Maybe it would be Junior's first word. She reached into the sling, pulled out a handful of quarters and fed another into the machine in front of her. That's when I realized Junior was a couple hundred dollars in change.

Okay. I *was* in the Twilight Zone.

A couple of rows of slots later, I decided to ask someone where they played poker in this casino. I leaned down to a clean cut young man in a Nebraska Cornhuskers T-shirt. Poised to crank another chance, he looked at me and said, "Yes!"

I looked behind me. Nobody stood there. I looked at the machine to make sure he hadn't just won. Two cherries and an orange. I looked back at his eager face. "I, uh, didn't say anything."

"I know, but you are my lucky charm. I haven't gotten two of any fruit all night. You come up and I got two fruits. Three are bound to be next." He fed the machine and punched the button. Two apples and a banana. He looked at me desperately as he fed the slot again. "Soon."

"I'm looking for the poker tables," I began.

The Cornhusker grabbed my wrist. "Please, not yet, I gotta pay off my student loans. I'm gonna hit it. Just stand there for a minute. Please?"

Feeling extremely stupid, but sorry for the kid, I nodded hastily. He fed the slots, muttering under his breath, for another few minutes. No jackpot. Good. Maybe my lucky charm had worn off and I could go find Ben.

Just as I was about to melt away, the machine dinged and quarters cascaded out in a roar. Cornhusker grabbed my shoulders, jumping up and down with glee. Then he snatched his backpack off the floor, counting to himself as he swept the money into the pocket.

"How much did you win?" I asked.

"Three hundred dollars."

"Not bad, how many quarters did you have to put in?"

"Five hundred . . ."

Not a bad return on his money, I computed as he continued. ". . . dollars."

Ack. He'd lost two hundred dollars and was excited? What was wrong with this picture? He was about to win himself broke feeding that slot. "Good luck," I said, ignoring his impassioned pleas for me to stay. I stomped off, having to drag the suitcase behind me, no doubt compromising the effect of my elder statesman disgust. I'd have to find the poker tables myself, because I was afraid to get near any more strangers. I wandered past the roulette tables, craps players and dealers whipping up blackjack. I watched them play for a moment and thought of Frank. Intriguing guy, mostly because he was the only male I'd encountered since I'd been in Las Vegas who hadn't propositioned me. Maybe he was gay. I whacked myself on the head with the heel of my hand. I was as bad as the rest of these freaks.

"Are you okay?" a male voice behind me asked. Uh-oh. Loaded question. I spun around. A guy about my age in an Armani suit with the body of a gorilla stood there.

I jammed my hands on my hips. "I'm not interested in getting naked, videos, or strip poker with someone who's not old enough to drink a margarita."

"Are you a hooker?"

"Didn't you hear me?"

"Listen, only the tourists do all those crazy things. The hookers are much pickier."

He cracked a smile, and only then I noticed that he was wearing an earpiece. "Aren't you kind of young to be wearing a hearing aid?" I couldn't believe I said that. This place was getting to me.

He pressed his lips together and raised his eyebrows. "You look lost."

"That's an understatement."

The corners of his mouth turned up despite himself. "Can I help you find your room?"

"I wish. I don't know where I am staying."

His eyebrows shot up again just briefly before adjusting themselves back to a perfect corporate look of interest. "Well, the casino prefers that you don't wander around with your baggage on the floor. Can I have the porters at the front desk hold it for you? Miss . . ."

"Cooley. Belinda Cooley." I shook his proffered hand. "You don't understand. I lost my brother. This vacation nightmare was his idea. Mr. . . . ?"

He didn't respond to my question. I guess casino security was tighter than the Secret Service. "Give Vegas time. It grows on you."

"That's what I'm afraid of."

The edges of his mouth twitched again. "Miss Cooley, can I help you get to your room?"

"Sure, you can, if you can figure out which hotel is holding our reservation."

"I see. Do you have any idea where your brother might have wandered?"

"Here in the casino to play Hold 'Em."

Mr. Casino Bouncer asked Ben's name and what he was wearing, guided me to a side chair, ordered me nicely to sit and wait while he turned away to whisper into his lapel. A few minutes later, I saw some of my gorilla friend's look-alikes making their way through tables. It wasn't long before I saw one of them haul a man sitting at a table in the center of the room to his feet. Ben was halfway across the room, flanked by two suits, before his perplexed look turned to one of frustrated fury when he caught sight of me.

"It looks like your brother's finished his game, Miss Cooley," my friend said in smooth warning. "Perhaps now he will be able to check you into your hotel."

"Bee," Ben warned. "I don't like being pulled out of a hand with a bunch of fish when I had nuts on the turn."

"Ben, since I have no idea what you just said, I can't say I'm sorry."

"Perhaps you should teach your sister to play poker, Mr. Cooley," my bouncer buddy put in. "Then she wouldn't be so eager to find her room."

"I'm sorry, Bee," Ben said, shaking his head at himself. "I did promise to teach you. I will. Let's go check in at the Lanai and then we'll get started."

The only thing I wanted to start was a hot bath. I thanked my personal Secret Service agent, whose associates had somehow melted away during our conversation. He nodded and stepped back, keeping us in his sights as Ben grabbed the suitcase handle from me and we headed toward an exit.

"Did you really have to call the goons on me?" Ben whispered as we pushed our way out into the neon-lit night.

"The head goon found me, Ben. I guess they thought I looked like a terrorist, lugging my bomb fixings around in a Burberry bag."

"That's weird, but I guess with Hold 'Em becoming such an international sensation, it makes sense that they would increase security in all the casinos leading up to a well publicized tournament like the one I'm in."

"Ben, why did you drop more than I used to make in a month on entering a stupid game?"

"How do you know how much it costs to enter?"

"You put me at the bar with someone who knew something about it."

"A player?"

"Used to be, apparently, now plays blackjack."

"I know it's a lot of money, Bee, but I'm going to win a lot more."

"Come on Ben, what are the odds? Most of the players are professionals or they've won their way to the tournament by playing a lot more than you do. I know you must play the odds when you play a hand, right? Play the odds here and get out before you get in too deep."

Ben waved off my advice. "Hold 'Em is not all about playing odds and experience. Instinct and heart have a lot to do with it."

"And luck, don't forget that. That is so easy to control," I added, sarcasm thick.

"Not everything in life can be controlled, Bee."

"You are living proof of that." I sighed.

We'd reached the Lanai where I would finally get my hot bath. I stepped into the driveway to avoid a trio weaving their way down the sidewalk. A loud honk behind me made me jump and Ben's hand closed on my arm, pulling me back up onto the sidewalk as a glittering iridescent white Hummer limo zoomed its way to the front door. We'd just made it to the front door as the door to the limo opened. Out came two pairs of long, tan female legs, one wearing silver and rhinestone strappy Manolo Blahnik sandals, the other some pink polka dotted Jimmy Choos, followed by their giggling blond Playboy bunnyish owners. A tall man hopped out after them, dressed in red leather jeans and jacket, black snakeskin boots and mirrored wraparound

Oakleys. Longish hair peeked out from under his black Stetson. For some reason, ZZ Top's *Sharp Dressed Man* sang in my head. It wasn't that this guy was that handsome—on closer inspection his nose was too big, his lips too thin and his jaw too thick—but he sure had a powerful charisma. Heads turned, and it wasn't just because he wore half a cowhide.

Ben elbowed me so hard I almost went down. "That's *him*!"

I was trying to figure out what movie star he was as other casino guests stopped and pointed. A couple waved and one man gave him a thumbs up. He ignored them, draping his arms around the shoulders of the bunnies, letting each hand dangle over a size D. Tacky. I groaned.

The Sharp Dressed Man paused and looked back at me over his shoulder. I could feel his glare through the lenses. "You got a problem?"

"No, but you do, two of them. And they are attached to your arms."

"You oughta mind your own business."

"I'm trying to, but you're in my way."

I think he was so shocked at being back talked that he reeled back a step, just enough for me to get through the door ahead of him, pulling Ben in my wake. I didn't stop until we arrived at the front desk.

"Bee." Ben wore a bemused half grin/half grimace. "I can't believe you just got away with that! You know who he is?"

"I don't care—" I could see him out of the corner of my eye, dragging his blondes along, glaring our way.

"That's him," Ben whispered heatedly. "That's Steely Stan Trident. The jerk I've gotta beat."

And the jerk Frank Gilbert warned was dangerous.

Five

I can't remember when a hot bubble bath felt any better than the first one I took in Vegas. Of course, it helped that our room turned out to be a suite and bigger than my apartment back home by half—two bedrooms, a sitting room, dining room, fully stocked bar, even a foyer. Did I mention the Jacuzzi that overlooked The Strip lit up brighter than Christmas from twenty floors up? That might have been why I thought I was in nirvana amidst the Giorgio scented bubbles.

I could get used to this, I thought as I wrapped myself up in an overly plush cabernet-colored robe.

Of course to do so, I would have to rely on my brother sitting in on high stakes poker games on a regular basis. I wasn't sure I could handle the stress. That was why we were in a suite—neither of us could afford such. I found out—after I'd nearly suffered a heart attack when the porter opened the front door—that Ben's last flight attendant girlfriend had treated him to a turnaround to Vegas in April and he'd played at the biggest table at the Aladdin. According to his story, he'd won a lot and lost a lot and went home even. The hotel wanted him back in the hopes that he might not be as lucky as the house the next time, so they offered him a free room. The strategy must have worked, or they wouldn't be passing out thousand dollar a night rooms with such wild abandon. When Ben registered for the tournament he'd called the Lanai and bemoaned the fact that he would be staying at his free suite in the Aladdin. The Lanai, of course, preferred a big spender be tempted to squander his free time gambling at their tables so they offered the same, a suite.

I wandered out into the spacious, tastefully decorated living area and took in the view that wrapped around nearly 180 degrees in floor to ceiling glass. It was already three o'clock in the morning but The Strip was as busy as rush hour in Houston. I looked at Ben's closed door. He'd dragged the suitcase in to unpack when I'd left to bathe. Surely he couldn't have fallen asleep already. I wouldn't be so lucky.

I knocked. "Ben?"

Hearing nothing, I turned the knob, bracing myself to find one of the coeds from the street or someone like her. Ben had never been known to go long without some girl on his arm, or rather, in his bed.

The bed was empty, save a piece of hotel stationery. Uh-oh. Snatching it up, I read Ben's chicken scratch handwriting.

BeeBee,

Enjoy the champagne I ordered. I'll be back soon. I went to find out what Stan was up to. The more I find out about the guy, the easier he will be to read at the table. I plan to beat him and make you proud. Consider it a research trip.

Your thorough brother, Ben

Make me proud? Make me crazy was more like it.

I could just see him gambling away our return tickets on a last ditch effort to beat Steely Stan. Jeez. With only a

glance at the champagne (Perrier Jouet, what was he thinking!), I grabbed the suitcase and wheeled it back into my
room. There I pulled out the jumble of clothes I'd so bravely
pitched in and took stock.

"This is what I get for being impulsive," I told myself
out loud. Now I had to live with the consequences, which
would be cordovan leather Steve Madden scrunch cowboy
boots with an eggplant suede jacket, an ocher silk shirt, tan
suede skirt. I didn't even pack the jewelry that matched any
of the partial outfits I had on. If I had any luck at all, that
would've happened by accident. Luckless, that was me. Oh
well, might as well go all the way into unmatchingdom. I
closed my eyes, dipped my hand into my jewelry pile and
came out with . . . oh no. Sucking in a deep breath, I slid on
the teal and gold chandelier earrings. I hoped everyone I
encountered was color-blind.

I almost put back on the unobtrusive denim mini and
black baby tee I'd worn on the plane, but then remembered
it had been touched by Cyrano's slimy hands. With a
shiver, I deposited it into the hotel laundry bag and stuffed
it into the side pocket of my suitcase.

I tied my unruly hair back into a bun at the base of my
neck, slid the room key into the pocket of my jacket, blew
out a breath and reached for the doorknob. So far this vacation was a blast.

I'd been waiting for the elevator for ten minutes. Ten
painful minutes trying to avoid the mirrors that lined the
wall opposite me. Once I'd eroded my confidence to sub
zero, I turned to look at the empty hallway. All I could
think about was all the trouble Ben could be getting himself into. The whole way up to our room, he'd talked about
the Stan guy like they'd had some longstanding, multigen-
erational feud. Granted, the guy was an obvious jerk, but if
you lost sleep about every one of those you encountered,
you'd die young. There was something Ben wasn't telling
me. Ben said there were claims Stan didn't play a clean

game (in other words, he cheated). After more prodding, he told me Stan's well publicized and clearly obvious womanizing got Ben's back up. I wanted to advise Ben to look in the mirror, but to his credit, I'd never seen Ben with his hands on two women's breasts at the same time. Maybe in the same hour, but I guess that was an important detail.

Finally, when I threatened to get on the next plane home, Ben mentioned that Stan was supposedly some kind of pill popper. I still didn't see what that had to do with Ben, except for the fact that he sold pills for a living, which you'd think would make him less critical of the guy if for no other reason than he might boost Ben's paycheck in an indirect way. Okay, I was stretching it a bit, but something was off. Why a drug abusing, skirt chasing poker champion would get his back up, I don't know. Ben was acting like he was employed as the flack for the World Series of Poker. It didn't make sense and I aimed to get to the bottom of it.

The longer I stood there waiting for the elevator, the further my imagination stretched. Finally, when my mind had drawn a picture of Ben choking Stan to death at the poker table downstairs, I went in search of the stairs. Twenty floors was a long way to go, but at least it was down and maybe the exercise would curb my anxiety. Good thing my Steve Maddens were comfy. I was huffing by the time I got to the tenth floor, so I barely heard the voices over my own wheezing lungs. I paused and bit down on my lower lip to keep from panting out loud. The voices, loudly angry, were both male and drifted down the stairwell from a few floors above me.

"I don't care what kind of problems you're having down there right now, Pete, discretion is especially important because of what is happening here this weekend." A deep bass threatened. "This is very important to the jefe. You cannot talk to him. You cannot talk to me. Got it?"

"But what am I supposed to do if I have problems with a new driver? He walked off the job and I swear he thinks something's hinky with the operation. We already lost a day because of it and two transfers. We'll lose money, he'll get mad," a whiny tenor proclaimed defensively.

"He's already mad. You coming up to him in the middle of the casino like that, blowing his cover."

"It wasn't in the middle of the casino, I caught him out of the way. I didn't know that idiot was stalking him or something. How could I know that?" The one named Pete raised his voice in frightened desperation.

"Listen, the jefe is a big deal here. People think he is some sort of a god. So that is why you have to cool it. I don't know what the stalker idiot heard but now he's my problem to deal with and I hate problems. If you don't quit arguing and shut up, I'll shut you up for good," a deep bass threatened. I heard thumping and a whimper.

My heart was racing, and not from my hike. The hairs on the back of my neck stood up. Part of me—obviously the smart part—told me to escape out the door with the big ten on it and run like hell. Some other part of me—obviously the same part that keeps finding the wrong men to date—made me crane my neck to sneak a peek upstairs. A balding head on a neck bulging with a couple of fat rolls hung over the railing. Not on purpose, I didn't think, since a pair of big hands were buried in those fat rolls, squeezing until the bald spot started to turn red. Rambo-ish dark-haired Bad Guy in a good suit loomed over the pudgy dude named Pete and squeezed harder. He glared at him with eyes so electric blue I sucked in a sharp breath.

Damn.

I shrank back against the wall. I tasted Iceberg Effusion on my tongue and sniffed again. I recognized it because, way back when, I'd spent about three hours smelling every men's cologne at the Dillard's counter to find the perfect birthday present for Ben. The crisp, hard-edged, almost threatening scent wasn't my brother but it certainly would fit the tough guy upstairs. I hoped they couldn't hear my heart that was now roaring. I swallowed hard and nearly choked. Fine, maybe I would die right there and spare the guy a second victim.

"Did—you—*Ack*—hear—*Blek*—that?" Pete forced out of his compressed airway.

Uh-oh.

"What?" demanded Electric Blue Rambo.

Pete groaned loud enough to make me think his throat was free of Rambo's hands. "That sound?"

"The only sound I hear is you trying to distract me from killing you," Electric Blue Rambo said. I swallowed my sigh of relief as he went on. "Listen, just because we are partners doesn't mean we like you enough to keep you around. Take care of things for the next couple of days without bothering us or you are taking the fast track to hell. You got that?"

I felt like I was caught in the middle of a gangster movie. Who says stuff like that . . . "fast track to hell"? It reminded me of The Godfather. Which reminded me of horse's heads in bed. I shook my head, trying to snap myself back to reality. It occurred to me that they were wrapping up their quaint little tête-à-tête. What was I going to do if they came down the stairs toward me? My Steve Maddens weren't soundless. Damn, should have worn the moccasins after all.

As Electric Blue Rambo (I assumed) made a few more loud thumps on Pete, I considered slipping off the boots and running the rest of the ten floors on socked feet. But before I could decide, Electric Blue Rambo advised his buddy to get lost and footsteps scuffled above me.

Damn. Without any further brain bending, I lurched for the door to the tenth floor, opened it and ran faster than I had when my sorority housemother caught me in the broom closet with a Sigma Phi. The door slapped closed behind me. I had no plan, a tight skirt, high-heeled boots and the world's longest, straightest hallway with absolutely no place to hide, but suddenly luck on my side. An older man appeared out of the elevator and began meandering down the hall. I escalated, slowing to a walk before I came even with him. As I heard the stairwell door slam open, I wrapped an arm around his waist and said loudly, "Uncle Jack! I've been looking for you all night."

He grinned at me and the alcohol fumes made my eyes water. "Oh? Where was I?"

Heart pounding, I refused to glance back. Instead I winked at "Uncle Jack." "Where you don't belong, no doubt, you rascal."

"This old dog might have seen his prime, but I've still got some go to me, girlie." He chortled, then frowned. "I might have some go, but I don't have a lick of memory. You must be Martha's girl, right? Be sweet and remind a silly old man of your name."

Thankfully, before I had to answer, he pulled up unsteadily. I could hear footsteps hurrying up behind us. "Oops," "Uncle Jack" said. "Here's my room. Almost passed it. That memory really is going."

I held my breath as his wavering hand fished in his shirt pocket for his room key. His gnarled fingers shook as they fitted the plastic card into the lock. "Uncle Jack" held the door for me. I was halfway through when my luck ran out.

"Excuse me," Electric Blue Rambo called out behind us.

I gently shoved my dear uncle forward, but the bad guy with the bad ass voice commanded attention, and he got it. "Yeah?"

I suddenly found a reason to primp in the mirror, yanking my hair loose to further hide my face.

"Hey, old man, did you come up the stairs just now?"

"No, went by the elevator, sonny."

"How about her?" Electric Blue Rambo scared me so much I couldn't look at him. I hoped he couldn't see my legs shaking. I cocked my head and examined my lip gloss, smoothing it with a pinkie. I smelled the Iceberg again and tried not to shiver as I saw him reach for me out of the corner of my eye.

"This is my niece, sonny," my gallant savior announced bravely if slurringly as he stepped in the way. "Paws off."

"No offense, I just wanted to know if she came up the stairs. I'm looking for something I lost."

I shook my head, not wanting to speak, partly because I thought my voice might sound like Minnie Mouse, but also because I didn't want to give Electric Blue Rambo any more hints to who I was other than my backside.

"Sonny, you're gonna lose something else if you don't skedaddle out of here right quick." With that "Uncle Jack" slammed the door in Electric Blue Rambo's face. Ta-da. Gotta love it.

I was so relieved, I threw my arms around his neck and gave him a peck on the cheek. It threw him a bit off balance and I had to steady him by his elbow. I looked closer at him and saw his watery blue eyes couldn't even focus. Damn. I couldn't leave the old guy like this. He was going to be harder to get away from than The Godfather pair.

"I'm sorry about that," "Uncle Jack" said, peering through the peephole to make sure Electric Blue Rambo was gone. "He was a rude young 'un, that's for sure. I never want to see you with a no mannered whippersnapper like that, you hear me?"

"Yes, sir." I smiled.

He smiled back, then sighed, shaking his head. "I'm sorry. I've already forgotten your name again, Martha's girlie."

I patted his shoulder. "It's Belinda." I couldn't bear to lie to the old guy.

I pointed at the clock on the bedside table. "It's late, I ought to let you tuck in for the night."

"You're not leaving yet, are you?" His watery blue eyes almost broke my heart.

"I can stay a few more minutes," I assured him, thinking it wasn't a bad idea to give the bad guys more time to get lost.

His eyes brightened at that. He was beginning to sway again. "I imagine you're of drinking age by now."

"Just barely." I hid my grin by coming around the couch, putting my hand on his shoulder and easing him back until the backs of his legs hit the loveseat and he plopped down. "What can I get you to drink, Uncle Jack?"

He chuckled. "You keep calling me that. You're entirely

too young to have as bad a memory as mine, Belinda. I'm Uncle Felix."

"Oh, I am so sorry. I get you and Dad's brother mixed up."

Felix sat ramrod straight. "I remind you of that no ac-count—"

Oops. I put up a hand. "Just in looks, Uncle Felix. I always thought Uncle Jack was so handsome . . ."

"Oh, well, in that case. I guess I don't mind."

He grinned, and I grinned back, pouring him every little bottle of whisky in the bar, with a little ice and no water. I poured myself a ginger ale.

As we made small talk about what he'd done while he'd been in Vegas, I sucked down my ginger ale fast enough to make him want to keep up. I poured us both another, relieved to see his eyes beginning to lose focus for longer periods. By the time he was on his third drink he'd forgotten I was supposed to be his niece and was recounting his life story. He told me about being widowed and his life back home as the postmaster of his Valentine, Nebraska town, population 2800. I was starting to like old Felix. I hoped I wouldn't kill him with alcohol poisoning.

Finally, he began snoring in the middle of one of the longer pauses in the conversation. I'd been there twenty minutes and hoped that was long enough for Electric Blue Rambo to have given up and gone on to give a hard time to the poor snoop who'd gotten caught eavesdropping on the mystery man. I tried to shake off the bad feeling about that. Rambo seemed pretty ruthless, but maybe he'd let the guy off with a small choke and a warning like he did with Pete.

Oh well, I didn't know any of them. I'd get to write this whole adventure off as the total of my excitement in Vegas, since the rest of the time I'd be chasing down Ben to keep his nose clean.

Speaking of which, I'd better get to the floor and find him. I glanced back at Felix and made for the door. I had my hand on the doorknob when I thought of something. I went back to the desk, found the stationery and wrote a note.

Uncle Felix,

Thanks for being my hero!

Your niece, B

I opened the door soundlessly and surveyed the hall in both directions. The coast was clear.

Since it seemed my luck had turned, and since there was no way in hell I was ever going in the stairwell again, I hustled to the elevator and pressed the down button. Thirty seconds later, the arrow dinged. I jumped in with a nod to the solitary woman inside, who pulled a wad of cash out of her bra and began counting. She ignored me as I surveyed her from out of the corner of my eye. She had on some calf-high knock-off boots and an outfit that was a kaleidoscope of colors and textures. We'd almost reached the casino when I looked up and saw the two of us reflected in the mirrored doors. We looked like we'd been dressed by the same clothier.

Swell. A couple hours in Vegas and not only was I acting like a working girl but I looked like one too.

Six

After an hour of scouring the hotel casino with no luck and not a little anxiety that I would bump into Electric Blue Rambo at every turn, I still hadn't found Ben. I had found people who remembered seeing him, not coincidentally, in the vicinity of the famed Steely Stan. I had a couple of players ask me if I was one of Steely's Squeezes (as I found out they were called). Woo-hoo. Great compliment. So now, not only was I looking like a whore, but I was looking like one of a jerk's whores.

Nice.

I decided not to ask around about Stan Trident anymore, although I had made some progress getting a location on my brother. While women see a resemblance to Colin Farrell, men for the most part either a) don't know who he is (as opposed to women of all ages who know every sexy bad boy star) or b) think Ben reminds them of their best friend or their favorite cousin. Must be a pheromone thing.

The last Ben sighting had been at a poker table that he'd gotten up from abruptly—never returning to finish his play. I thought maybe he'd been losing, but the woman he'd been playing next to assured me he'd had plenty of chips in front of him. He'd never returned to claim them or her (she'd made an interesting offer of entertainment after the game was over).

That concerned me. The money more than the woman. Ben found women without any trouble. In fact, that might be it after all—he might have gone for a pit stop and run into the coeds from earlier and gone up to our room for a quickie. Sex with a pair might be worth a couple hundred lost dollars. He was stupid that way. I went to the house phone and dialed our room. It rang three times without being answered before going to voice mail. I left a message that I would be up to the room in ten minutes and everybody better be dressed when I got there.

It took me nearly that long to hula my way through the roulette tables and surf my way past the slots. I didn't think that my amazement in the amount of money spent to make these casinos seem like the real paradise would ever wear off—in fact it grew each time I walked through a new room in a casino. I would notice something new, like the giant-sized blown glass surfer riding a blue glass wave decorated with lifelike bubbles and foam. Upon closer inspection, I decided it might not be glass at all but crystal. Sheesh.

I shook my head. It seemed horribly wasteful and irresistibly fascinating at the same time.

I was solo in my trip up in the elevator, proof, I suppose, that activity does slow down in Vegas somewhat in the wee hours before dawn. Considering the night I'd already had, I wasn't in the mood for a kama sutra experience, I paused with my room key poised above the slot and decided to knock. No squeals, calls or other noise. Goody, maybe Ben was tucked away safely in bed alone.

I slid the key in and pushed the door open to disaster.

"Benjamin Cooley," I shouted, letting the door ease closed behind me. "I cannot believe that you trashed our room for a couple minutes of wild sex. Do you know what this is going to *cost*?"

It's incredible what expectation does to a mind. I just

knew that the lamp knocked to the floor and the coffee table swept clear of its water glass, magazine and remote had the look of a pair looking for a place to couple.

Then I saw the blood smeared on the wall and noticed the cracked glass of the coffee table and knew reality had taken a wide detour from my expectations.

Swallowing a scream, I tried to get a handle on the thoughts that were careening around in my head. "Hello?" I called loudly. "Ben?"

I ran to Ben's bedroom; the door I'd left closed was now open. The comforter on his bed was wadded up in the corner, his clothes were strewn on the floor, the poker strategy books by his bedside riffled through and upside down on the pillows. I peeked in the bathroom. His shave kit was overturned in the sink.

I sucked in a deep breath as I spun around. An alarm went off in the back of my mind, but I ignored it. I rushed to my bedroom to see the suitcase overturned on the bed. Every zipper was open, every pouch pulled loose. My makeup was scattered on the bathroom floor. My shoes and clothes were jumbled on the bedroom floor, save for my Victoria's Secret bras and panties that were on a separate pile on the dresser, obviously having been pawed. Grr. So a man had robbed our room. Still steaming, I stomped back to the living area and saw the blood again. Had the freak robber not found any valuables, gotten mad, hit the table and hurt himself? I hoped so. But then a darker possibility crossed my mind. What if Ben were here when the robber broke into the room and Ben tried to stop him?

But if that were the case, where was Ben now? At the hospital? Surely if he'd called 911, they would have left me a message. The message light on the phone was blinking. I almost reached for it, then remembered to preserve the fingerprints. I ran to the bathroom, snagged a washcloth, picked up the receiver and pressed the envelope button with my knuckle. One message. From me. I slammed the phone down at the sound of my voice. Then, I picked it up quickly and dialed the front desk.

"Do I have any messages?"

"No ma'am room 2003 has no messages."

I don't know why I didn't report the break-in right then, but a weird feeling held me back. Maybe I didn't want to hand over my credit card for the cost of the lamp and coffee table. Maybe I'd just recognized the scent that had been bothering me since I'd walked through the room.

A men's cologne.

Iceberg Effusion.

The last time I'd smelled that scent this evening was when Electric Blue Rambo had caught me with Felix. I didn't want to jump to a scary conclusion, so I returned to Ben's bathroom and looked at the contents of his shave kit. I saw only the bottle of Balenciaga Cristobal I'd given him for his birthday. I smelled the crisp bite of the Iceberg again as I walked past the window. Damn. Whoever he was, he hadn't been gone long.

If he was gone at all.

Without thinking more about that, I walked to the door and left.

I ran to the elevators, pressed both up and down buttons and jumped in the first door that opened. The car was going up. I didn't care where I was going because I didn't know what I was going to do. I pulled Frank Gilbert's card out of my purse and considered it. Security. Hmm. I reached for my phantom cell phone. Damn Ben. I started to tear up for a second then squelched the urge. In the age of wireless communication, it was almost impossible to find a pay phone anymore. At the twenty-eighth floor, the doors opened and a corporate looking woman in a gray suit and gray pumps, carrying a briefcase hopped in. She looked so solid, so normal, so much like the people I'd worked with at my ad firm that I almost spilled the whole story. I opened my mouth when her cell phone rang and she answered in a baritone.

"Just tell the prick I'm on the way. If he wants us doing a Women of Wall Street gig at the last minute, he's just got to be patient. Try finding butt ugly clothes that *fit*, in Vegas, in an hour, for a rehearsal. Hell, I know he's a showman genius, but he's got to chill when it comes to reality. I could find a thousand diamond thongs and not one knee length gray plaid polyester skirt."

I was almost saved by a female impersonator. She severed the connection and shook her head at the phone in her hand. "Bosses are the bitch, aren't they?"

Huh. I could relate to that one. "You said that right."

I looked at the phone. Maybe she could save me after all. "Could I borrow your phone? I don't have one, and I'd be happy to pay for the minutes."

She handed it over. "Don't worry about it, comes with the job. Speaking of which, sister, you'd be better off doing something else. Your line of work is just too damned hard on the body. I did it for years and now I just dance. It's better money and better hours. Come by New York-New York and I'll see if I can hook you up with an audition."

Oh great, now I look like a transvestite hooker? "Uh, thanks for the offer, but I'm, um, really a woman."

"Duh." She hit her hand on her head. "I knew that. You couldn't fake those tits. They are way too natural and nice, if you don't mind me saying so."

I shook my head. I really didn't mind. I think Vegas was rubbing off on me. She continued. "No, there is a new show at our casino, it's girls dressed up like guys. They look the real deal, girl, then they strip and wa-la, there's real tits for all the world to see. The audience is floored. It's the coolest. Wish I were a real woman. And the best part for you is, my boss only hires girls with real ones. No silicone. Nothing fake. That makes the surprise so much better in the end."

I was really depressed now. I was a man-ish looking woman who looked like a hooker. I sighed and wondered why I continued to be polite, except that I kind of liked my new buddy. "Thanks, but I think I'm too old. I'm forty."

She hit my arm and I nearly fell over. "You're shitting me, girl! I would've never guessed it, and neither will my boss. Just fudge a little. By the time he hires you and sees those goods you got, he won't care."

She pulled out a card and handed it to me. Carey Beckwith. "Thanks."

"Call me, or at least come see the show before you decide. I'll get you in for free."

We were almost to the ground floor, so I quickly dialed Frank's number. A sleepy male voice answered. "Gilbert."

"Frank? This is Belinda Cooley."

"Uh . . ."

Oh great, he'd been so drunk he couldn't remember me. Maybe this was a mistake.

"Belinda Cooley," I repeated, thinking I might add, that mannish looking woman you sat next to last night at the Caesars Palace bar. But then I remembered I never introduced myself. "Uh, 'Debbie Dallas' from last night?"

Carey's eyebrows went up and she did a humping action against the wall. It looked so funny for a corporate maven to be doing the nasty that I giggled.

"Oh, yes, *Debbie*," Frank said, his cold voice warming. "Sounds like you had a better evening after I left. What can I do for you this early morning?"

"You said I could call you anytime," I reminded him, sobering and still not sure this was a good idea. The elevator deposited us on the ground floor and we exited, Carey following as I walked to an alcove against the wall. "I wondered if we could meet somewhere for coffee?"

"Sure, about ten?"

"Could it be sooner? Like in a half hour? I'm staying at the Lanai too. I could come to your room." I didn't like the way that sounded but I didn't want to talk about what happened in the middle of the casino. I didn't know when or where Electric Blue Rambo might reappear. Besides, I didn't know if I was being overly dramatic, imagining the danger of the whole thing, and if he'd laugh at me in public. Private was better. I held my breath as his pause stretched on. Carey shot me a sympathetic look, clearly misunderstanding the reason for my call.

Finally, Frank answered hesitantly. "Sure. Come on up. Or down, depending on where you are."

"I'll be right there. 2521. Right?"

I handed over the phone with a thanks that she waved off. "Those cold calls are hell. Really, girl, think about a new career. Call me."

She reached into her cleavage, came out with a handful of twenties and handed it to me. "Here. Tell the guy to take a powder. Being a working girl nowadays is just too dangerous."

I put the money back in her hand, touched at her kindness. "I promise I'll come see your show."

She grinned. "The show is pretty fun, always. Can't make any promises on this Wall Street woman thing, but I'd love to see you in the audience, girl."

On impulse, I gave her a hug and we waved goodbye. She was by far the best person I'd met in Vegas. Transvestite show girl, amateur psychologist. I guess that said it for the city. Of course, Frank could elevate himself above Carey within moments. I was quickly back on the elevator, headed to his room. Only time, and probably a few aspirin on his part, would tell.

"This is a surprise," Frank said, stepping back in his maroon terry cloth robe, from the door of his room to allow me to enter. He reminded me of my Aunt Telly who always acted like it was a surprise when we showed up, invited, for Thanksgiving dinner.

"Really, I'm sorry to wake you so early, and I wouldn't have done it except that your card said 'security,' you offered to help and I have a problem."

"Okay," Frank said from behind me as I hurried in and sat on the loveseat in his suite that was bigger and more expensively decorated than ours.

"What?" Frank asked as he sat in the chair opposite the loveseat. I looked around in awe, as he continued, crossing his legs at his ankles, "I'd have to guess you are on a floor below me? Some of those are the comp rooms."

For some reason I was distracted by his bare feet. Men's

feet, when bare, seem so vulnerable to me. That was a good thing in this case, because now I felt like I could tell Frank my problem without being intimidated. I looked again. Size twelve B, nicely kept, but not professionally pedicured. Feet that made me wish I'd noticed the hands that went with these nice big feet. They were currently hidden in the pockets of the robe, but I might find a reason for them to come out to play.

I stopped myself.

No, no, no. No fun for me. I had to find Ben and get to the bottom of the break-in.

I sucked in a breath and explained: "We are on the twentieth floor. And when I went up to our room for the second time tonight, I found it had been vandalized."

Frank sat forward, elbows on his knees. "What do you mean?"

I described the scene in detail and he didn't interrupt me, which led me to believe he might have spent some of his past as a cop. I'd been interviewed by a few of them, through no fault of mine and all of Ben's, but suffice it to say I had experience with the men in blue. Frank struck me as an ex-cop.

"I guess I should call the Las Vegas police." I said. "This has all been made more complicated by Ben, yet *again*, who made us leave our cell phones at home. They need to know he's missing."

"First of all, this casino is not in city limits, so the city cops wouldn't care. You would have to call the deputy sheriffs for Clark County, and let me warn you, Belinda, that you have to be careful who you talk to on the force."

"You sound paranoid," I offered, I admit, a little antagonistically.

He wasn't offended. You had to love that. He looked at me with that awesome intensity. "With good reason. Some well placed guys on the force are on the pad from the mob and from some drug runners, some operate their own illegal gigs. You don't want to be telling your story to them, because if this had anything to do with any kind of corrupt doings, they might want to cover it up instead of investigate. That might turn out to be dangerous to you."

"Come on." I said, "That sounds like an episode of *Las Vegas*."

Frank gave me a look. "Trust me, it's worse than any Hollywood imagination could dream up."

"I really don't have any other option. My brother is missing. My room is trashed. What am I supposed to do?"

Frank sighed. "Was anything missing?"

I shook my head. "Nothing of mine was missing, but I don't know exactly what Ben brought."

"You don't have a cell phone and neither does he," Frank mused. "Is there anyone back home, friends, family he might contact if he can't get a hold of you?"

"I doubt he would call Mom, she manufactures reasons to panic and Ben is her baby. She'd have the National Guard here if he got a hangnail. Dad tells Mom everything so calling him is like calling her. He has a couple of good buddies but I certainly don't know their phone numbers, and Ben knows I don't. He might call my best friend, though."

"Call her first, then call your parents and his closest buddy if you can get his number from information. Don't let on anything is wrong." Frank handed me a paper thin phone. Very high tech, very cool.

He watched carefully while I talked to Shana. She hadn't heard from Ben, obviously, and chastised me for not gambling yet. Mom didn't know we'd gone to Vegas and hadn't been able to get a hold of me and had called police to my house. She sent me on a major guilt trip. I started to give her my room number and Frank shook his head, scribbling his own instead as well as his phone number. I reluctantly read both to Mom, and finally extracted myself from the conversation.

"You really don't want my mom having your number. She'll call fifteen times a day."

"Better that than whoever roughed up your brother finding out about your mom and going to see her."

Yikes. "They wouldn't do that."

"We don't know what Ben was into and what they wanted from him." Frank pointed out.

Finally, I tracked down Sam Cuero, who asked how much money we'd won so far. I did tell him Ben and I had gotten separated and he just advised me to sit tight because Ben was probably "getting him some." Ah what a romantic. And to think I'd turned Sam down when he'd asked me out ten years ago.

I shook my head when Frank raised his eyebrows in question. "No luck."

"Okay, you need to check in periodically with them. Let's go back to the sequence of events. You said that when you found the room trashed, it was the second time you were there. Tell me exactly what you and your brother did between when I saw you and when he disappeared."

"After I left you, I was going to find Ben when a casino security guy stopped me and asked if he could help me. He sent some goons to find Ben at the poker tables." Frank drew his eyebrows together at that but rolled his hand to get me to continue the story. "Then we walked over here and as we entered the Lanai, the Steely Stan guy got out of a limo in front of us. I said something snide to him as he went in. Ben was obsessed with finding out where he was going and what he was doing."

Frank held up a hand to stop me and sat forward on the couch. "Wait a minute, Belinda. Why did you say something snide to Stan?"

"His limo nearly ran me over, then he gets out with a girl on each hip and a hand on each breast and walks over and through people like he owns the world. It just rubbed me the wrong way. It was tacky."

Frank narrowed his eyes and gave me the most intense stare I've ever seen. "Belinda, I warned you to stay away from Stan. He is dangerous."

Have I mentioned I don't like to be told what to do? Especially by virtual strangers. I straightened my spine and looked down my nose at Frank. His intensity was hard to fend off, and those bare feet were hard to ignore, but I tried with a look my mother perfected to guilt her little bad boy Ben into behaving. Frank just stared back. I don't think it worked as well on him. Or maybe I wasn't as good at it as my mom was.

"What happened next?" Frank finally prodded.

"So we checked in and rode the elevator up to the room. I went in to bathe and Ben left me a note that said he was going to check out where Stan had gone because he wanted to 'research' him to do better in the tournament."

Frank shook his head. "What is your brother really up to?"

I shrugged. "I really think 'researching' Stan *was* what he was up to. Ben is obsessive. Anyway an hour later he still wasn't back and so I dressed and went down the stairs because I got tired of waiting for the elevator."

Frank shook his head with a small smile, and his glance drifted to my legs. "Twenty flights? You must be in good shape."

I felt my cheeks warm. "Well, I didn't quite make it all the way." I hadn't decided whether or not to tell him all about what happened next but his eye contact with my knees so flustered me that the story in the stairwell spilled out in a rush.

Frank glowered, his dark eyes darkened. "Did these men see you?"

"Um," I began, really not wanting to go into the whole Felix episode. Somehow I didn't think Frank would approve. "My back. My profile, maybe."

"And what did they look like?"

I described both men as best I could. Of course, I'd seen Electric Blue Rambo a lot better than I had the short, fat whiner named Pete. I didn't mention the cologne connection. Frank was all about facts and I doubted fragrance would qualify as a fact.

"Look, I don't know if this is all connected, coincidence or you have a knack for being at the wrong place at the wrong time. And saying the wrong thing to the wrong person."

I crossed my arms over my chest. Humph. I thought I'd done pretty well getting away from the bad guys, but all Frank could do was criticize. Maybe *Frank* was the wrong person. Double humph.

He continued, "But the bottom line is: You can't go to police, some guys are on the up and up, some aren't and you don't know which is which. Some are linked to the mob and the Mexican mafia, but I also hear whispers that a couple are in Steely Stan's pocket. I don't know why he'd need them there unless he's running some kind of poker scam. But that would be hard to do since he wins at casinos and tournaments outside Vegas. So that may be nothing but a rumor. Still, Stan's up to something. And it's not good, because all these rumors have some grain of truth. And that's enough to steer clear of him."

"What about our hotel security. I'll just report the break in to them."

Frank shook his head. "Half the security force are moonlighting cops or ex-cops who went to work the casino for bigger money."

"What do you suggest I do then?"

"I'm not sure."

"Great," I said, jumping to my feet. "You're full of advice on what *not* to do. You can't tell me what *to* do while my brother is out there somewhere bleeding to death."

"You don't know if that was his blood or someone else's," Frank rose slowly to his feet. I was momentarily distracted by his feet, but fortunately my anger pulled my attention back to where it should be.

"That's where police expertise comes in," I retorted. "They could do blood tests and a real investigation."

Frank was glowering deeper and shaking his head stronger now.

"You tell me not to trust anyone in Vegas, but you want me to trust you, some drunk I met at a bar who has a stupid cryptic card that means nothing. For all I know you're an ex-cop who works for the Mexican mafia who will hold me hostage in this room while your compadres slice and dice my brother for fun."

Jumping to my feet, I strode to the door, trying not to think about the flash of hurt in Frank's eyes when I'd called him a drunk. I was so mad I was shaking. I was so mad I couldn't see straight. I grabbed the doorknob. Frank was behind me and put his palm on the door to hold it closed. I was so mad I was actually stronger than he was. I yanked the door open and marched down the hall.

"Don't do this, Belinda," Frank called low and hard.

"Call me Bee." I threw over my shoulder. "And watch me buzz away."

Seven

♦ ♣ ♥ ♠

As I stomped to the front desk, I forgot to worry about
Electric Blue Rambo jumping out at me from behind a pot-
ted palm. All I could think about was Frank trying to boss
me around like Toby did, albeit in a different way. Toby
was a smooth manipulator. From what I could tell of Frank
he was his name—frank to the point of being blunt. One
didn't wonder what Frank wanted because he spelled it out.
Toby was sneakier about getting what he wanted, but he
still got it. Same difference. I'd let one too many men control me. No more. I was forty now and I was independent. I
might die a spinster but at least I would go my own way doing my own thing.

I marched through the blue granite waves and polished
sandstone that was the lobby floor of the Lanai. A marble
dolphin leaping out of a wave almost caught my right
thigh. I detoured and nearly ran over a killer whale. Was
that onyx and quartz? Ack.

Thankfully, no one was in line. I approached the desk
clerk who looked up, her eyes widening. I probably had

smoke coming out my ears. "Yes, ma'am?" she asked cautiously.

"I have a problem and need you to call the police for me."

"Is there something I can help you with?" she asked.

I felt like I was dealing with a diplomat from the United Nations. Sheesh. I remembered that Frank said the casinos liked to equalize trouble immediately. I remembered that the last casino had not even liked the way it looked when I was wandering around with luggage. Blood and break-ins would be much worse. I took a deep breath and tried not to scream. "I . . . Just . . . Told . . . You . . . How . . . You . . . Could . . . Help . . . Me. Call the police."

"Oh yes, ma'am. You are in luck." *I bet I was.* She tapped something into her computer. Probably a red alert message and the casino goons would be on me momentarily. She nodded and spoke with a careful tone reserved for those not mentally stable. "There is a detective with the sheriff's department here right now checking out security for the big pro-am poker tournament that starts tomorrow night. I'll take you to him. Maybe he can help you."

She poked her head in the open door behind her and another young clerk appeared, giving her colleague a sympathetic look as she took over the computer. The first clerk beckoned me to come around the front desk and follow her through a door she opened by punching a code into the keypad above the knob. She led me down a hallway and opened another door with the same code, 7826, which I memorized. Who would've guessed reading all those Nancy Drews when I was thirteen was coming in handy.

She opened the door and motioned me to go ahead of her into what looked like a conference room. Two men in suits stood with their backs to us, bent over what looked like schematic blueprints. "Excuse me, Detective Conner?" my escort said apologetically. "This guest was asking for the police."

I walked past her as the taller man turned to look at us. His eyes were electric blue. I sucked in a breath and tasted

Iceberg Effusion. Uh-oh. This changed everything. I tried to rewind the conversation I heard in the stairwell in my mind, playing the bad guy as a cop to see if I had misunderstood anything. Nope. Electric Blue Rambo was still the bad guy. Just so happened he was also a cop.

That meant Frank was right.

"Are you Detective Conner?" Maybe he wasn't the cop after all. But he nodded.

"Daniel Conner, Clark County Sheriff's Department." He turned to the man next to him who was still bent over the papers on the table, more than happy to leave any police business to the police. "This is Wayne Cedillo, head of security here at the Lanai. What seems to be the problem?"

"I, uh . . ."

"Yes?" Conner cocked his head, drew his eyebrows together and looked at my earrings, my jacket, my boots. Gulp.

". . . had my wallet stolen." I finished weakly. I bet Nancy would've thought of something better than that.

"Really? Where did this happen? Perhaps in a room on the tenth floor?"

Conner remembered me. I had to get out of there as quickly as possible. "Well, you see I opened my purse . . ." I acted out what I was saying, unzipping the Coach on my arm and reaching in. Conner took a step toward me. I pulled out a tampon. He stopped with a grimace. I put it back and then sucked in a loud breath. Both men startled as I yanked out my wallet. "Will you look at that! It was here all the time. I can't believe that! What a ninny I am. I swear, I have to clean out my purse more often so I can find things in here. I am so embarrassed. I am so, so sorry to have bothered you gentlemen."

Cedillo shook his head in disgust and went back to the plans. Conner frowned, suspicion obvious. I had to find a way to confuse him so he wouldn't think I was the one who'd heard him in the stairwell. Suddenly I remembered what my mother told me when I asked her where she hid our Christmas presents—always hide something in plain sight, because no one will look for it there.

"Are you sure there isn't anything else you'd like to talk to me about?"

I cocked my head. "Yes, there is."

Conner looked like a panther ready to pounce as I continued, "Your voice certainly sounds familiar. Have we met before?"

He blinked. I'd surprised him. Good. "Maybe," he said. "I might have seen you and an older man going into your room earlier this morning."

I forced a hearty laugh. "Oh yes, Uncle Felix is such a character. By the way, what was going on in the stairwell that you were so concerned about? Now that I know you are a policeman, the whole incident is much more exciting."

That got him. He opened and shut his mouth soundlessly. Cedillo looked up, curious. Finally, Conner found his voice, "Police business. None of your concern."

"Oh, I get it." I winked and giggled like an airhead. "I'll let you get back to work now."

I wiggled my fingers and scooted out the door. Conner was looking more bemused than suspicious now. I'd hid my guilt in plain sight. I crossed my fingers behind my back as the desk clerk lead me back down the hallway. I hoped that would be enough to keep Conner off my trail.

*T*hree cups of coffee hadn't helped. Neither had the supersized cinnamon roll with a gallon of glaze. I still couldn't come up with anything better than "I'm sorry," so I paid my tab and took the elevator to the twenty-fifth floor.

I paused in front of 2521. What if apologizing wasn't enough? I would be alone with a missing brother, a bad cop, no plan and—the worst—no cell phone.

Holding my breath, I knocked. I waited. I knocked again. Finally I heard the lock tumble. The door opened and Frank stood there, holding a steaming mug and dressed in faded Levi's and a white T-shirt. His feet were still bare. He wore the quintessential poker face as he opened the door wider and stepped back in an invitation to enter. "Look what buzzed in."

I shuffled my way in as he closed the door behind me. "But what you didn't tell me is what kind of 'Bee' you are. There are killer bees and bumble bees and honey bees. But I guess they all sting now and then, don't they?"

I knew I deserved it. "I'm sorry."

His dark eyes warmed. "Honey Bee, it is then."

I flopped onto the loveseat. "You were right."

"You were right too." Frank said, walking across the room to look out the window. "I am an ex-cop and I am a drunk."

I shook my head. "I'm sorry I said that."

Frank's gaze met mine. His eyes were shadowed with sadness. "I'm not. I needed to hear it and I haven't had anyone have the guts to tell me. And I promise you, I'm trying to stop." He walked to sit opposite me. "Okay, why don't you tell me what happened."

I went through it all. Frank's intensity built during the story. He leaned forward, with his forearms on his knees. I could see muscles bunching when he clasped his hands together as he listened. When I came to the end, he remained tense, but the corners of his mouth turned up. "That was pretty smart. I imagine he wouldn't expect anyone to be quite that brave. I'm sure it didn't eliminate you as his witness but it certainly threw enough uncertainty in to bump you off the top of the list."

His smile faded and he pinned me with a hard look. "Look, I don't like that you left out the part about the old man earlier. You've got to trust me. And it isn't a good idea to go into a stranger's hotel room, over the hill or not. There are a lot of freaks in Vegas."

"That's why I left that out earlier," I said. "It wasn't so much I didn't trust you, I just didn't think you'd approve."

"Ah, I see, you operate on the approval motivation. I'll remember that *Honey* Bee."

"Very funny," I muttered, squirming in the loveseat and looking again at those feet. Damn.

"Okay," he said, giving me a strange look. "We need to make a plan. First, let's go back to your room and take a look at things. Maybe you will notice something different. Maybe I'll see something you didn't. We need to hang a 'Do Not Disturb' sign out so the maids don't go in there. Then, we need to come back here and go to bed."

"What?" I looked up from those sexy toes. His eyes were dancing.

"You need some sleep. A family of five could pack for a month long trip in the bags under your eyes."

Oh well, so much for thinking he wanted me.

I suddenly did feel like I was eight hundred years old. Frank went into his bedroom and came out with some black lizard skin Luccheses on. Ooolala, almost better than naked feet.

"You're going to have to change clothes. What you have on right now is, um, rather distinctive."

I started to explain that I didn't usually dress like this, that I wasn't color-blind, fashion challenged or looking for a new career, but I was just too tired to go into it. Instead, I mumbled, "All my clothes are in my room."

"You'll have to wear something of mine." Frank paused to appraise me as neutrally as a tailor would. Still, his roving gaze had an effect; I felt parts warming and concluded I was decidedly hard up, being boyfriendless only three days. Pretty scary. Frank disappeared into his room and came out with an outfit that would make the critics on TLC's *How Do I Look?* cringe—red and orange plaid pajama pants, a purple Lakers T-shirt, a blue Dodgers baseball cap and some forest green house shoes.

"This work for you?"

I shook my head. "No, sorry, I'm not a Lakers' fan."

Frank glared. And I put up two fingers that said scout's honor. "Really, it's sacrilegious to be a Houstonian and wear anything that says 'Lakers'."

"Perfect, then Conner will never guess it was you."

Oops, I stepped right into that one. Sighing, I took the hideous outfit out of his arms and shuffled into the opposite bedroom. I tried not to look in the mirror as I changed clothes. The cap I wouldn't do. I didn't wear caps.

I walked out of the bedroom and Frank nodded brusquely in approval and motioned me over to him. He snatched the cap out of my hands, roughly wound my hair in a wad and stuffed it under the cap as he jammed it on my head, ignoring my protests. "This Conner cop might be having your room watched. Or he may be watching on the security cameras. I am being hypervigilant about this but we can't take any chances until we know a little more about what's going on."

We took the elevator down to the twentieth floor where Frank made me stand in a corner of the elevator lobby while he slapped duct tape on the security cameras. How he knew where the lenses were, I didn't know. We raced to my room and I let us in. Everything seemed the same, trashed, ugly and somehow even more scary. Frank put a finger to his lips when I tried to talk, then went through methodically and silently, taking a digital camera out of his pocket and recording the scene, extracting an evil looking knife out of his boot to scrape some of the dried blood off the wall and into a plastic evidence bag. He was the cop at work. I certainly didn't want to mess with him.

He ordered me to collect my clothes and he headed for the front door. I saw my reflection in the mirror above the Jacuzzi, which was all it took to properly motivate me. I threw all my scattered things in my Burberry and ran to keep up with him as we raced back down the hallway and into the elevator that just happened to be waiting. Frank was a guy like that, even the elevators worked for him. For me, they went on vacation.

I opened my mouth in the elevator, but he shook his head. I clammed back up. It wasn't until we were safely back in his room that Frank spoke. "Do you know how much money they spent on building this hotel and casino?"

I shook my head. "I see the opulence—the crystal sculptures, the precious stone floors—and I wonder but I can't even begin to imagine. It's mind boggling."

"Okay, if they spent that much on decoration, don't you think they went all out on the security? There is a lot of money at stake at the tables here every night. Don't you think they want to protect that?"

I nodded. Frank continued, "Then it would be feasible to assume that the elevators and all the rooms are bugged."

My eyes widened as I looked around. "Then why are we talking in here?" I whispered.

"I've swept the room already, and disconnected all the bugs."

"You found some?"

"Yes, but I expected to. This is a room they give to visiting dignitaries, to the highest of high rollers, to the owner."

"You'd think that it would be a penthouse."

"Everyone else thinks that too, that's why it's in the middle of the hotel instead of the top. Much more difficult to guess and to infiltrate. The doors around it are dummies."

"Which are you, the high roller or the dignitary?"

"Neither."

"Okay, then why are you in their suite?"

"Because the Lanai's owner owed me a favor."

"Who is the Lanai's owner?"

"He is a silent partner who is also invisible."

"So, why are you here?"

"Because I owed the owner a favor."

I sighed. His face was closed. "You aren't going to tell me any more than that, are you?"

"No."

"Frank, what is a security expert?"

"It can be a lot of things, but I would say it is someone whose goal is safety of people, of things, even of time."

I shook my head. Frank was speaking in riddles. I wasn't good at those in the best of times, and being awake for thirty-six hours definitely wasn't one of them. As I watched the sun rise over The Strip, I felt the last bit of energy drain out of me.

"I need to go check into another room," I said, walking to the front door where I'd left my suitcase.

"No you don't. It's too big a risk. You stay here tonight." Frank looked at my hesitant face in exasperation as he sat down at the desk in front of a laptop computer. "Look, this place is bigger than most houses. The bedrooms are on opposite sides of the floor. There's even a lock on the door. The best part is, you don't even have to change to go to bed."

I couldn't help giving that a weary smile. Nodding, I dragged my suitcase into the bedroom. I paused at the door. "Frank?"

He looked up from his typing.

"Thank you."

"I haven't done anything you should thank me for yet, Honey Bee." His crow's feet crinkled. "But I will before this is all said and done. I will."

Eight

♦ ♣ ♥ ♠

I heard Frank talking before I opened my eyes. I tried to roll over and winced, my muscles sore and loose like I'd been beaten by a giant meat tenderizer. Man, I had to get in better shape if this was what riding the elevator too many times did to me. Or maybe this was what forty felt like.

I buried my face under a pillow for a few minutes and tried not to think about that.

Frank's voice was all I heard from the living room so I presumed he was either talking to himself or on the phone. I sucked in a breath and got brave, sitting up and swinging my legs over the bed in one smooth motion. I was a scary sight in the mirror, hair a matted mass, mascara smeared under one eye, crease marks on the opposite cheek. I considered showering, putting a decent face on and dressing before I went out but since Frank wasn't interested in me that way, I didn't bother. I mean, the bags under the eyes comment hurt at the time, but I had to say it completely dispelled the sexual tension, which was a relief (and a lot less work, frankly). The weird thing he'd said about giving me something to thank him for might have been read as a double entendre for someone who didn't remember that comment. That someone wouldn't be me.

I wrapped my robe around me and padded out on bare feet to the living area. The sun was at about noon. Frank was in front of the laptop with his cell phone at his ear. I missed my cell phone. I smelled coffee and saw a steaming mug, and my mouth started to water.

"Hold on, let me get that information for you," Frank said into the phone. He handed it to me. "Tell them what Ben looks like, including any unique identifying marks."

What was this? Was he finally giving in and reporting Ben missing to the police? "My brother is, uh, forty years old, about six feet tall, weighs about a hundred and seventy pounds, has black hair and green eyes. He, uh, has a mole behind his left ear and a tattoo of a giraffe below his belly button." Don't ask, I issued in silent warning to Frank whose eyebrows had risen.

"Race?"

"No, I think he just works out at the gym and plays rugby."

Frank hid a smile behind his mug as he took a sip.

"No, ma'am. I mean: what is his ethnicity?" The woman asked on the other end of the line.

"Oh, sorry." My cheeks burned. "Caucasian."

I heard some papers rustling across the phone line. Finally, she spoke, "We have two John Does matching that general description that have come in in the last twenty-four hours. Of course, neither had a tattoo."

My heart clutched. I stared at Frank. He looked sorry and snatched the phone out of my hand. "What was that?" He nodded brusquely. "Okay. We may come down anyway. Thank you."

I stared at him. This was too much for me to process B.C.—before coffee. "Was I just talking to the county morgue?"

"Yes." Frank was in full cop mode, no gentleness, no "I'm sorry for waking you to talk about your brother's corpse." "I've called all the hospitals in the area too and so far the morgue is the only possibility."

"Why? Neither Doe had a tattoo."

"She said that neither has been autopsied, and the check-in dude is some minimum wager who misses a lot. They just got him to get hair color right. I think we need to take a look."

I fell into the couch, rolled into a fetal position and buried my head in my hands. I felt his hand touch my shoulder. "I'm sorry, Bee, but investigation is a process of elimination."

I groaned.

"Are you okay?"

"I NEED COFFEE," I said through my fingers.

"Ah, a woman after my own heart," Frank said, his hand leaving. I could hear him over in the bar area. "Black, cream or sugar?"

"All of the above. Any way it comes."

He chuckled, returning to waft the cup under my nose. Peeking through my fingers to make sure it wasn't a ruse, I sat up, took the proffered cup and had a sip. I already felt better. Of course, now I was hungry. "I just realized I haven't eaten in . . ." I paused, remembering the quesadilla we'd shared while we waited for our flight, ". . . eighteen hours. Wow. That's got to be some kind of record." I saw his indulgent grin. "I like my food."

I jumped when a knock sounded. I looked at Frank in alarm. He grinned wider as he walked to answer the door. "I like my food too."

"Room service," announced the young man in the café uniform of surfer shorts and a lei. The smell of bacon wafted in and I was afraid I would cry with joy.

As the waiter rolled the table in, Frank signed the ticket. He tipped him and dragged two chairs over. "You know, most women I know would be suffering from a case of the vapors, unable to eat for worry over their brother," Frank teased.

"Then you hang out with the wrong kind of women," I said as I shoved my napkin in my lap. "Besides, Ben's seen me hungry enough times to know I shouldn't be out in public when I'm in this state, much less trying to find him. You know, food is a number one priority for him too, which makes me wonder why he wasn't wanting to take me to one of Vegas' famous restaurants last night. He must have been really distracted."

Frank nodded as he uncovered eggs Florentine, croissants, a heaping platter of bacon, sliced mango and chunked pineapple. "The more little things like that you remember, you need to tell me. The better I know Ben, I can piece this thing together better."

We ate in famished silence for a while. Then, after I'd had seconds of everything, I pushed back my chair. "I'll shower and then we can go."

Frank nodded. I noticed for the first time he was still wearing what he'd had on at dawn when I collapsed. "You didn't go to sleep, did you?"

He shook his head but waited to answer until he pushed the table out into the hall. Once the door was closed, he spoke. "I wanted to do some research on Stan. On this tournament. On some other things."

From his cryptic tone I knew Frank wouldn't tell me more. I was beginning to read him pretty well. Still, I tried, "What things?"

He just smiled absently and returned to his laptop. I disappeared into my bedroom, showered quickly, thinking with a bit of regret about the cozy Jacuzzi in our room downstairs. Since Frank's suite was much nicer, I was betting he had a pretty awesome setup in his bathroom. Hmm.

I blow-dried my hair, but having no patience to wait for the wavy mop to be totally dry, tied it in a bun at the base of my neck. I brushed on some mascara (to hide any bags, you know) and some peach Dior lip gloss. The clothes, now that was a problem. I was again regretting my mass raping of my closet at home. I hung pieces up in a closet so big it seemed wasteful in a hotel and didn't get to anything

I was willing to wear to the morgue until I came to the end. I'd forgotten I'd thrown in a Christopher Deane sundress with a swingy calf-length skirt in stripes of deep burgundy, dark gray and light pink. Since I was a bit sensitive about all the call girl misunderstandings, I covered its strapless top with a white cotton long sleeve button down I left open, tying the tails around my waist. The Kate Spade strappy sandals with lover heels and silver braid and black pearl earrings I had at home matched the ensemble (a Houston boutique, Rouche Jovan, had given me the entire outfit as a thank you for a successful spring ad campaign), but I didn't pack those, of course. Reviewing my slim options, I decided on some oversized plain silver hoops and flat silver jeweled slip ons that would be better than heels when fleeing down stairwells from bad guys.

Frank looked up from his laptop when I opened my door. He shook his head. Damn, those bags were probably showing again.

"How has Conner seen your hair? It was up like this when I saw you at the bar."

"I pulled it down when he saw me with Felix to hide my face. I don't think he saw me in the stairwell, but I guess he could've caught a glimpse. I had it in a bun then."

"Then you need to wear it differently. Anything that might trigger a memory enough for him to suspect you is risking danger."

"I just wear it two ways—up or down."

"Come here," Frank beckoned, rising from his chair. I went to him and he pushed me down where he'd been. He ran his fingers through my hair, grazing my scalp. I have to say I'd never felt a man do anything so erotic in my life. I bit my tongue to keep from moaning.

"Am I hurting you?" he asked.

"Uh, no." I cleared my throat. "What are you doing?"

"French braiding your hair."

"You know how to French braid hair?"

"I have a daughter."

"You're married!" I spun the swivel chair around so fast

that I ended up way too close to him, eyeball to groin, my legs between his thighs. I'd noticed before he smelled of warm Dove soap. He still held my hair, and it started to burn where it was pulling at the roots. "Ow, now you are hurting me."

Frank released my hair, took a half step back and said, "I'm sorry but I don't think I asked you to try to choke yourself to death with your braid."

"Well?" I demanded.

He stepped forward again, and spun me back around. "No, I'm not married."

"Divorced?"

Frank didn't answer, just started combing his fingers through my hair again.

"Had a child out of wedlock?"

"No!" he said, offended. "Look, I don't talk about my kids a lot."

"Well, I'm not the one who brought it up."

Frank's fingers went motionless for a moment, then he chuckled quietly. "You're right. Huh, I wonder how that slipped out? I'm never so careless. I suppose I owe you a small explanation then."

I waited while he braided. Finally, he said, "Gretchen is eight and Henry is ten."

"Where are they?"

"In California."

Bingo, I thought.

Holding the end of the braid in one hand, he reached with the other into a pocket of his soft leather briefcase to extract a rubber band.

I finally asked, "In California, with their mother, maybe where you used to be a cop?"

He paused halfway through wrapping the rubber band around the end of the braid. "You just asked three questions in one breath."

"Don't feel obligated to answer in one," I generously offered.

"I don't think I even need a breath. I'm done talking for now."

"Why?"

"Because I just told you more about my life than I've told any woman in the last decade."

"That's because the women you hang with are too busy having 'vapors' to pay attention to what you have to say."

Frank spun me around, stepping back to review his handiwork. Nodding once, he strode to his bedroom. Guess that was the end of the kid conversation. I wasn't giving up there though. I'd get more out of him later.

After a few minutes, which I used to call for any messages from my room—there were none—he emerged wearing a black leather coat. Pretty sexy, but I wasn't letting on I thought so.

"Don't do that."

Uh-oh. He caught me staring. "Don't what?"

"Call from a landline for your room messages. Use my cell phone."

"Oh, I'm sorry."

"Someone could be tracing the checks on your room phone. That's a long shot but still a possibility. Because you weren't registered together, whoever tangled with your brother might not know about you, but they would know he was staying with a woman that wasn't his lover. And they of course will know your bra size."

"Cute," I muttered self-consciously.

"Let's go."

As we made our way through the casino to the parking garage, I watched for Conner or his whiny associate. I didn't see either, although I did see the casino security chief I'd met with Conner. He looked at me curiously, so, on impulse I wrapped my arm around Frank's waist and caressed the pockets of his Levi's. Cedillo shook his head in disgust. Frank nearly jumped out of his skin at my contact.

"What is going on?" he whispered in my ear. I could feel his muscles under the denim. Oops, I shivered.

"The head of security who was with Conner last night is over there." That's all I had to say, Frank was hip to the farce. He reached over and slid his hand along my waist and gave me a kiss on the ear. The security chief turned away.

Finally we turned the corner out of sight and I dropped my hand like Frank's rear was on fire. Truth was, I was the one heating up and that complication certainly wasn't going to do me any good. Well, it might do me some good, but it wouldn't do Ben any. Frank chuckled but stayed silent as we rode the elevator to level four of the parking garage. More potential ears in the wall, I assumed. This whole fiasco was going to make me paranoid.

"So I guess those two remember you, even in different clothes, different hair and with a different guy," Frank observed as we exited and walked across the asphalt, me slightly behind him as I had no idea which of the dozens of cars were his. "This makes it difficult to protect you. Unless you stay completely under wraps."

I shook my head. "I can't find Ben that way."

"No, but I could. Somehow, though, appearances notwithstanding, I don't think you'd make much of a hothouse flower."

I slid to a stop, which on flats, one can do in a cool, rather dramatic way. Maybe I should start wearing flats more often. "What does that mean? I think I've just been insulted."

Frank, wearing his great stone face, dug in his pocket for his keys. "Not at all, hothouse flowers are the most beautiful, but they also are high maintenance and sit around under cover, doing nothing.

"While you might be two of the three, I don't think you'd do well sitting around under cover, doing nothing."

Ignoring the two compliments he'd given me, I went straight for the negative. "You think I'm high maintenance?"

Frank pressed a button on his key ring and a Hummer beeped back. Security must be a good gig. Cool.

As if he'd read my mind, Frank opened my door for me

and said, "It's a rental, goes with the room, so don't get any ideas."

"What kind of ideas; like you might be independently wealthy, like you might be the most successful 'security' dude in America?"

"No," Frank retorted in a dry tone, as he slid into the driver's seat and started the engine. Hubba-hubba, those cylinders sounded good. "Ideas, like you might like to drive."

"Oh," I muttered, crossing my arms over my chest, completely deflated.

We made our way through the traffic on The Strip, and I realized after a while, Frank seemed to take a lot of unnecessary backstreets. Again eerily sensing my thoughts, he said, "I just want to make sure we aren't followed."

"How do you read my mind?" I asked, suddenly worried, considering where my mind had been at times today.

Frank smiled. "It's a good thing you don't play poker, because your face says it all."

"That's not what my brother claims."

"Aw, he was just trying to sell you into coming to Vegas, although why I can't imagine, since you don't seem like the Vegas type at all."

I wasn't sure if that was a criticism or compliment, so I didn't respond.

A half hour later, we parked outside the Clark County morgue. All institutions give me the heebie-jeebies and the county building was the worst. At the basement, we marched up to a woman shaped like a muffin. I'm not kidding, she was big on top and small and square on the bottom. Anyhow, she led us through to where the coroner's office was and made us wait. After about ten minutes, Frank excused himself. I don't know what he said, but immediately upon his return we were led into a cold room full of numbered drawers. A tall, exceedingly thin man with small, washed out blue eyes walked out of an adjacent room. "Hello, I'm Dr. Vassey."

We shook hands all around. Dr. Vassey said in a surpris-

ingly ultra deep baritone, "I'm sorry your brother is missing. I do hope we can't help you."

I cocked my head. Frank offered no help as he was
looking off with great concentration at the wall.

Dr. Vassey walked over to drawer number forty-six and
slid it open. The long mound on the flat metal panel was
covered with one of those paper sheets they make us wear
when we strip naked at the gynecologist. An arm slipped
out from under the cover. I automatically reached out to put
it back on the table. When my hand touched the cold, dead
flesh I gasped. I've never seen or felt death before. It was
startling and horrible like nothing else. Maybe because our
minds expect flesh to be warm, and it isn't when the heart
hasn't pumped in a while. Then skin seems cold enough to
have been refrigerated.

"Is the air conditioner on too high?" I asked with a gasp.

"First timer, huh?" Dr. Vassey winked at Frank, who
was looking a bit concerned at me.

"He's okay. A little frostbite won't hurt him," Dr. Vassey
cackled.

Nice. Dr. Vassey pulled the blue cloth back with a flour-
ish, and I started shaking my head immediately. Nausea
rose and I covered my mouth with my hand to stop it from
getting any ideas. Frank wrapped his arm around my
shoulders. I started crying.

"He looks like he was in so much pain," I sobbed, looking
at the lips pulled back from his teeth in a horror grimace.

"I'm so sorry, Bee," Frank murmured onto the top of my
head.

"Me, too. I wish I could tell his relatives," I murmured
back.

Frank pushed me back to look me in the face. "What do
you mean? Isn't this Ben?"

I sniffed. "No."

Frank drew his eyebrows together, pulled in a breath
and let it go. "Okay. Let's see the next one, Doc."

Dr. Vassey, looking like he was one of the few Americans who enjoys his job, reviewed his list and strode over

to drawer fourteen. Frank walked next to me and grabbed my arm to keep me from getting too close this time. This drawer was about as high as my forehead and at first, all I could see was the corpse's peaceful profile.

"Oh no!"

Frank again came to hold my shoulders. "Is it Ben?"

Dr. Vassey was looking hopeful. Maybe he got points toward the county Christmas party for every John Doe accounted for. Maybe he liked to see sisters of dead guys bust a gut. He offered a stool. "Here, Ms. Cooley, we want you to be sure."

I shook off Frank's arm and climbed the four steps. Vassey had put me way too close to the dead dude's face and I gasped again. Frank grabbed my calf. Hmm.

"Nope. It's not Ben," I said, retreating down the steps.

"You're sure?" Vassey asked, disappointed no doubt, that I hadn't thrown up my brunch.

"As sure as a twin sister could be."

As Frank thanked Dr. Vassey, a door at the other end of the room slammed open. Two men in scrubs marched in, pushing a gurney. The shorter of the two apologized, "Sorry, doc, but it's been a busy night. We gotta get rid of this one so's we can go pick up two more."

Vassey motioned them on. They stopped right next to me and the short one pulled out drawer number two. They grabbed the corpse by its feet and arms and slid it onto the slab. The covering on the body slid off and I gasped. It was getting to be an irritating habit, I realized, but this time I had good reason.

"Wait. I know this one!"

Nine

"**I**'m sorry, Ms. Cooley, but this man is slightly older than your brother," Dr. Vassey said patiently, obviously thinking I was addled from my close encounters with the unliving.

Tears were building in the corners of my eyes. I tried to blink them away as I looked into the face of the man who saved me. Had I doomed him to death?

"Who is it, Bee?" Frank asked quietly. I could feel his intense focus but couldn't look away from the face of the septaugenarian who would never return to Valentine to find a second love ever again.

"It's Fe—" I began, my voice breaking into hysterical sobs before I could finish his name.

I looked apologetically at Dr. Vassey, who appeared quite pleased with his consolation prize. The two delivery men scooted out, handing the coroner a sheaf of papers.

"How did he die?" Frank asked.

"Felix Quinn," Dr. Vassey read. "Age seventy-two. Found dead, fully clothed in his bed. Presence of prescription nitroglycerin in the bathroom. Apparent heart attack but some question as there were signs of small struggle in hotel room. Security officer took a report that the gentleman was in the company of a woman in the early morning hours before he was found dead."

My heart jumped to my throat. Were they trying to pin this on me? I looked at Frank and I could have been looking at an iguana. Iguanas don't blink, and Frank didn't appear to either, at least not in cop mode.

"Now, this couldn't be the guy you knew, honey," Frank said. "His name was Farouk, right?"

"Oh, right. Farouk."

"Too bad," Dr. Vassey said. "You probably couldn't have helped the detectives, although I doubt they will spend much time with this one. Old guy dead. Call girl. Likely history of heart problems. They'll probably write this one off without visiting the room."

I looked down and dried my tears, feeling more threatened. I felt so guilty. "P-poor guy."

"I got a dozen more like them if you want to cry on their heads too," Dr. Vassey offered like he was hosting an episode of Name that Slab.

"Thanks, Doc, but we got to go. Her brother is still missing."

"Ah right, that." Dr. Vassey said, taking Frank's proffered hand. "Good luck."

We nodded our thanks and got out of the sub-zero room as fast as we could. Frank shook his head when I opened my mouth to speak in the elevator and then in the lobby. I bit my tongue all the way to the Hummer.

"Do you think they killed Felix looking for me?"

"Not necessarily," Frank said, his dark eyes now almost black. "But it is a helluva coincidence."

"Poor Felix." I held my hand over my mouth to keep the sobs in. "If I killed him, I'll never forgive myself."

"Stop that kind of talk, Bee. It doesn't do the old guy any good, you are the one to worry about now," Frank said, negotiating around a bus slowing in front of us. "But this changes things. We have to operate on the assumption that

Conner is hunting down his witness, and that he is pretty much ruthless. That means you have to stay in hiding."

"Great idea," I agreed.

Frank swung his head around so fast to look at me that the Hummer swerved into the neighboring lane. We heard a couple of honks. "That doesn't sound like you. You must be really scared."

"Sure I'm scared, but the best place to hide is in plain sight," I reminded him. His mouth tightened but he didn't interrupt me at first, "So first I'll register for the tournament—"

"Too late, entries are closed," Frank put in.

"In Ben's place," I finished.

Frank shook his head. "They won't allow substitutions."

"I won't have to be one. He registered as B. Cooley. I am B. Cooley. I'll just adopt his address and phone."

"And you'll sure make it easy for Conner to find you."

"He'll know who I am and where I am, but what can he do about it? He is consulting on security for the tournament. Any player who is hurt or killed or disappears during the event will certainly reflect poorly on him, won't it? He would be sabotaging his cover career to protect the undercover, illegal one. Whoever the hell it might be."

Frank pulled the Hummer into the parking garage without answering, swinging it into a space and killed the engine. Only then did he turn to look at me. "You've certainly thought this through and argued it like a pro. Are you an attorney?"

"No, unemployed ad exec."

He gave me a wry grin. "Even better. You sold this one to me. Although I reserve the right to change my mind at the first sign that Conner is getting desperate enough to hurt you 'in plain sight'."

I didn't answer, but Frank must have taken it for an assent, because he nodded briskly and got out of the car. I almost reached for my door handle, but then I remembered what he'd done the last time we'd left the car, so I waited, fidgeting in my seat, unaccustomed as I was to this rather old-fashioned gallantry. He came around and opened my door. Once I was out, he touched my shoulder. "Bee, understand that I'm agreeing to it, but I don't like it. And there's one part of the plan you haven't covered: how are you going to learn Texas Hold 'Em by tomorrow night?"

I smiled. "You're going to teach me."

The poker tables at the Lanai were in the middle of the casino. The bouncers wouldn't let any nonplayer near enough to the tables to see the cards, but we could see the players, if not the action. My first lesson was to watch the body language from afar.

"Soak up the rhythm of the play," Frank advised. "There are little things you will see here and might not understand you're seeing them. But when you play, your mind will click them into place. You are a visual and tactile learner. That will be an easy way to teach you. Show you, then let you play the cards."

"How do you know what kind of learner I am?"

"By how you reacted at the morgue. Some people can't stand the sounds, some people can't stand the smell. You had trouble seeing and feeling. You're a tactile and visual learner. The best way to teach you to play will be to show you, only telling while you are seeing and then let you play."

We watched, although I didn't know what I was watching for. Frank pointed to a table with one flamboyantly dressed middle-aged woman and six men of varying ages from early twenties to senior citizen. Three of the men wore mirrored sunglasses. I noticed that every time it was the woman's turn to bet, one of the men would tap his fingers on the table, or would stare at her, or would blow out a big sigh. I didn't notice as much of the same behavior when a man was betting.

"Why are they trying to intimidate her?" I finally asked Frank.

He grinned. "You noticed that, huh? Good. You might

have a knack for this after all. You're very intuitive and observant. They are intimidating her, partly because of the
societal gender gap—and remember that is worse if you
are playing with people from certain parts of the world,
like Eastern Europe or Asia. Also, they are intimidating her
because it is part of the game and they are trying to intimidate each other as well. The reason why it is becoming
more and more obvious in her case is that she is letting
them. Watch how she is making her bets faster, how she is
starting to bounce her leg under the table—a nervous
habit. See how she is peeking at her cards repeatedly, even
though she's got to remember what she has by now. They
are down to The River."

"What's The River?"

"The last community card thrown out by the dealer. I'll
get more into semantics upstairs, for now just watch."

He fell silent and let the last round of bets take place.
We, of course, couldn't hear them but we could see her
push her cards into the center.

Frank shook his head. "They talked her into folding,
and I bet she had something in her pocket to stay in the
hand that long. Okay, first thing, look at your cards one
time, memorize them and never look at them again. Only
novices and nervous Nellies look at their cards over and
over. If you get distracted and can't remember just fold, because your repeated peeking will change the game so
much, encouraging all kinds of bluffs and semibluffs, that
you won't be able to play.

"The second thing she taught us is to never let them see
you sweat. That leg bounce, even though it was under the
table, was evident to any veteran poker player. Suck it up
and stay as still as you can. If you need an outlet, chew gum.

"Third, and most difficult to master, is don't let anyone
speed up your bet. Having said that, you don't want to take
so long that the dealer has to hurry you. That sends a whole
different message. You can do that if you are trying to send
a message to the table, but that's only after you've got a
better handle on the game. If you use it wrong, it just shows

you are a novice, again. So if you want to show you aren't intimidated, stretch your bet a little longer than normal, but not too long."

"Sounds complicated."

"Not if you let yourself 'feel' the rhythm of the game."

We watched as the woman shook her head at the dealer, stood and left the table. "Tapped too hard on the aquarium, guys," Frank said under his breath. As I looked around for the fish tank, Frank chuckled and leaned over to whisper to me. "Those guys made a mistake. They put too much pressure on her when they could have intimidated her just a little and let her stay in the game. A fish is what veteran poker players call a poor player. And, using a fish is much more profitable for the whole table than scaring it away. A fish will give you money, but only if it stays in the game."

As Frank pointed to another table to watch, I was overcome with an anxiety attack. There was so much to learn and so little time. I almost gave up, but then I remembered the blood on the wall, the trashed room and my only brother. Damn his hide, but I loved him. I guess the only thing I had to lose was a game. He might be somewhere fighting for his life.

I sucked in a fortifying breath and listened to Frank. "See the guy with all the chips at this table?"

"How did he get all those?" I asked. In the five minutes or so we'd been watching, he hadn't played a hand.

"I've had an eye on him since we came in. He's a stereotypical player known as a 'Rock.' He's a tight player who plays very few hands, only great ones that are virtually guaranteed to make him money. Now the catch here is, sometimes to be a good Rock, you have to play like any other player every now and then, or else when you place a bet, the rest of the table will say, 'Oh crap, he has pocket aces' and all fold before you can make any real money. I bet if we watched long enough, we would see him bluff a hand or two. Or perhaps play one hand like a Maniac just to confuse the table."

"A Maniac?" Sounded scary.

"A Maniac is a very loose player, does a lot of hyperaggressive raising and bluffing when all he has is muck in his hand. A lot of people who are gambling addicts are maniacs because they are just into risk and not the strategy. A Maniac will actually lose more than she wins. But someone who plays mostly like a Rock but acts like a Maniac at strategic times will be very dangerous, because she will be unpredictable."

Frank looked at me. My thoughts were written all over my face again. "Okay?" he asked uncertainly.

"Sure. It's clear as mud," I answered.

"Just keep watching. It will come together when we go upstairs and play."

I sighed. Playing with Frank sounded fun right about now. I caught a whiff of the testosterone heated Dove again and watched his hands tap out a rhythm on the bar. I swear the man was getting to be irresistible. I think I was definitely hard up. Perhaps they had a pill to dispel sexual attraction at the hotel gift shop. Frank obviously didn't need one.

For some reason, for the first time since I'd conned the poor guy into helping me, I considered that I might be taking him away from work. "You know, Frank, I shouldn't monopolize your time like this. If you have work to do, please don't let me stop you. Ben is my problem, not yours."

Frank met my gaze with a grateful one of his own, then broke it to look back at the poker games again. "I have the time. I'm kind of between cases."

Cases? "Are you a private investigator?"

"Not exactly."

"What *exactly* are you?"

Frank's gaze met mine again. "Your Texas Hold 'Em tutor."

"And expert in avoiding the question," I added. "Well, I appreciate your help. It really is none of my business what you do."

Hmm. But I really, really wanted to know. I absolutely hate mystery.

Apparently, Frank didn't mind being one, though, because that was the end of the conversation for him. He nudged me and pointed at the table we could see the most clearly. "See that?"

The dealer was shaking his head at a man who'd dropped his head nearly to his chest. The rest of the table was either glaring at him or shaking their heads. "What happened?" I asked.

"The guy splashed the pot."

"There are certainly a lot of sea and water analogies in Hold 'Em," I murmured.

Frank nodded. "When you bet, always push the chips you are betting in a stack in front of you. Never, ever throw them in the pot. That's what he did."

"Poor guy," I said. "He just didn't know any better."

"Maybe, or maybe he just wanted to get away with gypping the pot and hoped he wouldn't get caught."

"Huh," I said, "I guess this game is never what it seems."

"Yeah, it is in the end."

"How's that?"

"While the players might, the cards, they never lie."

Ten

While I was still pondering the possibility that black-jack players may lie a little too, Frank motioned me to follow him. "I think you've seen enough for now. We'll go play and then the next time you watch, you'll catch more."

We made our way back through the casino, past a live troupe of hula dancers in traditional muumuus being accompanied by a ukulele. I had to hand it to whomever researched the makings of a Hawaiian themed hotel. Everything I'd seen was pretty authentic, or as authentic as a natural paradise could be in Sin City. I'd know more than the average Jane, I suppose, my best friend having grown up on the Big Island of Hawaii. Shana is constantly harping on any stereotypical portrayals of her home state. I learned more firsthand when we'd visited her parents three years ago. Seeing all the cultures that made Hawaii unique portrayed so well in the Lanai suddenly made me want to move there. Hey, maybe I would, considering I had no career anymore. And maybe one less brother to worry about.

I choked back a sudden sob. Frank stopped, put his

hand on my elbow and scanned the area for what might
have set me off. "What's wrong?" he demanded. "Did you
see Conner?"

I shook my head and dashed away a tear from the corner of my eye. I broke free of his grip and marched on.
"No. I just thought about the future for a moment and the
recent past caught up with me and bit me on the butt."

Jogging to keep up with me, Frank chuckled. "You Tex-
ans sure have a way with words."

While we waited for the elevator, Frank asked, "So I'm
betting there's more than just your surprise trip to Vegas
and your brother's disappearance, isn't there?"

I sighed. What the hell. He already thought I was the
queen of eye bags, he might as well know I was a loser in
love too. "Good bet, gambler. This week I turned forty, lost
my fiancé and cratered my career in that order."

My tone must have been about dirge level, because
Frank looked at me carefully. "Your fiancé, did he die?"

"Ha! I wish. I found him banging his barely-legal ad-
ministrative assistant on his office desk. We'd dated for six
years."

"Damn, I'm sorry, Bee. Remember, all men aren't ass-
holes." Frank's crow's feet crinkled as he flashed a rueful
grin. "Of course, I don't know for a fact it's true, but I've
heard it said."

I couldn't resist smiling too as we entered the elevator.
Frank waited for the couple who rode up with us to vacate
on the tenth floor before he asked, "So what happened with
the ad career?"

"Well, it's my fault. Toby was the head of the agency,
you see. I tried to be professional and stick it out. I gave it
four hours after I threw his ring at his private parts, but I
couldn't stomach that image of the two of them springing
up in my mind every time I saw his door closed. Besides, I
couldn't bear the pats of sympathy on my shoulders as my
colleagues walked by. You'd think at forty I would've been
a little more mature."

Frank's eyes darkened. He didn't look sympathetic, he

looked angry. "You were betrayed. And you're proud. That is not something to apologize for."

I offered a small smile in thanks, and then voiced what had been popping up in my head over the past couple of hours.

"You know, it's funny, I love the ad business, and I've worked in it since I graduated from Southern Methodist eons ago. But maybe I'm ready for a change. Of course, that's the way I feel one minute, and feel totally adrift another."

"The rug's been pulled out from under you this week." Frank motioned me to go ahead of him through the open elevator doors on the twenty-fifth floor. "We'll find Ben and then you can figure out what you can do when you grow up. Maybe be a world class poker player."

I laughed out loud at that one. "Ha! If I survive one hand in this tournament it will be some kind of miracle."

Frank slid his keycard in and held the door open for me. "Let's get busy on creating the eighth wonder of the world, then."

I gasped when I walked into the suite. A poker table complete with chips and cards sat in the middle of the living room. "Where did that come from?"

"Can't have miracles without an angel or two in the wings."

I shook my head as we sat down. Frank poured two glasses of iced tea from the bar and brought them to the table. "I don't know if you noticed down there, but you can have a drink at the table but not *on* the table. Usually, the casino keeps a drink cart of some sort nearby."

I shook my head. "I think I'll be too nervous to drink anything."

"Wrong move. Definitely keep a drink there. Try to talk to the waitstaff before the tournament and see if you can order 'the same' or 'another' when the waitress comes by the table. That way, no one knows what you are drinking—you could be sucking down straight vodkas for all they know. You hope they assume that, anyway. It's just one hand in the mind game."

We sat down. "Remember, Frank," I said as I watched him slide the deck out of the box and start to shuffle. "You have to go back to kindergarten with me. I don't play cards, aside from Old Maid with my cousin's kids, and I have never gambled in my life. I don't even buy lottery tickets."

"Why not?" Frank asked curiously.

"It must be an offshoot of good ole Catholic guilt. Or perhaps it is the product of an upbringing where I was told life was fair. Intellectually, I know it isn't. Emotionally, I can't give up hope that one day it will be. So, I feel like if I won the lottery, then the natural consequence would be that something bad would happen to me."

Frank dealt as if there were nine players at the table. He didn't look at me, but his crow's feet were crinkling. "What if the something or somethings bad happened first? Maybe you should go buy three lottery tickets right now. You could win without any repercussions."

"Hmm," I murmured. "I never thought about it that way. But why three instead of four?" I held up fingers. "One, Ben is missing. Two, I lost my job. Three, Toby threw me over for a girl young enough to be my daughter." Ouch, that hurt saying it aloud.

"Which in the end is a good thing for you," Frank put in.

I shrugged. "I suppose. And, four, I turned forty."

"I didn't count the birthday as a bad thing because I consider turning forty an improvement for any woman." Frank said it lightly but with a shadow in his eyes that made me think the ex-wife might be younger than forty. A lot younger.

"Why do you say that? Because of the extra 'bags' we carry around?"

"You're never going to forget that are you?"

"Not likely."

"Guess I'll have to find a way to make up for it."

I tried not to read more into that statement, even though he'd hitched that teasing right eyebrow when he'd said it. "Teaching me how to sit in at the tournament long enough to give us time to find Ben would be the best way."

"Okay, first you need to get in the right mindset for Hold 'Em. I call it guarded cockiness. You've got to be realistic in this game, you have to be able to count the cards and weigh the calculated odds, but you also have to hope to win every hand. It's confidence that you want to exude so you can knock other players out of the game when the cards won't."

"Without tapping too hard on the aquarium, of course," I added in sudden inspiration.

Frank's eyes lit up. He pointed with the deck at me. "You're good. Keep it up."

For some reason his flattery embarrassed me. I squirmed and swept my hand around the empty seats. "You haven't introduced me to the rest of the table."

"Actually, I've never taught anyone to play poker quite this way before, but since you're smart and observant, this is a crash course and we have a lot at stake, I think it might work."

"Just don't tell me it's strip poker, because I've already had that offer in the last twenty-four hours."

Frank's head snapped up. "From who?"

"Oh, just some hard-up kid. He was kind of cute."

"Smart kid."

I squirmed in my chair again. I wasn't used to an appreciative man in my life. Ben was a good guy, but way too preoccupied with himself to dish out many compliments. Toby, well, I shouldn't even go there. Just suffice it to say that Toby would have considered even a mild compliment from a stranger as encroaching on his property. He probably would've tried to go search the poor guy out to threaten him. For a long time I'd thought his protectiveness was cute, lately though, I'd begun to realize that's all I was to Toby—one of his things.

I was nothing to Frank, so of course he wouldn't go offer to deck the kid. But his response was so unexpected that I was . . . uh . . .

"Let's get started," I said quickly, before I figured out exactly what I was feeling.

Frank, who'd been scribbling something on a casino notepad, shot me an odd look out of the corner of his eye. He finished what he'd been writing and shoved it my way. "There is the list of hands that can win, from best to worst. You can refer to it for an hour then I'm taking it away." Royal Flush, Straight Flush, four of a kind, full house, flush, straight, three of a kind, two pair, one pair and high card "kicker," which means you have the highest single card on the table.

"How long are we playing, anyway?" I asked in alarm as I read through the list again.

"Until I think you have a decent handle on it," he said.

Yikes. "That might not be until the start of the tournament."

"Oh, I'll let you have a little nap. I don't want you too tired for the tournament and besides, all you learn will be cemented into your brain by sleep," he assured me.

"Great, then you can really call me blockhead."

Chuckling, Frank waved at the table. "I've dealt extra hands so that you can see how the number of players changes the expected odds and the possible plays. You can expect to win a lot less with fewer players than with more. With more cards in play, full houses will win with regularity. With two players, called playing 'heads-up,' winning with a pair is common, and even a high card will claim the pot. You need to stop me and ask questions if I go too fast or use lingo you don't understand."

I looked at my hand rankings cheat sheet again. "What are the suit rankings? If two players both have identical royal flushes, which suit wins?"

"Good question. But the answer is, both flushes win and split the pot. In Hold 'Em all suits are equal, which should make it one less thing for you to worry about."

I nodded silently and reached toward my cards.

"Stop." Frank said. I froze. "First you need to set out your blind. Look for the dealer button. That's in front of me. The player to the left of the dealer is the small blind, or half the minimum bet, the one to the left of him is the big blind, or the minimum bet for the first round. In Hold 'Em, blinds are used to seed the pot instead of an ante, like in other types of poker and gambling games. We will play ten-twenty. So ten is the small blind; twenty is the big blind. To stay in the game, the rest of the players will have to come up with at least twenty."

"So what is the advantage of being the small blind? If I want to stay in the game, I'll have to ante up another ten anyway. Right?"

"Right, but you have the advantage of seeing what everyone else bets. If the five guys after you all raise, and all you have are a two of hearts and an eight of clubs, you should fold. If everybody just calls, and you have a pocket ace, Queen then you might go ahead and call."

"A pocket ace?"

"In your pocket means what's in your hand—the two cards you were dealt."

I nodded, shoved one white chip in front of me, then picked up the two cards dealt face down at my place. Frank put his hand on mine to shove the cards back on the table. His hands were warm and broad with nice long fingers. Hmm.

"Remember," he said, tapping his thumb on my wrist. "Never pick your cards up off the table. Never. Just raise the corners, shielding them from others. Look at them just long enough to commit them to memory and let them back down again. Picking them up not only risks flashing them to others, it also signals you as a novice or a fish. Don't look at them again."

He lifted his hand off mine. Internal sigh. I needed to get my focus back on the game. I made a mental promise to ignore the maleness of Frank from now on for Ben's sake. I flipped up the corners, keeping my hand between the table on my side and his side. Queen of clubs and a three of clubs.

"Better," Frank approved, glancing at his cards. Then reaching around the table and putting each player's chips out as a call. "We're going to assume that all these guys stayed in to see The Flop. It doesn't happen that often, but I want you to see how the cards play out if it does. So you need to call the big blind bet too for instruction's sake."

I put another white chip on top of my small blind. "What's The Flop? Sounds painful."

"Sometimes it is," Frank agreed, as he took one card off the top of the deck and laid it face down off to the side.

"What's that?"

"The burn card. Between each round of play, the dealer discards a card off the top of the deck on the off chance that anyone saw it during the deal or the last card up." He threw the next three cards down in the center of the table face down, then scooped them up and flopped them face up: a five of hearts, four of clubs and seven of clubs.

"That is a semipainful flop. Someone could be working on a club flush. Also a straight or a straight flush are possible. Someone with a low pocket pair could get lucky. It's kinda risky to rely on one of those to win you a pot with this many players, though."

"So, how many cards are you going to be flopping out there in all?"

"I'm sorry, I skipped that, didn't I? I guess I don't make a very good teacher."

"It probably depends on what you are teaching," I suggested.

He raised his right eyebrow. Oo-la-la. I didn't mean that. But . . .

Ben was missing. In less than thirty hours, I was playing in a tournament whose finals would be broadcast on national TV and I didn't even know how many cards made a hand.

Back to the cards, Bee.

"Only the first three community, or shared cards, are called the flop. There are two more community cards dealt, the fourth called The Turn or Fourth Street and the final called The River or Fifth Street. You can use any three of the five community cards with your two cards to create your hand, or use all five cards up. That's called 'playing the board'," Frank explained patiently. He seemed like he might be patient in everything. "Bee? Did you get that?"

I nodded so hard I felt like a bobble head. Someone needed to slap some sense into me. I should've brought Shana after all.

Frank sighed a standard I-don't-get-women sigh, burned a card and threw the next card out. The Turn, I told myself. King of hearts.

"Now that would be a scare card for anyone who was working on a straight or a flush, meaning the odds are pretty good that someone would have a pocket King and now a high pair and likely knock the others waiting for The River card out of the pot. But we'll see."

Frank had everybody check the bet, meaning everyone held tight. "If that ever happens in a hand, which is unlikely at the level you'll be playing, stay in. It doesn't cost you anything to see The River, and it's likely that no one has anything in his pocket better than what's in yours."

Frank burned a card and threw the next card face up. Three of diamonds.

I gasped.

Frank put his hand over my mouth. I smelled the musk-morphed Dove up close. I sniffed. Yum.

"Don't do that!"

"What? Don't breathe?"

"No, Bee, don't make any noise at all when the cards are thrown. None. Zero. Swallow your tongue."

Hmm. I bit my lower lip.

Frank was watching me sternly. Good thing he wasn't reading my mind now. "Better," he said. "Now usually, we'd have another round of betting. It could happen that some people fold now, as the cards have spoken and the only thing they might have left is a bluff. Some players might raise and possibly reraise the bet again before turning their cards."

"We'll just pretend that happened, and turn everyone's cards. Show me what you were all excited about."

I showed my three of clubs and Queen of clubs. Frank

shook his head. "You should have been crying. With that in your pocket after The Flop you had hopes of a straight flush, at least a flush after The Turn, and an outside chance for a Queen to make a high pair. Still, you might win. Let's see."

As he turned each hand over, he asked me what I would have done . . . fold, check, bet or raise. I was very slow at first, but by the fifth player's bet I was a little more comfortable. Three of a kind and a full house both beat me in the end, though.

Frank dealt another six hands like that, asking what I would've bet once we saw each player's cards. I felt a lot more comfortable. Then he dealt only four players in the game and I felt like I was learning it all over again. My pair of threes was much more likely to win at a four-hand table. I had an ace high kicker once and won.

"We can talk about probability and odds now. It's straight math. Hopefully, you were on the business side of the ad business."

I shook my head apologetically. "Creative end, VP of high concept ideas and copy."

"Well, don't sweat. If you graduated from junior high you can figure probabilities with a fifty-two-card deck, the cards you need as a fraction of the cards still out there."

"Oh geez, now not only do I have to 'read' other players' body language, project my own confidence or insecurity depending on my strategy, memorize my cards, but I also have to do mathematical probability in my head?"

Frank put down the stack of cards, rose and pulled my chair out. "I think you need a breather. Come here."

I followed him to the window, where he left me looking out over the sun setting on The Strip while he poured me a glass of Pinot Grigio. How he'd managed to get a bottle, not to mention remember that was what I drank last night, I'll never know. He handed it to me. I noticed he didn't pour himself one. Guess he was keeping his promise. So far.

I thanked him but mustered my willpower and waved

off the glass. "I think if I have to do algebra, I need a clear head."

He put the glass to my lips and I couldn't resist a sip. Ah, nirvana.

"Look," Frank said, leaning his rump against the windowsill. "All this strategy I'm teaching you are all just tools. You don't have to use all of them all the time. Furthermore, you *shouldn't* use all of them all the time. Sometimes you won't use any of them. Sometimes you just rely on your gut. It's the ability to be flexible, to be able to play a mathematical hand and then a pure instinct hand that will make you an exceptional player. A lot of players, mostly those who play a lot on the Internet, play purely by figuring the odds and probabilities. That might work well when you can't see your neighbor, but it won't work as well when you can. This is still, in the end, a game my granddad played without graduating from grade school. It is still a game of people at the mercy of the luck of the draw that have to rely on instinct more than fractions."

"You're just telling me that to make me feel more confident."

"I'm not. You can't tell me that if you were sitting next to a true Rock, who computed the odds of every hand and never played out until he had the nuts, that you wouldn't fold every time he even called?"

"I'd fold for sure."

"See, then he wouldn't win much on his guaranteed-to-win hand. It wouldn't have as much value as it would if he'd played out a couple of borderline hands before and lost a little, right?"

I shrugged. "I guess not."

"So the best advice I have for you for tomorrow is: Be unpredictable. No excuses, because in that you have an automatic advantage."

I cocked my head. "What do you mean, I have an automatic advantage?"

"You *are* a woman, aren't you?"

Eleven

♦ ♣ ♥ ♠

Just when I was beginning to think Frank was the almost perfect man, save the ex-wife mystery and secret security job and alcoholism (hey, I did say *almost*), he had to say something chauvinistic.

I stomped to the bar and jammed down my wineglass. The liquid splashed out onto my hand. "I hope you were joking," I said self-righteously.

He blinked. "Of course I wasn't joking. Play to your strengths. It's the trump card most women don't use in Hold 'Em. They try so hard to 'be like a man' in order to get respect at the table, and they end up losing. Play like a woman and win, is what I say."

He was serious. And he was looking seriously sexy—with his dark blond hair standing on end in places where he'd run his hand through it when I'd asked something stupid, his intense dark eyes boring into me, his fingers caressing the felt on the table. I realized it had been much safer for me to be mad at him.

I looked away and sighed. "Okay, Frank. I'll play like a woman if you tell me why you really quit playing poker."

"I was tired of mind games."

There was a lot between the lines yet nothing I could read. Maybe I should go back and talk to Summer or Winter or whatever season the bartender was. I bet she knew more than she was saying.

I reeled my thoughts back in. I could do that *after* I found Ben.

His cell phone rang, and I jumped. Unfazed, Frank flipped it open and answered. He passed the phone to me. "Who is that young man?" Mom asked. "Have you found a new boyfriend already? I knew it wouldn't take you long, dear, you are so attractive and smart, any man would be lucky to have you. What's his name?"

As always with Mom, she asked about five questions in one breath without waiting for an answer. It was convenient in this case because I didn't want to answer any of them. I chose the easiest. "Frank answered the phone, Mom."

"Frank, a good solid name. Is he Catholic?"

"Mom, why did you call?"

"I was just checking to see how things were going. I looked on the Internet and I got a lot of gambling tips I can pass along to you, for slots, for roulette, for craps."

"Thanks Mom, but I think I'm only going to be playing a little Texas Hold 'Em."

"Really? Poker? Good for you. Is Frank going to play with you?"

I grinned, unable to resist. "I don't think Frank wants to play with me."

He raised that rascally right eyebrow and nodded. Uh-oh. I had to look away. Mom was still talking in my ear, "Ben says that Hold 'Em is fun. But he says he might not be able to play in that tournament you told me you two went to Vegas to participate in."

Whoa. "Mom, I thought you didn't know we were coming. You talked to Ben about the tournament before we left?"

"No, dear, Ben called about a hour ago."

I jumped up off the couch. Frank made it to me in two

strides and put his ear close enough to hear Mom. I tried to calm the tension in my voice. "Mom, what did Ben say?"

"Oh, this and that. He said he couldn't talk long. He wanted to know if I'd talked to you. Silly, since you two are right there together. You aren't on the outs with each other, now are you?"

"No, Mom, we aren't. It's just Vegas is a big place." I hoped she couldn't hear my thundering heart. "We do our own thing mostly. We aren't attached at the hip, you know."

Mom giggled. "I guess you did spend enough time together in utero."

Oh geez. Frank stifled a snort. I tried one more time. "Mom, did Ben say anything else?"

"Well, he didn't tell me about this Frank. I'll have to get after him about that. A new beau in his only sister's life and he can't even mention him."

I sighed. Frank was chuckling silently. It wasn't helping at all. "Did he say where he was calling from, Mom?"

"No, Belinda, he didn't. I did ask him to turn down the TV, though, which he didn't do. It was so loud I could hardly hear what he said. And he sounded like he'd had a few drinks. In the middle of the day, and he was loopy."

Frank and I shared a look. Frank scribbled *caller ID* on the pad on the desk. I shook my head and wrote back, *no, Dad thinks it smacks of Big Brother*. Frank nodded, disappointed.

Mom was rattling on about Maggie in her garden club getting her gallstones out. Frank made a hurry up motion with his hand. "Okay, Mom, thanks for calling. Anything you want me to tell Ben for you?"

"Yes, dear, tell him I didn't appreciate the way he hung up on me like that without saying good-bye. It was rude."

Frank and I looked at each other again. "That doesn't sound like Ben."

"To tell the truth, I got the impression someone came into the room, probably a girl, and he didn't want her to know he was talking to his mommy. You know our Ben."

"Why did you think that, Mom? Did you hear anyone else?"

"Not really. It was hard to tell, the TV was on so loud. It was the Game Show Network, I could hear Bob Barker, which I thought was silly because Ben hates game shows. Probably the girl talked him into it."

Hmm. "Okay, Mom. If you talk to him again before I see him, give him Frank's room number. I'm not sure he has it."

"You're staying with Frank!" Uh-oh. Mistake. I groaned. "Isn't that moving a bit fast, Belinda? You can't have known each other more than a day. I'm worried about you. Of course, you aren't getting any younger and I do want grandchildren, so maybe moving fast isn't that bad an—"

My turn to hang up on Elva. "Bye Mom, love you."

I punched the button to disconnect as she kept talking. Frank was doubled over, shaking, and I was afraid he was having a heart attack. Finally he made a weird noise, straightened and turned to me with a straight face. But his crow's feet were still crinkled and his eyes were dancing. The jerk. He'd been laughing.

"Thanks."

"You did a good job under difficult circumstances. I think if you can handle that, the Hold 'Em tournament is nothing."

"I've had forty years of experience with Mom and barely forty minutes of poker."

"We learned two good things," Frank said, sobering completely as he returned to cop mode. I wish I could shift gears as cleanly as he could. Men had a special talent for compartmentalization, which I envied. And Frank was a real expert. "Ben is alive, or was an hour ago, likely being held hostage and drunk or, a less likely but better scenario, injured in a hospital on morphine. Then he would call your room and let you know. Check your messages again. Just in case."

I dialed. No messages.

"Okay, let's get something to eat, then I've got the best Hold 'Em book ever written for you to read while I do a little digging around about Stan and Conner."

I shook my head. "I think I should go watch some more Hold 'Em."

"Not without me you aren't."

I really hated being bossed around, especially when I knew he was right.

"I'll help you dig then."

Frank shook his head. "This digging is going to be too dirty."

I raised my eyebrows. "Who says I don't like getting dirty?"

I watched as his right eyebrow rose ever so slowly. "Okay, I'll feed you then we'll go get dirty."

The best thing I had to say about Las Vegas so far was that the food was sumptuous. Our room service brunch had been four star quality as was our dinner at the premier restaurant in the Luxor, whose food, décor and atmosphere put us so in Egypt that I wouldn't have been surprised to see a Cleopatra at the next table. I wasn't one given easily to fantasy but this town had a way of putting reality on hold.

After dessert of Zabadee el Mishmish, Frank picked up the tab, despite my attempt to grab it from our pharaoh server. "I owe you a thank you for all this time you are spending with my mess."

"There'll be time for that later," Frank promised.

Tease. Or maybe it was just wishful thinking. I'd never know because I couldn't get the guts to look at him.

We strolled back up The Strip. "Las Vegas was literally a natural oasis for thousands of years for the Indians—Ute and Paiute. Its artesian well made it a lush valley in the middle of the desert that wasn't discovered by modern man until about three hundred years ago. Some Mexican traders happened along and named it 'Las Vegas'."

"Which means fertile lowland in Spanish," I said, craning my neck to look up one of the towers of the Excalibur.

Frank nodded, impressed. "It's ironic that the first settlers were Mormon, who set up a way station for mail and supplies here. But true to Las Vegas' nature today, greed is what grew the town, when lead was discovered in the nearby hills. The Mormons eventually left and the mining struggled along. Finally the railroad came through, and it was Block 16 that put the stop on the map. There prostitution, gambling and liquor were legal. A defining moment in its history, I'd say. Otherwise the desert oasis might have faded into oblivion along with the mines. It's had its ups and downs but at each turn, Sin City has been the master of PR, taking advantage of every opportunity—Hoover Dam, the atomic bomb, Hollywood's fascination with the mob. It is the ultimate American success story. Opportunism at its most exaggerated."

His comment couldn't have been better timed, as we were passing the expansive, overdone fountains of the Bellagio. Of course, our hotel, which was next door, wasn't any less overwhelming, with its waterfalls, manufactured tropical mountains, smoking Kilauea volcano and sandy beaches that made up the front gardens leading to the hotel and casino.

"So where do we start?" I asked, turning down a bamboo walkway bordered with orange hibiscus, white plumeria and green ferns. They were so real looking, I decided they had to be fake.

Frank redirected me to follow him up The Strip. "We start by finding Abel. He's my contact with the local authorities. He might be able to tell us about Conner. Then, we'll look up Deidre. She'll tell us more about Stan."

"Who's Deidre?"

"One of Stan's ex-wives."

"She lives here?"

"He lives here."

"That seems weird, for some reason. Too obvious, maybe. A professional gambler living in Las Vegas."

Frank didn't comment, just kept walking up The Strip, past Barbary Coast, Flamingo and Harrah's. I had to double time it to keep up and was grateful I'd put on flat shoes again. "So how many ex-wives has Stan had, anyway?"

"I guess no one really knows for sure, but him. I know of three."

"Wow." I said, "That amazes me, considering I couldn't keep even one relationship together tight enough to get to the altar. I wonder how someone does more than I did three times."

"Some relationships shouldn't see the altar," Frank said, looking straight ahead.

He could have been talking about his marriage, my engagement or one of Elizabeth Taylor's many assignations, for that matter, but it was clear by his tone that whatever he meant wasn't up for discussion. I nodded vaguely and tried to keep up. I was huffing and puffing by now, having decided after this and last night's stairwell extravaganza that I was going to have to work out at the gym before I ever came to Vegas again. And they say you have to get in shape for a ski vacation. Ha.

We crossed the street and wound our way around such a labyrinth I was grateful I was with a Vegas veteran. We'd just passed one dark pathway when we heard a low voice. "Yo, Frank."

Frank slipped into the shadow, dragging me in with him. I couldn't see anything but the silhouette of a man on the pathway.

"How've you been?" Frank asked.

"I'm okay," the voice said. "But my sister, she had to have a hysterectomy."

"Here." Frank dipped his hand into the inside pocket of his leather jacket, pulled something out and handed it to the man. "Let me help your family."

"I will accept this for my sister."

"Thank you," Frank said.

"How have you been, Frank?"

"I've been fine. But my friend, here, hasn't. Her brother went missing while they were visiting on The Strip. We're not sure, but a county cop named Daniel Conner might have had something to do with his disappearance."

"Why do you think that?" Abel turned his attention on me, although I couldn't see his eyes, I could feel his focus.

When I hesitated, Frank nudged me. I had to trust Frank on this one. I sucked in a breath and told the story of the stairwell and the room behind the front desk. Then, because I figured I didn't have anything to lose, I mentioned the Iceberg Effusion. I was glad I couldn't see Frank's eye roll. I expected Abel to ignore it. Instead it was what he addressed first.

"We ought to have more women investigators. They always notice things we machos overlook. That, the Iceberg, is important, it is provable evidence—not enough to turn a case, but enough to build the strength of one—but more importantly, a link that Conner wouldn't think he's leaving."

Wow, who knew.

"Conner is dangerous; he is smart and careful and rich and political. He works for some big jefe and can pay off those in the right places on the force to keep him operating. I'm sure the jefe pays off plenty too. Conner is on the fast track to high up in the force. I hear he may run for Sheriff. I think he won't."

"If he's really smart he won't." Frank put in.

"True," Abel said. "Although that is his punto flaco. He is vain and likes attention."

"We'll remember that. Anything else?"

"I don't know who the jefe is, but aside from casinos who employ him to consult on security, he also consults security for Fresh Foods."

"What's Fresh Foods?"

"A giant produce supplier for the Southwest, based here in Nevada."

"What do you hear about it underground?"

"NAFTA made the company. It is a relatively recent success. They get their product from Mexico."

"I hear an 'and.' Is there something illegal going on?"

"And, that's all I can say *ahora*."

"Thanks, man," Frank said, reaching across the dark to shake Abel's hand.

"De nada." Abel said softly, *"Tienen cuidado, amigo. Su novia es muy hermosa."*

"Oh, *gracias*," I blurted in surprise, *"Pero, no soy su novia."*

Abel drifted away, tsking under his breath. *"Es una verdadera lastima."*

Frank put his hand on my elbow and directed me back onto the neon-lit sidewalk. We turned toward the south end of The Strip. "What was that all about at the end?"

"He said to be careful," I said quickly, trying to mask the blush that crept up my neck. "And, your girlfriend is pretty. I told him I wasn't your girlfriend. He said that was a crying shame. I thought you knew Spanish."

"If I knew Spanish that well I'd have talked to him in Spanish. It's safer. I just might have to keep you around as my translator."

I shot him a wry look out of the corner of my eye. "You have a lot of ESL candidates in your security business?"

"Good try," Frank snorted as he stepped forward to hail a cab zooming toward us down Las Vegas Boulevard. "I'm not biting."

"So how do you know Abel?" I asked. "If he's a good cop, how come you bribed him?"

"Good has a different degree of meaning here in Vegas. Plus, I gave the money to his family, not to him." He ignored my raised eyebrows as he continued. "And, the reason I know people here is a lot of people from L.A. end up in Vegas for some inexplicable reason."

"Next closest freak show," I said.

Frank looked at me sharply as a cab screeched to a stop next to the curb.

"Sorry," I said, not meaning it. "Guess I just insulted your hometown."

Muttering something about nosy women, he opened the door to the cab and pushed me in.

"Where are we going now?" I asked.

"The club on the corner of Ivy and Deen," Frank told the cabbie.

"What's it called?" the cabbie demanded.

Frank scrunched down in his seat an inch or two. "Fresh Fantasy," he muttered.

I rolled my eyes. He pretended to ignore me.

The cabbie floored the accelerator. We careened down the next street and off The Strip. After a few more sharp rights and a sharp left, I couldn't have found the place again, so I made a mental note not to lose Frank. We skidded to a stop in front of a men's club with lots of action out front. There were women of various ages in various stages of undress in various poses, trying to get work among the men loitering outside. Some were trying to get the job done right there against the building wall.

"Ack, I thought Vegas was being touted as the new family vacation spot," I said, unable to resist the temptation to look.

"That's only The Strip. The rest of Vegas is pretty much what Vegas has always been."

Again, I wondered if I weren't in an alternate universe as we walked past the hookers like they were hawking fresh flowers instead of themselves. Frank knocked once, then twice, paused, then three times more on a side door and it opened.

"Been here before?" I put in snidely. Why I'd feel out of sorts about that I don't know. It just seemed like Frank had more class than this, but I didn't know him. Not really.

Frank didn't answer and I sulked behind him as he talked in a low tone to a no-neck bouncer. We were shown down a dark hallway that smelled of sweat, sex and strawberries. He used the same knock on a door that had "Deidre" carved into the wood like someone got bored with their pocket knife. Steely Stan's ex. Wow, guess being married to him was pretty bad, if this was a better alternative.

The door finally opened and a drop dead gorgeous twentysomething redhead in a rainbow jeweled string bikini that barely covered her triple D nipples and a thong stepped back to let us enter. Frank's eyes never left her face. I found that incredibly hard to believe, since I couldn't help looking at her perfect body. Maybe he was gay.

Of course, maybe he hadn't gotten there yet. Her cat green eyes, plush lips and porcelain skin took a while to properly appreciate, I'm sure. "Long time no see," Deidre muttered, kissing Frank on the cheek and returning to the mirror where she picked up a bottle, sprinkled some oil on her thighs and began smoothing it on. Strawberry wafted through the room.

"Why strawberry?"

Was that me? I couldn't believe I asked that out loud. What was coming over me? The alternative universe was making me brave.

"Aw, my boss thinks it's the sexiest fruit. Chocolate covered strawberries and all that crap." Deidre had a voice like a chain saw. It made you cringe. Maybe God was fair after all.

"Why not chocolate then, a real aphrodisiac?" I offered.

"Oh, believe me, the asshole tried that, but most of the girls couldn't handle it. It's just too damned sweet and heavy. When it mixed with the sweat, it made us sick to our stomachs. At least strawberry keeps us feeling fresh."

Whoa. I guess every job has challenges one doesn't consider.

Frank looked from me to Deidre and back again. "You done with your oil consultation?"

We looked at each other and shrugged.

"I heard you and Stan broke up."

"Yeah, right before the bastard starts winning millions playing fricking poker. Wouldn't you know? Of course I did get to enjoy a little, since he started raking it in before he ever won his first tournament."

"What do you mean?"

Deidre sprinkled oil on her stomach and rubbed. "He was flashing around wads of hundreds like they were singles. It was way more money than he should've had then."

"Where was he working?"

"As a dealer at the Galaxy."

"Was he working a casino scam?" Frank asked, still not watching her hands as they moved around to her bare rump.

"I don't think there. He didn't really hang out with people who worked there. The people he started running with weren't low level scam artists. They were slick. Smart and scary. It was something bigger. Maybe he's out of it now, though, now that he's so rich and famous on his own."

"You're never too rich," I murmured one of Toby's mantras.

Deidre shrugged. "I was then. I didn't like those types and I told Stan. He told me that's where the money was coming from and if I didn't like it I could leave. It wasn't until the night I found his truck full of porn that I finally did."

It seemed somewhat ironic that a stripper would have qualms about porn.

"You think he was peddling skin flicks?" Frank asked.

"Worse than that," Deidre whispered, her hands stilling and her eyes full of real fear and anger. "Snuff films. From Mexico. They were killing these girls and they were begging for their lives in Spanish. I can still hear them in my nightmares."

Twelve

♦ ♣ ♥ ♠

"Mexico. That is the only common denominator we have found," Frank mused once we were back in his room at the Lanai.

"Maybe Conner worked for the Galaxy too, at one point. That would be another connection," I suggested, sitting down at the table and absently shuffling the cards.

Frank dialed a number, waited for an answer then pressed in a series of numbers before hanging up. Tension electrified his body as he paced from the window to the bar and back. "Maybe we are digging holes nowhere near where your brother is buried."

I gasped. He ran to the table and put his hands on my shoulders. "Cop lingo. I don't mean really dead and buried, Honey Bee. I mean where he's being kept in hiding. I'm sorry."

I wasn't used to a man saying he was sorry and meaning it. Ben said it and didn't mean it. Neither Toby nor any man I'd ever dated seriously had ever even said it, referring to himself anyway. Huh. I tried to voice what I was feeling. "I just am trying not to think too hard about Ben. I'm taking it one step at a time in trying to reach him. But every now and then I get an image of him in a room, with a blaring TV, trying to get me a message through Mom, without worrying her, and his kidnapper comes in, finds him on the phone and kills him."

Tears pricked at the corners of my eyes. I blinked them away. "But I can't think that way, can I? Or I'll have no motivation to go through with this damned tournament."

Frank's phone rang. He held one finger up to me to hold my thought. He answered and listened, then said, "Don't you guys have to log in your extra jobs? Can you check if Conner ever did consult work for the Galaxy casino? Sure, I've got all night."

It would be a break we'd been waiting for. I didn't realize I was holding my breath until I started to get light-headed. Finally Frank spoke again, and I blew out my breath. "He didn't. Thanks anyway. Listen, do you know anything about any snuff film industry south of the border?"

He stalked across the room as he listened. A minute later, he hung up. "The snuff industry is supposed to be an evil fantasy. Most law enforcement officers don't believe it exists. But Abel says he's only heard that the Texas Rangers suspect the unusually high number of girls disappearing in the desert on the other side of the border over the last couple of years might be proof that there is such a thing as a snuff film industry. One that's run by Americans and starring Mexicans."

I shook my head. "It's tragic but I don't see what it has to do with Ben or Texas Hold 'Em."

"Neither do I," Frank said, frowning like he'd been expecting something different. Very different.

"So what's our next step?"

Frank, obviously expecting company, went to the door. In drifted two women and six men who all shook Frank's hand and handed him a twenty dollar bill. I recognized one of the women as Spring from the bar at Caesars, she nodded to me. Frank introduced me. "Thanks for coming to give Bee here a crash course in Hold 'Em tournament play.

She knows the basics. Have a seat and don't treat her any differently than you would a stranger sitting next to you at a table on the floor downstairs. She's gotta learn the hard way. So go get after it."

Everyone introduced themselves. Frank let each pick a seat number out of one of his baseball caps. I got the empty chair next to Spring. "I see Frank is sober," she said as we peeked at our pocket cards. Ace/clubs, ten/diamonds.

"I've kept him so busy, he hasn't had time to drink," I said, not realizing how it sounded, and unable to clarify for fear of giving away more than I should about the investigation.

Spring winked. "Good for you. He's a good man and has just been looking for a good reason to quit."

I didn't know what to say to that. I doubted I was his good reason, just like I doubted he'd quit for good. But after The Flop of Jack/diamonds, four/spades and eight/diamonds, I didn't have time to doubt anything but my skill, or lack thereof, at Texas Hold 'Em.

*F*rank disappeared sometime in the first hour but I didn't even see or hear him leave. I found that playing with real people instead of empty chairs honed my focus and interest in the cards. Perhaps there was a bit of type A in this type B girl after all.

I won a hand or two, enough to still be in our single table tournament two hours later. Spring hung in there with me, along with another man who said he'd been playing poker on the Internet for ten years. He was predictable, though, one of those Rocks who'd just happened to get enough good cards to win little bits of money after scaring everyone at the table off the bet from the beginning. I think he'd only stayed in seven hands all night. He was one of those people who wouldn't be able to hang in with the blinds if he had a bad run of hands.

Spring played like the antifish I was supposed to emulate. She was good. Completely unpredictable, and she won some big pots because the men didn't believe she knew what she had.

I took mental notes and tried to keep up.

Finally the Rock used his last chips for a blind and lost the hand. "Time to play heads up," called the man who'd assumed the job as the dealer to speed things along for us.

I was dealt pocket aces, both black, and was the big blind, so I raised. Spring raised her eyebrows, but raised with me. I went all in on The Flop, which was ace/heart, ten/heart and Jack/heart. All I could see were the aces. Spring had a few more chips than I did, so she called. The Turn was a King/heart and The River was a blank—three/club.

Spring had a royal flush, beating my three of a kind handily. Frank walked in right then. "Taught her something, didn't you?"

Spring nodded as she collected her chips. Frank paid her a hundred and twenty dollars for first place, giving me sixty for second. I thanked everyone as they drifted out but Spring paused in the doorway. "Bee, you have an instinct for reading people. Don't forget that when the cards are screaming at you. I imagine you might have seen me catching the flush at The Turn, but it was too late. If you'd waited to go all in until then you might have chosen not to and we'd still be playing. Be patient. Another thing, I started to trust your reads of people and use them. Be careful that others don't do that at the tournament. When you can afford to, do something out of character: pretend a wrong read on a player and lose a hand if you catch someone at your table doing what I did."

I thanked her. Frank looked proud. "Where did you go?" I asked, looking at the clock and surprised to see it was already midnight. I thought I smelled whiskey, then remembered one of the men had been drinking Chivas Regal. I looked at the mess of glasses left at the bar and wondered if it were hard for Frank to be around it. I walked over and began cleaning up.

"Snooping," he answered finally.

"What did you find out?"

"That you are too damned sexy to leave alone for long."

Uh-oh. I peered at him. Frank was leaning against the back of the couch. His eyes were more bloodshot than they had been earlier, and he wore a goofy grin.

"Did you have a drink or two, Frank?" I asked carefully.

"One of the guys was getting suspicious when I was sitting at the bar with a Perrier and asking a lot of questions." He stood and leaned across the bar to tickle the end of my braid. Whoosh. It was him I smelled, not the players' empty glasses. "I ordered the drink to make it look right. He was a good source."

"I don't even want to know what he said right now. You just need to go to bed. I don't want you to sacrifice yourself just to find out some spare information for me."

"I'm not doing this for you." He argued. "I'm doing this for you."

Okay. I put my arm around his shoulders while he busied himself trying to undo my braid, and guided him to his bedroom. His biceps brushed my left breast. His fingers tangled in my hair. Oh dear. I tried to get some distance between us, which was hard because half of his two hundred pounds was leaning against me. Finally we reached the bed and I snuck out from under his arm as he leaned in for a kiss. He fell onto the mattress with a groan. Even as toxic as he smelled, it was tempting, but I refused to do something at least one of us would regret in the morning.

"Honey Bee?" He mumbled something indecipherable into the pillow. Good thing I didn't hear it.

"Good night, Frank." I said, as I shut the door.

I slept like the living dead. I guess I wasn't too afraid that Frank would sleepwalk his way to my room and fulfill whatever male fantasy he might have entertained last night because I'd left the door to my bedroom open, which let the morning light in on my face to wake me. Of course, it wasn't *that* early. I shielded my eyes from the sun and saw 9:43 on the clock.

Gripped with sudden panic that I had only nine hours until the tournament started, I leaped out of bed and hot-footed it to the bathroom. I showered in record time, slapped on some makeup and then tackled my daily fashion dilemma. I'd packed my Lucky jeans skirt, which I had been saving. I needed to be lucky today, so I pulled it on. I grabbed a sunflower colored halter top from Bebe and fit some gold hoops in my ears and the same shoes I wore yesterday. That would have to do. I was both shocked and amazed to realize I didn't much care if I matched or not today. Being vogue seemed to have dropped a few notches on my priority list.

"Ready for your big day?"

Frank sat in front of his laptop, tapping on the keys. He took one hand off the keyboard and pushed a coffee cup toward me then went back to typing. I wondered how long he'd slept. As I reached for my cup, I could see he'd shaved and he smelled like fresh Dove. He wore his requisite Levi's and a black T-shirt. He didn't meet my eyes. Guess we were going to ignore last night.

Men.

I sipped my coffee without answering. Frank kept typing. "Nervous?"

I made a noncommittal sound. "What are you doing?"

"Snooping."

Oh great. We were back there. I bet he didn't even remember what he'd heard last night. I had to try. "What have you found out since we last reconnoitered?"

Frank looked up with a raised right eyebrow. Wrong choice of words considering what he wanted to do last night, but I held his gaze coolly. He closed down his computer. "There's plenty of time to compare notes. Let's go to the Galaxy and see if any of the staff over there remembers when Stan was a working man."

The Galaxy was on the northern side of The Strip. We rode down the elevator in silence, a chasm between us. I wondered if it was because he was embarrassed about drinking or whether he'd found something out he didn't want to tell me. Either way, we had to clear the air—I just didn't know how to start. Frank was as intense in his stony silence as he was in his unflagging interrogations.

We stopped at the bakery for another coffee and croissant that we ate under one of the coconut palms outside the casino. I think Frank chose the table adjacent to the waterfall so its roar would preclude any opportunity for conversation.

I tried to let the incident go, as he most certainly preferred, but my resolve lasted only ninety seconds before I couldn't stand it any longer. I would never be able to live with myself if my dilemma was to blame for pushing Frank back to booze. I leaned forward and raised my voice over the cascading water. "Frank, I'm worried about what happened last night."

He looked up sharply, a hint of surprise showing in his eyes before he hid it. "Don't worry, it won't happen again."

Uh-oh. What wouldn't happen again? He wouldn't make a pass at me again or he wouldn't drink again? I didn't want to close the door on the attraction building between us, so I figured I should clarify. But, what if he meant the drinking and didn't remember making a pass at me? I tried some careful semantics. "I just don't want you to sacrifice yourself to help me."

"It wouldn't be any sacrifice to make love to you, Bee."

Oh dear. My face flushed as tingles spread through my torso, igniting small fires that I tried to put out by squirming in my seat. That only made them worse. His dark eyes danced as he sipped his coffee poker faced. He was better at this game than I was. I finally looked down at the bottom of my coffee cup and mumbled, "I didn't mean that."

"Good," he answered succinctly.

I didn't have the guts to pursue the conversation further, so we finished our croissants in silence.

We'd started back toward the Galaxy before Frank spoke again. "They ruled Felix Quinn's death a homicide."

I stopped in my tracks and nearly took out an octogenarian couple behind me. Frank caught the old gal before she careened into the street. The old man grabbed my right boob and righted himself with a grin so wide, I didn't feel guilty. I apologized, and they tottered off. "What killed him?" I stage whispered.

Frank's mouth was tight. His eyes smoldered. "Smothered to death. They are looking for the call girl he was last seen with who goes by the initial B."

That was what I got for being nice. Damn that note. And guess I should burn the eggplant suede. I swallowed hard and tried to stay cool. "How did you find out?"

"I called our buddy, Dr. Vassey, who was more than happy to tell me. And then I listened to the morning news."

"Are they saying who last saw him with a call girl?"

"Not exactly. They are saying an anonymous witness. I think it's a smoke bomb, designed to flush you out so Conner can find you." Frank paused. "How do they know your first initial? Is Conner guessing, or have they forced it out of Ben?"

"I, uh, left a note to Felix."

Groaning, Frank hit his head with the heel of his hand. "Why?"

"I felt sorry for the old guy. He was so lonely."

Frank just shook his head. "You've got to stop thinking about everyone else and worry about yourself."

"I'm not as worried about them knowing my name as what I look like. They could look at the security cameras and see me flying down the hallway and into his room," I mused, wondering how this would compromise my ability to nose around.

"And then they would see Conner coming out of the same stairwell and stopping at Felix's room. I think it's safe to say that he dispensed with said security tape, or reviewed it prior to reporting it 'anonymously,' to make sure no one could be identified with any accuracy. Still, this is a bold move on his part. He is getting desperate."

"Good, then maybe he'll get sloppy and give us a chance to catch up with whatever he is cooking up."

Frank stopped, turned and looked hard at me. For an instant, I expected him to accuse me of really being a call girl and killing Felix. After all, he'd never met Ben. I could have fabricated the whole disappearing brother scenario. I withstood his scrutiny. "You're tougher than you look," he said, finally.

"Maybe I'm tougher than I thought," I admitted.

He smiled then, crow's feet crinkling. I knew we were okay again, but I really did want to have a serious talk with him about the drinking sometime soon.

"Maybe we both are," Frank said softly.

Thirteen

♦ ♣ ♥ ♠

Walking into the Galaxy casino reminded me of the time I took my cousin's kids to Disney World. I remember there was some tortuous rollercoaster that sped through the pitch black tunnel, dodging falling asteroids, stars, aliens and manufactured planets at the speed of light. I remember telling my nine-year-old second cousin, as she screamed bloody murder, that I had paid for this, so it had to be fun. I'd ended up wearing someone's vomit and deciding that theme parks were designed for the masochistic. I had the same revelation as I dodged a twelve foot tall ape from *Planet of the Apes* who tried to hand me a coupon for an eatery.

As Frank and I wound our way through the slot machines, my hand brushed the hand of a player. I jumped—his skin was cold, gummy and creepy. I looked down to apologize anyway and gasped. It was a Martian from *Mars Attacks!* Fortunately, it was a wax figure and not the real thing.

An elderly man sitting at the opposite slot machine cackled with glee. "Watching folks do that is more fun than feeding this thing quarters. Cheaper too!"

I rolled my eyes. Everyone has their own brand of entertainment, I suppose. Frank put his hand in the small of my back to move me on. It wasn't the only time we passed wax figures. Chewbacca and R2-D2 were standing at a craps table. A dead ringer for Neil Armstrong, in full astronaut regalia, was sitting at the bar.

I'd wondered a couple of times during my trip to Las Vegas if I weren't in the Twilight Zone. Now I really was.

"This would not be my first choice of hotel or casino on The Strip," I told Frank.

He shrugged, pointing at a costumed group of tourists. "There's a lot of Trekkies out there. And, I think the alien craze is just behind the poker craze in popularity. Just think, playing poker next to an alien. Must be someone's dream come true." Sure enough, at one of the Hold 'Em tables was the alien that popped out of Sigourney Weaver's stomach. I'm not kidding.

"What's the plan?" I asked Frank. Time to focus.

"I'll go ask around at the poker tables. I'll assume that he dealt Hold 'Em but who knows." Frank looked around. "Go over to that Space Shuttle bar and chat up the waitresses you think serves the poker tables. Maybe we'll get lucky and one of them will have been here when Stan was dealing."

I nodded. Interesting that I was the one to go to the bar. He was trying. Or maybe he was just hungover.

I wandered over. At eleven in the morning, it was kind of early for a drink, but apparently I was one of few who thought so. Only one stool was available, and of course it was next to Neil. I tried to ignore him but he was looking right at me.

"Creepy, huh?" said a cocktail waitress wearing Spock ears and a Starship Enterprise uniform. I wasn't sure if she was referring to herself or the astronaut. I went for a vague. "Got that right."

"Yeah, I don't know how they make their eyes look so real. It's almost as if they follow you," she continued. "Someone told me it takes a whole month to put in their hair. It's real, you know. Even the hair on their arms and stuff."

Of course I couldn't resist looking at Neil. He was holding his helmet under his arm and seemed to be smiling at me. Hmm. His hair, shot with just a bit of gray at the temples, did look pretty real.

"Cool," I said, again trying not to offend her since she seemed so proud. "But I guess you'll get so used to it once you work here for a while that you don't notice him anymore."

"Oh, no, I won't," she grinned haplessly. "I've already worked here five years and I'm not used to him yet."

I laughed more at my luck than her comment. Bingo. She'd worked here with Stan.

"Can I get you something to drink, darlin'?" She asked. I shook my head and she did too. "Nah, you don't look like an early morning drunk. I guess you're just biding your time while your baby plays Hold 'Em, huh?"

"How'd you guess?"

"Not hard. *Everybody* plays Hold 'Em now. It's like a national addiction. I wouldn't be surprised if they take out half the blackjack, craps and roulette tables and put in more poker tables by next year."

"It sure is all over the TV anyway, especially that Steely Stan guy. Has he got charisma or what?" I winked at her.

She leaned in with her secret. "You know he used to work here?"

I gasped and held my hand to my chest. "Here? In this casino?"

She nodded. "I waited on the table where he was the dealer."

"No kidding?" I leaned in too. "What was he like? I have such a huge crush on him."

"Everybody does, darlin', at least anyone with estrogen." She giggled. "He is even sexier in person."

Gag. If you like raving chauvinistic egomaniacs with spastic fashion sense, he's a prize for sure.

"It just seemed like destiny when he got that sponsorship

and could quit and play Hold 'Em professionally. Nobody deserved it more."

I nodded. Uh-huh. "Who sponsored him?"

She looked at me a little suspiciously. Wrong question. Guess I should have asked how big his schlong was instead. "Some vegetable company," she muttered, desultory.

I shrugged like I couldn't care less and held my poker face. Good practice for tonight. I guess it worked, because she went back to extolling Stan's virtues, which revolved around how many times he pinched her ass in a night.

Vegetable company would likely translate into produce supplier. Likely Fresh Foods. But what was Fresh Foods doing sponsoring a poker player? What does a televised royal flush do for spinach sales?

Even though it didn't make sense yet, this was a big break, a connection that might mean something someday.

I wanted to jump up and down and wave my arms at Frank, but instead I had to keep the dingy waitress in conversation for another ten minutes until someone at a table did just that to get her attention for a drink. She trotted away with a promise to return with more about Stan.

Since I figured I'd already gotten all she knew of value, I made a break for it. Frank was playing at a table in the dead center of the room, so I loitered as close as I could get and tried to catch his eye. He looked everywhere but at me.

He was either learning a lot of good stuff or he was winning. Either way it looked like I would be cooling my heels for a while. I visited the gift shop, but since a Martian toe ring didn't particularly appeal to me, I wandered on. What did people who didn't gamble do in Vegas, anyway? I guess one could go to see Cirque du Soleil or Carey in the Women of Wall Street, but if I just went from show to show I think my butt would get sore from overuse. Of course, come to think of it, poker playing involved a lot of sitting, but maybe the adrenaline rush of winning would provide a brief aerobic interlude. I suppose there was shopping here, but unless you came from the Ozarks, I can't imagine they would have shops here that you couldn't find within a couple hundred miles of your own hometown. I took the elevator up to the fifteenth floor for the heck of it and tried to catch a peek in a room to see if the beds were in the shape of flying saucers.

When a security goon ambled by and gave me a long look, I decided I'd worn out that form of entertainment. I hightailed it to the elevator lobby, hoping the news didn't have a full description of the call girl killer. I didn't know how ballsy Daniel Conner would be.

I jumped in the elevator before the doors even fully opened and scurried to the far corner, nearly impaling myself on the cart that the poor bellboy tried to pull out of the way. I murmured an apology. We traveled in embarrassed silence until the doors slid open on the second floor. No one got on, and I couldn't see anyone waiting from where I stood, but I could hear a man's urgent whisper. "I told you, I just need a little more time."

The bellhop, who could likely see the whisperer, drew his eyebrows together and shrugged. The elevator doors shut just as the man whined, "Pleeese."

Those long ee's certainly sounded familiar. I looked at the bellhop's name tag. "Ahmad? Did you happen to see that guy?"

He nodded.

"What did he look like?"

Ahmad drew his eyebrows together again.

"Was he a white guy, short, fat with a balding head, wearing a bad suit?"

Ahmad nodded.

"Was he talking to another guy, tall, handsome, black hair, blue eyes, good suit?"

Ahmad narrowed his eyes. "Why?"

Uh-huh. He spoke English as well as understood it. I might have asked a little too intensely—it might have been slightly unnerving. He'd probably be reporting me to the security goons as soon as we hit the lobby. I had to go for the Oscar. I jammed my hands on my hips. "Come on, Ahmad, tell me, please. The fat guy's my husband, see, and I know he's having an affair with that man." I paused to sob. Ahmad looked sick. I grabbed his arm just as the elevator came to rest at the first floor. "Please, tell me the truth and I'll let you go."

Shaking his head madly, Ahmad was trying to flop his arm loose of my grip and roll the cart out at the same time. I jumped on the cart and let him roll me out of the elevator. He looked panicked. "I no see other man. Fat man talked to someone behind corner."

Damn. It might have been Conner, it might not. It had definitely been his fat friend, Pete, though. The more I heard that whine in my mind, the more I was sure of it. I jumped off the bell cart and spun around to press the up button. I can't say I didn't consider going to find Frank and tell him, but I didn't do it long. I knew if I had any chance of seeing who Pudgy Pete was talking to, it had to be now.

The elevator slid open and I had to resist the temptation to push a trio of elderly women out of the way. They tottered into the elevator and took so long, the doors started to close. I threw my arm out, and when that didn't stop the doors, I jammed my torso through. The doors bounced off my right boob. I jumped in before they snapped shut.

"Oh, dear, are you alright?" One of the nice old gals asked. I felt bad for breathing down the grannies' necks when they were so considerate of me.

"You've got to be careful," another added. "You'd better take care of a chest like that, right, girls?"

Huh? I looked down at that part of my anatomy, and noticed the whole group had already beaten me to it. Four gray heads nodded in agreement. I was speechless.

"Are you a dancer, dear?" the third granny asked.

"Uh, no, ma'am."

"What do you do for a living?"

"Nothing right now."

They all tsked. "You might look into dancing then. We were dancers here in Vegas in the boom in the fifties. Vegas was living high off the craze for the atomic bomb. Remember those wigs that were shaped like mushroom clouds, we wore with our bikinis, girls?"

They all nodded and started reminiscing. I was still dumbstruck. Finally, the one pushing the "door open" button remembered I was standing there. She took her arthritic finger with its three inch crimson nails off the button. "What floor did you want, dear?" I pressed the second floor button as we started to move.

"We're here for a reunion and just went to see that new show 'Women of Wall Street.' What a blast. Talk about a surprise ending!"

I forced a smile. I'd changed my mind about Vegas.

The Twilight Zone had nothing on this place. Nothing at all.

The second floor looked deserted when I walked off the elevator. The black iridescent carpet decorated with sparkles emulating stars started to waver as I looked left and right. Was it a special effect? No. I realized I felt light-headed and let out the breath I didn't know I'd been holding. I was going to have to stop that if I wanted to stay conscious.

I didn't hear anything except my blood roaring in my ears. That was when I understood that it had been stupid to come up here alone. I tiptoed unsteadily to the right where a narrow hallway lead to what I assumed were conference rooms. I peeked around the corner, then I backtracked and went left where the ceiling opened up to a large area that could've been lifted from the set of *Close Encounters of the Third Kind*. I peered at a space pod hanging from the ceiling and wondered if it was really moving or if I was holding my breath again.

A hand snaked around my waist from behind. I screamed. Another hand clamped down on my mouth. I bit the hand and snapped my heel up to kick at the body.

"Oof." The hands freed me. I spun around to see Frank sinking to the floor with his hands on his groin.

I fell to my knees and touched Frank on the shoulders.

His eyes were closed. I slid my hand to his face, and he moaned again.

"I am so sorry. I didn't know it was you!"

"I was stupid. You did what you should," Frank grunted, opening his eyes. "I'm just glad you didn't have those damned high-heeled boots on."

"I hope I didn't permanently damage you," I said.

Frank looked down at his crotch and gingerly turned his left hand over. My incisors had left a bloody brand on the inside of his middle finger. Ouch. The bigger ouch was still being cradled by his right hand.

"I'm not so worried about you being alone anymore. You are your own weapon. Killer Bee after all." Frank smiled ruefully. "I saw you waiting for the elevator downstairs, but didn't get there before the doors closed. Then I saw you'd stopped at the second floor. I came up the stairwell. I guess I surprised you."

"Yeah, I thought you were Pudgy Pete."

"Thanks. I've been called a lot of things, but those descriptions are new."

"No, Frank, I mean the guy Conner threatened in the stairwell at the Lanai."

"What made you think he would be here?"

"I thought I heard him when the elevator stopped on this floor. The bellboy described him, so I came looking for him."

"And what were you going to do if you found him?" Frank asked, his eyes darkening to black. I gave him a weighty look at his crotch. He narrowed his eyes. "This isn't a joke anymore, Bee. If you thought you heard him, you should've come to me first."

"Don't start talking to me like I'm a stupid child," I warned.

"Why not? You're acting like one."

I stomped off, angrier at him than I ever remember being. I wanted to pull my hair out and scream. I wanted to give him another swift kick, on purpose this time. I nearly ran across the star-studded carpet, around the corner and down a hallway full of small convention rooms. I heard him behind me, but I'd had the advantage of having already been on my feet and not having throbbing private parts.

I skidded around another corner, wishing my decorative shoes had more grip. This investigating business was going to force me to resort to practical footwear if I expected to outrun bad guys and my own bossy accomplices. I saw the stairwell door marked "Employees Only, Service Access," and despite vowing never to step foot in one again, I flung myself through the door and down the stairwell. I heard the door slap shut and slam open behind me, and I knew I only had about ten seconds on Frank. I jumped the stairs two at a time, promising myself once I'd reach the open air, I could hail a cab and disappear. That would show him.

At the ground, I yanked the door and raced through. Uh-oh. Instead of putting me out on the street, the stairs dumped me at the loading dock. Unless I hailed a passing laundry truck I was going to have to hoof it a bit longer to stay free of Frank. I was beginning to wheeze. I paused behind the dumpster, leaned my hands on my knees to catch my breath. I felt something brush my hair and looked up. I was staring at a hand protruding from the trash heap.

Now, most girls would have screamed like frightened ninnies, but not me. I'd seen enough of those stupid wax figures inside to know one when I saw one. I touched a finger. It felt like Neil Armstrong's, except a little chubbier. William Shatner-like maybe. So, their wax Captain Kirk was kaput—maybe his real hair had started to fall out or something.

I heard footfalls. It was too late to run, and I was tired anyway. Frank came around the corner of the dumpster, stopped in his tracks and pointed, open mouthed.

"Oh, Frank, chill out. It's just a wax figure." I reached up and grabbed the hand and pulled.

Out came a disembodied arm, bloody and very human.

Fourteen

♦ ♣ ♥ ♠

"**B**ee, we have to get going. Bee, I'll carry you if I have to, but it won't be pretty. Your skirt will be up over your head. Everyone will see your panties. I hope you wore your best today."

I was wearing my ugliest boy cut undies that made my butt look big. "No, don't carry me," I heard myself say. I felt like I was coming out of a fog. I blinked at Frank and tried to remember where I was. "What happened?"

Frank took my face in his hands. "Are you okay now?"

I looked down. I was standing. On dirty concrete. I noticed I'd been sloppy painting my toenails because I had red spots on the skin on my toes. I looked at Frank. "Did I pass out or something?"

"No, you just went into shock. You were mentally out of it. It was fascinating, actually, I don't know that many women who can do that and stay standing."

"Why did I go into shock?"

"You found a dead body."

It was coming back to me, along with the croissant for

breakfast. I swallowed carefully before correcting him, "I didn't find a body, just found an arm."

"The rest of Pudgy Pete is in here," Frank tapped the dumpster with his knuckles. "In pieces."

"How do you know?"

"I took a peek. I wanted to make sure the live one with the carving knife wasn't in there with him."

"I guess he's not or you wouldn't have given me an option about flashing my panties, huh?"

Frank shot me a wry grin. "I think you're good to travel now, so let's book it."

I put a quelling hand on his arm. "Wait, shouldn't we call the police?"

"You are such a good citizen. Please resist the urge here. I will tell you what I've learned about Conner later, but suffice it to say he's badder than we think and his bosses think he's better than he is. Deadly combination, as Pudgy here found out."

"But we don't have a choice but to report it somehow. The security cameras will see us."

"I might be wrong. Pudgy Pete could have coincidentally taken the wrong exit out of the casino and met a random killer who favors dismemberment. But I bet I'm right and Conner or his cronies had something to do with this, and if they did, the security cameras have been disabled so they couldn't record the crime."

"Oh." I felt stupid.

"So, let's just go through the parking garage around to the right and out to the street. Act normal."

"It's hard to act normal with blood on my toes," I grumbled as we ambled, a little too slowly for my taste, through the parking garage. I felt edgy—I saw Conner every time I saw a shadow. I grabbed Frank's arm at the first three people we encountered. We were just alongside a row of cars, about to reach the alleyway between the hotel and the street when a man came out one of the side doors to the casino and headed down the alleyway. He wore a good Armani suit like Conner wore; he had close-cut dark hair like Conner's; he was about Conner's height. Paranoia? Nope. He turned to look our way and in a flash, I pulled Frank to me, smashing his lips into mine.

"Conner," I mumbled against his mouth.

"Again?" That right eyebrow arched. His eyes twinkled. Crow's feet crinkled.

"It's the real thing," I whispered furiously.

"I'll say," Frank murmured as he kissed me and kissed me and kissed me so long and so thoroughly forty Daniel Conners could've walked by and I wouldn't have seen any of them.

I finally pulled back for some air and Frank said, "So that was Daniel Conner. Doesn't look like his ID badge photo."

That's all he could say? "So while you were kissing me senseless and putting your hands . . ." I paused to shove said hands off where they still rested on my hips and batted them back into his territory, ". . . where they have no business being, you were really just watching Conner walk by and comparing him to his cop picture?"

Frank's eyebrows drew together, confusion obvious. "A guy can't do two things at once?"

Men! I stomped back toward The Strip. Frank pulled me to slow me down, but I shook loose. He leaned in. "Not so fast. Watch where Conner goes and let him get farther in front of us."

We could see his black hair gleaming almost blue in the sun. He got a lot of second glances from women; he deserved them. He was good looking, but also projected that irresistible arrogance typical of people in power positions. Toby had the same thing in spades. The similarity suddenly bothered me. "I want to wring his neck and make him tell me what he's done with Ben."

"Cool it, Killer Bee. You'll get your chance," Frank promised as we inched along.

"I just hope it isn't too late," I murmured.

* * *

Once Conner had disappeared back into the Lanai, and we were back in Frank's room, Frank made me call Mom (Gladys in the crochet club had to have a colonoscopy, Dad left his chainsaw out in the rain, she hadn't heard from Ben again, how was my new beau and when was the wedding?). I wanted to go downstairs and get some dirt on Stan, but Frank suggested I not go out until I would be protected by the tournament.

I despised being told what to do, but I could see his logic. Besides, I had to wash the blood off my feet and get the smell of his musk morphed Dove out of my nose anyway.

I walked out of my room, having decided on an ultra flashy gold lamé halter top, cubic zirconia chandelier earrings that went to my shoulders, black satin slacks and jeweled four-inch Manolos for my debut at the poker table. I'd put my chestnut curls half up and half down. It took forever, but was worth the suffering. Frank whistled appreciatively from his seat at the desk. "You look great, but maybe you'd better save that for the championship night."

"I thought I'd make a splash now since I might not make it to the final round, or even beyond tonight." I offered. "Besides, I thought the more people notice me tonight, the less likely Conner is to do anything to compromise me."

"Smart girl." Frank bowed his head in approval. "That hadn't occurred to me."

"You're not caught in his crosshairs either. That tends to sharpen your senses."

Frank nodded grimly.

"So, are you going to tell me why Conner is even worse than we thought?"

"He's a busy guy, donates to the right politicians, does favors for the right bosses. He actually hasn't been on the Clark County force all that long, but has risen in the ranks quickly due to his high case-closure rate. He was an investigator with the Border Patrol but left that job right before a still-ongoing internal investigation into smuggling within the ranks was begun."

"We already knew he was bad, now he's worse." I swallowed and tried not to think of Ben in this guy's clutches. He didn't have much of a chance. Pete certainly didn't. Don't think that way, I told myself. "I wonder who they were trying to warn by cutting Pete up in little pieces?"

Frank met my gaze with surprise. "Most law abiding people wouldn't have realized that was a warning."

"It's kind of obvious." It takes more time to hack him up than just stab him and fling him in the big box. "Maybe they took photos and showed them to the suspicious driver?"

Frank raised both eyebrows and nodded. "Keep using that criminal mind of yours and we might have this thing solved by daybreak."

I nodded toward his computer. "Any luck finding proof of a Fresh Foods sponsorship?"

"Yes, I've found a handful of media references that make the connection. But if they are sponsoring him to get free plugs, they aren't making the most of it. Out of a hundred stories I only came up with four references."

"Maybe Fresh Foods has a poor PR department."

"Maybe they didn't fork over the money to get media attention."

"Why then?" I asked.

"Two possibilities I can think of," Frank said. "One, Stan knows something he shouldn't and they are paying him to keep quiet about it."

"It doesn't make sense, the publicity would be opposite of what they would be looking for. Plus, he's independently wealthy now with all his poker winnings, so he has less incentive to keep quiet, other than he might be afraid for his life."

"Right," Frank agreed. "Holes in that plan. It's still workable but not perfect. The other possibility is Stan is helping the company *do* something it shouldn't, and that is why they 'sponsor' him. Maybe they've taken a page out of your mother's book and are 'hiding in plain sight.'"

Hmm. "But what would a produce company be doing illegal?"

"Smuggling: drugs, people, or if we believe Deidre, porn."

"But what do plums have to do with poker, have to do with some dirty cop who kills, have to do with a spacey casino, have to do with an arrogant Hold 'Em champion, have to do with a dead pudgy guy who couldn't 'handle the operation,' have to do with my brother?"

Frank shrugged. "Is your brother into drugs?"

I shook my head, offended. "No! He's a pharmaceutical salesman."

Frank cocked his head as I realized the irony of my statement. He continued, "Is he in any financial straits which would force him do something he might not ordinarily do?"

"Uh . . ." I paused. "He owes some money for a failed business deal a while back, but he's paying that off, legally."

"Would he tell you if he were cutting corners?"

I laughed. "Are you kidding? Ben is not one to suffer silently. If he were bad off, he would come beg me to double mortgage my condo or lend him my savings to get him out of debt. It would be a lot easier than messing around with bad guys. Ben always takes the easy way, trust me."

That placated Frank, but I was restless. We hadn't talked about our visit to Stan's ex and what that produced.

"You think what Deidre really saw was a snuff film?" I shivered despite my promise to myself that I would be nonchalant.

Frank's mouth tightened. There was something he knew and didn't want to tell me. Finally, he sighed. "I did some research on the Internet last night. I found a masters thesis about the possibility that snuff films actually do exist, and as real murders, not ones simulated on video. The PhD student quoted an anonymous source as reporting a rumor of a Las Vegas dealer who sells snuff films for $100,000 each. Buyers get the original. You wouldn't have to sell many of those to stay rich."

"A Las Vegas dealer. That's almost too coincidental."

"Coincidence is rare," Frank said.

We sat in silence for a while. Frank stared out the window at dusk on The Strip. "I wish I had better sources in the county. If I had someone in Vice to ask about this snuff dealer rumor we might have a handle on whether that angle is a wild goose chase. Abel told me to keep away from all the guys in Vice, apparently Conner lines their pockets on a regular basis. Of course we could always talk to a porn dealer," Frank joked. "If we knew one."

"I do."

Frank's head swiveled around so fast I was afraid he'd given himself whiplash. "What?"

I'd remembered our encounter with Cyrano. Who knew I'd really use that card? I hoped it was still tucked away in that skirt I'd wadded up in the corner because it had cooties. "I met a porn dealer, or porn producer, at least."

Frank had puffed up like a lion whose lair had been invaded. "And how did you happen to meet a porn dealer?"

"He wanted to make me a star."

Frank grimaced.

I went into my bedroom to retrieve Cyrano's card and handed it to Frank. He looked at it thoughtfully. "I don't want you to have to talk to him, but these guys have cop radar. If we double-team him, he might suspect a sting.

"I'll figure something out, but first, we need to get you to the tournament. Maybe Ben will be there checking in and our problem will be solved. Maybe the bad guy will try to nab you as you check in. I'll threaten to pull his fingernails out and he'll lead us to where they're torturing Ben by making him watch endless *The Price is Right* reruns."

I couldn't resist a smile. "You can be a real goofball."

"Not usually, I think you bring out the goof in me," Frank admitted.

I'm a bit of an introvert, so big crowds of people aren't my thing. One strike against this Hold 'Em tournament from the get-go. Crowds not only waited in line to check in, but throngs gathered on the sidelines to catch a glimpse of the pros playing. No sign of Stan yet, but I was guessing he would wait to make a grand entrance. I wouldn't have thought that some stupid card game would draw fans, but then again I can't believe people pay to go to the zoo either. Man, that place smells. I sniffed. My place in line was actually starting to smell pretty rank too, since the woman next to me was holding a baby whose diaper was well past due for a change. I wondered how she was going to juggle the newborn and her hand, but that wasn't my problem.

Unless of course she was sitting next to me. Which, knowing my luck, she would be.

"You're at table forty-one, seat six," the registrar informed the little mother. She took her seat assignment and packet and started to move off. "What will you be doing with the baby?" her registrar asked as I moved to the front of my line.

"I'll be taking him," she said, jutting her chin out in challenge.

"No you won't, unregistered people aren't allowed inside the barriers."

"He's six months old. I'm breastfeeding. Don't tell me that you would deny a child his right to nutrition because of a rule that couldn't possibly apply to infants."

The registrar shook her head and consulted behind her hand with her colleague. "I'm sorry ma'am."

"I guess the Lanai," the mother raised her voice to a crescendo, "is prejudiced against nursing mothers. I'm sure NOW and the La Leche League will be interested to hear about this. Maybe we can file a restraining order against the casino to keep the tournament from taking place."

The poor registrar's face had gone from pale to flushed and back again. She called on a walkie talkie and whispered to my registrar. Suddenly, they both looked up beyond me and smiled. I sucked in a breath, praying for patience. Iceberg Effusion! I started to look back and suddenly Daniel Conner was at my elbow. Ack. Of all the dumb bad luck. I looked quickly forward, swallowed a scream and forced myself to breathe normally. Frank had gotten a call and had gone around the corner for better reception. He wouldn't be able to save me if Conner suddenly grabbed me by the hair and dragged me out to the dumpster.

I had a second to escape, if only I could just creep away unseen. Conner hadn't seemed to recognize me—but he was focused on the dispute next to me. He spoke in low calm tones and all the women seemed placated, probably more by his physical beauty than anything else. Apparently, the Lanai chose to forgo a lawsuit and bad press and let the nursing mother play.

My registrar sighed and turned to me just as I was about to slip into the crowd. "Sorry to keep you waiting. What's your name?"

Conner was whispering into his walkie-talkie. I held my breath. I smiled at the registrar. She raised her eyebrows impatiently. "Yes?"

I muttered my name fast. Conner turned his back to me, pressed his hand to his free ear and kept talking.

I leaned down to the registrar and quickly whispered, "B. Cooley, Houston, Texas."

Conner froze for an instant, then spun around, eyes narrowing at me. I steeled myself, smiled wide, held out my hand and exaggerated my drawl, "Hi, handsome, I'm Bee."

"We've met," he said smoothly, kind of like a snake must talk to a mouse before it swallows it.

I shook my head slowly. "I don't think so, because I would've remembered a gorgeous pair of baby blues like yours."

A little uncertainty crept into those baby blues even though his voice was just as confident. "You lost your wallet, except you didn't. Remember?"

"I'm sorry, I haven't lost my wallet in Vegas, but I will if I get to talk to you again." I winked. Ick. I hope I wasn't overdoing it. "And what room are you staying in where I should go report if I notice anything of mine missing at all?"

He narrowed his eyes at me again, clearly getting my

sexual innuendo. He wasn't interested, thank the good Lord. "I guess I was mistaken," he mumbled, turning away with only a single glance back.

I knew he was not at all sure he was mistaken, but he certainly wasn't going to try to shake me down about the Felix encounter in front of these women. My registrar was smiling smugly at me, clearly gratified by his rejection of my advance. Little did she know I was more gratified than she was. She held out a glass bowl. "Draw your seat."

Still watching Conner out of the corner of my eye, I reached my hand in and grabbed a paper. She took it from me and read: "Table forty-one, seat five."

Uh-oh. "Is that—"

Her smile grew. Bitch. "Yes, that is right next to Amy Downs, the lady who just checked in with that sweet little baby. Good luck in the tournament, Miz Cooley."

Fifteen

♦ ♣ ♥ ♠

By the time I turned away from the check-in table, the number of onlookers had doubled. I suppose this signaled the approaching arrival of the star pro—Steely Stan. Other pros had arrived to a smattering of applause from the crowd. But they were clearly waiting for the main man.

I looked over heads for Frank. There was no sign of him. I'd kept an eye on Conner, who'd kept an eye on me as he consulted with some suited goons, pointing at the tables in the adjacent ballroom. I tried not to let his presence bother me, because he seemed to have a shark's sense for blood in the water. A couple of the players waiting with me helped distract me by striking up conversations. A chatty bunch, these poker players, I guess it's more fun to know the person you'll be taking money from later. I used the opportunity to get as much information as I could about Stan, but none of them knew any more than I did.

"How many of these have you played in?" a balding accountant from Nova Scotia named Ringo asked me.

"It's my first," I answered, looking over him for Frank.

"Wow, you sure are jumping in with both feet."

"And sure to find myself in way over my head, I'm sure," I said, trying to warm up to all Hold 'Em's water analogies with one of my own.

"I don't know," he offered, "if you're brave enough to start at something this big then you'll probably make a helluva Hold 'Em tournament player."

"I hope so."

"Where are your shades?"

"Huh?"

"Your sunglasses." He motioned to the clutch purse I held in the crook of my arm. "They can't fit in that tiny thing."

"I don't have any." Panic threatened.

"Don't worry if you don't have them tonight. Most of tonight is looser play, so luck plays a bigger part than skill, I feel. But the game changes as time goes on. You'd better get some shades by day three, if you're still in there. Things get serious then. There's a lot of money at stake and some of these pros are experts at reading even a blink."

"Okay, thanks for the advice, Ringo," I said, shaking his hand and trying not to let my knees knock together. *Where was Frank?* The tournament officials were beginning to herd us into the ballroom where 200 poker tables were set up and waiting. "Good luck."

I lingered with the last stragglers, but still no Frank. Just as I was about to slip into the ballroom, I heard a burst of catcalls and applause behind me. I turned to see Steely Stan making his way through his fans, TV cameras following. I noticed he ignored them all as he sauntered by with a woman on each arm (different ones from the other day). His only acknowledgement of propriety was he kept his hands on their shoulders instead of their breasts. He wore a black leather jacket, black jeans and a red silk shirt unbuttoned to reveal a thick gold chain with a gold poker chip in a nest of nasty chest hair. Ick.

"Man, aren't you glad he's not sitting at your first table?" the scrawny thirtysomething guy behind me whispered.

I reached in my clutch and pulled it out just as the dealer tossed out the first pocket card. The second followed. I set the marker on the two and pinched up the corners. A pair of sevens, all red. This was a good pocket pair, according to the book Frank had given me. Maybe this marker would be lucky after all.

In the end it seemed way too easy. The pro was a total Rock who signaled his good hands from miles away. He got knocked out in the first two hours. Yegor wouldn't be buying Grey Goose tonight. Of the rest of the table, only three gave me a run for my chips. A man sitting in seat four might have actually nosed me out if it hadn't been for fate known as Amy and Junior. Amy had been playing pretty damned well for a woman juggling an infant. A Queen fell on Fourth Street with a Queen and a pair of sixes on the flop. I had only a pocket eight and an ace. Somebody likely had a full house, or easily four of a kind. Junior was hungry, so Amy tucked him under her shirt for a little snack. The D man couldn't keep his eyes on the game so driven to distraction was he by Junior's sucking. I decided to bluff. I raised. Everyone folded. I won even though there were better hands out there, because when Seat Eight showed bad etiquette by asking what I had in my hand, I used worse etiquette in showing the table my cards. Seat Four gritted his teeth and Seat Seven kicked the table leg. I widened my eyes and apologized for my bad poker manners, but I'd taken the opportunity to use a lesson Frank had taught me—sometimes you had to act stupid to win smart.

Amy and I ended up heads up in the last round. I had unsuited ace and Jack in the pocket and even though Frank and the book both told me this wasn't a hand to play, I decided to try it anyway. Amy raised and I called. We had Queen, ten, four all unsuited, on The Flop. Amy raised. I wanted to bounce my leg, I wanted to tap my fingers. I stayed still and waited for the right time. Just as the dealer was about to urge me along, I reraised and she went all in.

The River card was a King. I got lucky—Amy had pocket Jacks.

I thanked a sleeping Junior for his help and shook Amy's hand. "I'm going to be watching you, Bee. You are one cool customer," she said. "I hope you beat the pants off Steely Stan."

Her comment reminded me of the Internet players who'd wished the same result for Ben. My eyes misted.

"Are you okay?"

"Yes, just thinking about my brother. He really wanted to be here, doing this. He really wanted to beat Stan in the worst way. I didn't want it as bad and still don't understand his intensity about the guy."

Amy shrugged. "He's the guy we all love to hate in poker. I think those of us who've played for a long time are sorry that he would have to be the one to ride Hold 'Em's sudden wave of popularity. Right now he is Mr. Texas Hold 'Em to the world, and most of us would rather have a different ambassador for the game."

"I can see that," I said.

"On the other hand, Stan is larger than life, an easy person to put on a magazine covers and expect to sell lots of copies. If some dweeb won the World Series of Poker, it might not be as popular as it is. Still, I hate that he put people out of jobs once he made it big."

"What do you mean?"

"My sister used to work for Fresh Foods, a produce supplier. They've sponsored Stan on his World Series bids since he was a nobody. Once he won his first title, a lot of people were fired at Fresh Foods and replaced by people hand picked by Stan. It must have been some sort of power trip."

"Sounds like it," I said vaguely. Hmm. I smell something fishy in the produce section. "Was your sister one who was fired?"

"Yes, she and all the other quality control experts. Stan told the company he wanted the quality of the produce to match the quality of his game. Gag me."

"Quality control? What did your sister do exactly?"

"Randomly open boxes to make sure the right fruit was in the right box, that there were no spoiled fruits, that kind of thing."

I nodded and made sympathetic noises. I wanted to ask her for her sister's name and phone number, but I couldn't without getting her suspicious. And besides, I really didn't want anyone else to die. I'd have to ask Frank how to proceed. "Amy Downs, good to meet you."

"Bee, what's your last name?"

"Cooley."

" 'Bee Cool' Cooley. I see a championship in your future."

Frank was shaking his head in disbelief when the tournament officials finished taking my information to move me into the next round. "I guess the marker was lucky after all."

I nodded. "Even better than winning, I stumbled into some more information about Stan and Fresh Foods." I related the story Amy told me.

"I don't think tracking the sister down will do any good. From her casual tone, Amy told you all the sister knows. If they replaced the quality control department, it certainly means that Stan wanted his guys in place so they could bring in something illegal. Or else they just blamed Stan."

I held my head in my hands. "How complicated is this going to be?"

"Consider this: Stan is just the figurehead and Conner is the real bad guy. We already have enough circumstantial evidence to link Conner to Felix's murder and to Pudgy Pete's demise."

"I guess the best way to find out would be to talk to Stan and see how he reacts."

Frank shook his head. "Too dangerous."

I arched my eyebrows at him. "Not if I do it in front of the TV cameras."

"Just keep playing like you're playing and you just might

get the chance." Frank guided me to an alcove off the lobby. "Now, you need to call your buddy Cyrano. I've rented another room for the night. Tell him if he'd like a preview of what you can do, he can meet you at room 1969 in one hour."

Yuck, just pretending was going to make me sick. "What if he's too careful to come?"

"Oh, he's careful alright, but he's also a pervert. Perverts can never resist a free show."

Sixteen

♦ ♣ ♥ ♠

Frank was right. Again. Cyrano was cagey on the phone when I invited him over. He offered money up front if I'd come to him, but I told him I was worth more and I'd give him a free preview to prove it.

A half hour later, there was a knock on the door. I looked again toward Frank who shoved a thumbs up around the drapes he hid behind. Steeling myself with a deep breath, I walked slowly to the door. Slimy Cyrano who was wearing another five thousand dollars worth of clothing. The guy had to be loaded. I wondered if this was business or recreation. He surveyed the room thoroughly before stepping foot into it. I tried to remember Frank's warning that if Cyrano wasn't the snuff film dealer, he might know who was. Either way he might be more than just creepy—he might be deadly.

"Exquisite sequins," he fingered one right at my nipple. I jumped and swallowed a squeal. The drapes moved and I quickly guided Cyrano to the couch, our backs to the window.

I had to remind myself I was doing this for Ben. If he

made it out alive, he was going to owe me for the rest of his life for this one.

"Would you care for a cocktail?" I asked.

He ignored my question. "When do you begin?"

"Uh, I just need to get a little warmed up first," I answered.

Cyrano's beady eyes lit up. I couldn't begin to imagine what fantasies my casual words inspired. Whatever it was it made him lick his lips. Ook.

"Remember, I would love to pay you triple if you come now to my studio."

I leaned toward him, as nauseating as that was, and asked, trying not to appear too smart with my higher math, "That's great, Cyrano, but that would make it, like, eighteen thousand dollars, right?"

He nodded.

"Well, earlier tonight I met this guy and he offered me twenty-five thousand just for me and one of his guys in a video. He said that they would be acting out some scary things but it was all just pretend. And, I'd get to travel, to go to their studio in the desert somewhere. It'd be kinda like those Sports Illustrated swimsuit shoots I think."

Frank and I had come up with this story after he'd called Deidre about the setting for the snuff film she saw. It had been set in the desert, which would jibe with the Texas Rangers' theory on the disappearances of the young Mexican girls.

Cyrano's face clouded. He shook his head—at himself more than at me. He looked undecided about what exactly to say. "I would not recommend doing that."

"Why not? Sounds like pretty easy money and I'd get to keep it all myself."

"Because you might not live through it, you stupid girl," he snapped.

"What do you mean?" I tried to swallow but couldn't through the lump in my throat.

"Have you ever heard of a snuff film?"

"Um." I tried to act like the airhead I was supposed to

be. "Isn't that porn where they simulate murder during the act?"

"Sometimes it isn't simulated, you understand me? The man you talked to would take you somewhere and never bring you home."

Cyrano was jittery and angry. I wasn't sure if it was directed at me or his competition. "What did this man look like?" he demanded, narrow eyed.

Uh-oh. I shrugged. "Average white guy."

I didn't know exactly how far I could push him. He was getting more agitated by the second, a box of explosives about to blow. I looked at the drapes. They were still. No help there. I crossed my legs and let my skirt hike up. He looked at my thighs, briefly distracted while I asked, "So you know him?"

"By reputation."

"Aw, maybe it's just a bad rap."

"A bad rap they try to attribute to me," he spat out suddenly. "Is this a set up?" He lunged for me and I leaned back out of his reach. "Is there someone here, listening?" He jumped up and ran to the bedroom. He flung open the door, looked in and ran back to me, reaching over the couch to grab me around the throat. "Are you working for him or the cops? Are you wearing a wire?" He stuck his hand down my halter top. If I hadn't been so scared, I might have thrown up dinner.

Before my adrenaline even reached my fingertips, Frank had yanked Cyrano off me. He planted the porn promoter's face into the carpet, stuck his knee in his back and handcuffed him.

My mouth dropped open. I couldn't find words for a moment. "Where did you get handcuffs?"

"My back pocket." Frank looked at my chest and I realized then that my halter top was ripped open to my belly button. Cute. I pulled the pieces together and tried to act self-righteous.

"And why do you have them? Are they standard equipment in the security business?"

He cocked his head at Cyrano. "If they aren't, they ought to be—I'd say he was pretty secure now."

"I don't think it's legal to have handcuffs if you aren't a cop."

Both Frank and Cyrano said, "Yes it is."

Okay. Well, I had to try a different tack to find out Frank's secrets.

"Who the hell are you?" Cyrano grunted. "You aren't her brother Benjamin. I just met him once, but forgive me if I say don't think he'd have the balls for this."

"Watch what you say about Ben," I warned, although I kind of agreed with him.

"Her brother is missing," Frank told Cyrano, as he hoisted him up by his designer leather belt I swore was an S.T. Dupont and deposited him on the chair. "Do you know where he is?"

"How would I know where he would be?"

"You might have heard among your colleagues," Frank said.

"I want you to understand something." Cyrano cleared his throat. His expensive taste, formal manners and aristocratic accent made what he did almost otherworldly. "This man who does these snuff films is sick and is not *my* anything. What he does is immoral."

Ha, I guess even morality is relative.

"What's more, I have no idea what he looks like nor do I know his name."

"Maybe he doesn't exist," Frank offered. "Maybe the films don't exist beyond an urban legend."

"Oh at least one exists. I saw it. A few months ago, he sent a boy to meet me. He had an iPod that showed the movie like a music video. I got a preview as an advertisement. It was for sale for a hundred thousand dollars. And it was real. The sex, the death." Cyrano was ashen. It had to have been worse than horrible to turn the stomach of professional smut distributor.

"And you told this to authorities?"

"Yes, I called the FBI. They didn't believe me, probably still don't, because of course I had no evidence. They traced the number that he called from and it was one of those prepaid phones you can buy at Wal-Mart with a twenty dollar bill and no identification. And the whole affair has put a damper on my reputation. I'm afraid they are watching me now. You and your brother were the first time I'd tried anything extracurricular in months and now, look, I'm in the mess all over again."

I could tell Frank was frustrated. For as disgusting as Cyrano was, his story rang true. "Who did you talk to at the FBI?"

"I didn't call local police, because you never know who is corrupt and who's not. If I'd happened to get one of the ones expecting a bribe, I would have been angry, because they are just too expensive. It was worse odds than the craps table. Therefore, I just dialed a California FBI office. I can't remember the agent's name."

Another dead end. Frank shook his head.

"Why do you think Benjamin is with them?" Cyrano asked me. "Is he mixed up with this style of entertainment?"

"No, I think he was just in the wrong place at the wrong time."

"What do you know about Steely Stan?" Frank asked, playing a hunch I thought.

"He's famous and he's feared here in Vegas."

"Feared? Why?" I asked.

"Because he's ruthless and not just in cards. I hear he's been acting more and more like a cornered tiger."

"But why?" Frank asked. "He's at the top of the hottest gambling game in the world, wouldn't an expected reaction be arrogance instead of desperation?"

"Maybe because he's about to lose his sponsor and maybe he's afraid he won't be able to sustain the lifestlye he's become accustomed to on his winnings alone."

"But why would Fresh Foods want to drop him?"

Cyrano got a hard, faraway look. "Maybe because Fresh Foods doesn't like the image he has begun presenting."

In the end, we let Cyrano go. We both thought we'd gotten out of him all we could, and frankly I think we both liked him in a weird, "I have a freak as a friend" kind of way. He really did care enough about me that he didn't want me to die, even though he wanted to watch me on video doing icky things.

Vegas was not black and white, that's all I can say. And it was either morphing me or warping me. I wasn't sure which. Either way I was going home changed.

Frank and I were back in his suite when he told me where he'd been while I went to check into the tournament. "I was talking to a colleague of mine who was researching Steely Stan Trident. His real name is Donald Sipowecki, age forty, born and raised in a small town outside of Detroit. He changed his name ten years ago and settled here. Smart guy, graduated from University of Michigan in accounting, which would explain his razor sharp ability to calculate odds in Hold 'Em. It's my experience when someone changes their name, it's not because he didn't like what Mama gave him, he just is running from things."

"What 'things' was Donald running from?"

"Accusations, but no charges apparently, of duping some seniors out of their savings for a moneymaking scheme. Accusations, again no charges, of pilfering from a company he worked for after that. Three out of wedlock children whose mothers are looking for alimony. Guess none of them play Hold 'Em or they might have recognized him."

"None of that is accusatory in this case, though." I pointed out.

"Except his tendency toward opportunism. He's not some criminal mastermind, just a guy without a conscience who likes to make a buck illegally when he can."

"So what do you think that means in this case?"

"I think it means that I need to get my guy to delve more deeply into the Fresh Foods connection. If Stan holds true to pattern, Fresh Foods' sponsorship was another opportunity."

"And Ben somehow got in the way of his opportunity and that's why he's being held captive."

"We don't know that for sure. We can assume whatever we want based on how we read Stan's comment to you tonight, but at this point we only have evidence linking Conner with Ben's disappearance. We don't have anything yet linking Conner with Stan. Of course we can assume he is the one they were talking about in the stairwell."

"So what do we do now?"

"I called from my cell phone and left a message for Stan at the front desk, giving the dummy room number. I said that I wanted to talk about Donald. It'll shake him a bit. Likely make him paranoid, distracted, less careful."

"What if it makes him hurt Ben?"

"Actually, it will make him less likely to do that, because he will be confused about Ben's compadres. It will cause some infighting, which is always good to produce among the enemy."

Hmm. Now Frank was sounding like a soldier. Maybe he'd been a military cop in California. I wish I had a faceless "colleague" to go research him.

"I need to do the same with Conner but I wanted to wait until you'd made your first appearance at the tournament." Frank slid his cellphone out of his pocket and dialed the front desk and asked to leave a message for Detective Conner. "I think he left something of his in the dumpster behind the Galaxy."

"Now let's wait and watch," Frank said, as he put his phone away.

"But what if he goes and takes the body away?"

Frank shook his head. "I called and reported it from a pay phone earlier. He knows the cops found the pieces of Pete. So, this will make him very nervous and very confused. He'll probably suspect one of the men in blue is on to him."

"Since we've shaken them up a bit, they might try to move Ben. I can't get to Stan's room, it's a keyed penthouse. But we can follow Conner. I've got a friend who just came into town and I've put him on Conner's tail."

"Won't a cop know he's being tailed, especially a dirty one?"

"He won't know this guy is there," Frank assured me. "He's the best in the business."

"The security business," I sighed.

"Exactly."

"Now I guess I'll turn in," I yawned.

"No, now I guess you'll turn into a real poker player." Frank got up and started a pot of coffee.

"What?"

"Tomorrow night is a whole new game, Bee," he explained, coming to sit down next to me. "The way the tournament tonight was set up, some people qualified with no money in, some, like Ben, paid up front, and others came just to see the pros. With that mix, it played more like a home game. No one could really bluff effectively because few folded, and luck was a major factor. Don't get me wrong, you played well, you read body language and stayed cool. But get ready for the heat to get turned up.

"Tomorrow every player will smell the money. You may be at a table of all pros. They will underestimate you. Use that. Act a little sloppy; slurp down drinks. Try to lose a few hands where you can afford to so you can bluff them later. The rest, just do what you did before. Calculate the odds, but remember, anyone can do that. Read the body language. That is your big gift."

Three knocks sounded at the door. I cocked my head at Frank and tried not to let my heart race out of control. Had Conner found us? But Frank smiled. "Don't worry, it's just the same group that taught you last night. Tonight, they are going to play a different game to warm you up for tomorrow."

Seventeen
♦ ♣ ♥ ♠

I slept until one o'clock in the afternoon, which wasn't bad considering we'd stayed up playing Hold 'Em until dawn. I shuffled out into the living room and knew I was alone. I had a moment of panic when I realized how much I'd come to rely on a man I'd only known a couple of days. That was not a good thing. Relying on a man had never done me any good.

Besides, I really didn't know Frank Gilbert. He could be using an assumed name, like Stan, for all I could prove. I didn't know what his motivation was in helping me find Ben besides being bored or nice or both. Or neither. He could be Conner's sworn enemy, out to bring him down. He could be someone Stan beat at a poker tournament once who vowed to get even. He could be another snuff film supplier here to take out the competition.

Why finding out he was any of those things, besides the last one of course, would make me feel better, I didn't know.

I wandered over to make coffee and saw his note.

Bee -

Went to go rendezvous with my man.
Have some coffee. Read Hellmuth's book again.
Above all, stay put!
I'll take you to lunch in a bit.

- F

Hmm. I hated to be told what to do. I decided to forgo the coffee in favor of dressing, going downstairs and nosing around. I washed my face, threw my hair up, pulled on my low rise Calvin Klein jeans, a white silk shirt and the jeweled thongs that were becoming my uniform shoes. Vegas had changed me, I realized as I made my way to the elevator. I'd forgotten all about earrings. I don't think I'd been this fashion lax since I was ten years old.

I got in the elevator and joined a half dozen people inside. We were about halfway down when a voice from the back said, "Hey, it's Bee Cool."

I looked back. "Hi, Amy."

"This woman is going to beat Steely Stan," Amy announced to the captive audience.

A couple of people murmured, "Oh, you made it through the first round?"

Now I understood why my mother always told me to put on clean underwear because you never knew what was going to happen when you went out of the house. Sure enough. I hadn't put on makeup or even earrings, thinking I was in a city full of strangers. The tournament had changed that. Great.

"We'll be watching you, Bee Cool," one of the men said, as I waved and escaped into the lobby.

I'd been unlucky to run into Amy but surely she was the only one who'd recognize me. I relaxed as I made my way to the casino to get some dirt on Stan. I'd planned to sit at a Hold 'Em table and talk up the dealer who was bound to have heard stories about Stan before he got famous. I got some chips and joined a $10-$20 table with eight players and an empty chair next to the dealer, who was a man. I was tired of hearing about Stan's pheromones from his female fan club.

"So I guess you know Steely Stan, huh?" I asked as I peeked at my pair of eights.

"Not personally," he answered, tossing off the burn card.

"I heard he used to do what you do for a living."

He looked at me sharply. Uh-oh.

"He was a Hold 'Em dealer at Galaxy, right?" I clarified carefully, pushing some chips forward to raise the bet.

"Uh, yeah," he answered, throwing down The Flop and a lot that was unsaid.

"He didn't have *another* job, did he?" I said, raising again as I looked at the unsuited eight, deuce and Queen Flop.

"Not an official one," the dealer answered.

Ah-ha. Now we were getting somewhere. Just then I heard, "Bee!"

Damn, I looked up, along with the rest of our table, to see my Nova Scotian accountant friend, Ringo, waving from three tables over. He pointed at me. "There's the woman who's going to win the tournament! Bee Cool! Woman with ice in her veins."

What bad timing. My dealer clammed up immediately, giving me a narrow-eyed look that reprimanded me for trying to get dirt on Stan to use against him in the tournament. My whole table looked at me and folded when Fourth Street dropped another eight. Double damn.

I collected my couple hundred dollars in chips and left the table, walking past Ringo. "Nice to see you again, Ringo. Have you been talking to Amy?"

"Who's Amy?"

"I think she came up with that silly nickname for me."

"What are you talking about? I came up with that myself. You said your name is Bee Cooley. You are one cool customer at the table, so the 'Bee Cool' thing is obvious. I got my money on you."

"Thanks, Ringo."

For the first time in my life I could see why movie stars

resented fame. Talk about cramping my style. Cranky, I waited in line to cash in my chips when a hand swooped in and grabbed me out of the line.

I glared at Frank. "What are you doing?"

"What are you doing?"

"Doing what you told me not to do."

"Exactly." Frank blinked, apparently unaccustomed to women stating the obvious. "Why?"

"Because I felt like it."

Frank leaned in and whispered harshly. "You felt like dying today?"

I narrowed my eyes and used Toby's favorite term. At least I learned something in five years. "Don't be melodramatic."

"Certainly when you grabbed a disembodied arm, you realized this is no soap opera."

One of the men I recognized from the elevator walked by, curious and concerned at the tension between us. He put his hand on my shoulder. "You okay, Bee Cool?"

Frank looked at him like the guy'd grown horns, then at me like I'd put them there. "Who?"

I reassured my gallant fan with a thankful smile and he wandered away. I turned back to Frank, shrugging. "I guess some people I met at the tournament knew I made it through the first round and came up with a nickname for me."

Frank ducked his head, shaking it and saying in a low tone, as he put his hand on the small of my back and moved me toward the elevators, "Then we really need to get out of here. You're suddenly famous and I don't want to be recognized with you. I won't be able to get any investigation done as Bee Cool's dude. We'll be in worse trouble if Conner IDs me and finds out what room you're staying in."

"I thought you were buying me lunch?"

"I'll get you room service."

I made a face.

Frank pulled me into a private alcove out of the foot traffic, struggling to keep his patience. "Look, you need to lie low, especially if people know who you are. You don't go playing Hold 'Em at the casino where you're doing a tournament. That just gives the opportunity for someone who might play against you tonight to learn your game. You don't see any of the pros here. If anyone wants to play outside the tournament they'll go to another casino, and not the one next door."

"Oh." I felt stupid, then brightened. "But I almost got some good information." I told him about the dealer's almost revelation.

Frank's eyes darkened. "Bee, you don't know who this guy is, or if he was calling Stan right after you got up and he'd have Conner there to grab you. Maybe I'm being hypervigilant, but I don't think so. Two people have been killed. One of them could have been you."

Poor Felix. Wrong place, wrong time. Poor me. Wrong place, wrong time, wrong brother. Poor Ben. I didn't know how to explain his dilemma. Usually he created his own drama, but I honestly couldn't see any connection other than maybe wrong hobby, wrong obsession with Stan. Maybe there was more, but I almost didn't want to know what it was.

"Why don't you trust me, Bee?" Frank asked, watching me closely.

"I just don't know why someone who doesn't know me would risk his life to help me."

"It's a fair question. Suffice it to say I had my own motivation to begin with, but it's changed now that I know you better than you think I do. It's more about you and less about the other thing. That's all I can say right now."

Great, more mystery. I believed him, though. It was hard to resist those eyes when they bared his soul, however briefly and however succinctly. "Okay, let's go back to the room."

"Separate elevators. I'll meet you there. No funny business. If I have to hunt you down again, it's going to involve tying you up so you can't go anywhere."

"You do have those handcuffs," I teased as I got into an elevator.

Crow's feet crinkled and chocolate brown eyes warmed.
He looked damn cute—it was probably a good thing we
were putting some distance between us for a few minutes
or I might be tempted. The elevator doors shut, and I
sighed.

*T*en minutes later, Frank still wasn't back to the suite
and I was worried. My fertile imagination came up with a
thousand scenarios, each one worse than the next. I was
embarrassed to realize in the middle of it that I felt sorry
we hadn't consummated the simmering sexual attraction
between us.

How base, how petty of me.

If he showed up in one piece I was going to jump his
bones.

A knock sounded at the door and I started, knocking a
lamp to the floor with a thump. Then I froze. I couldn't
breathe, but my pounding heart was demanding some oxy-
gen. What should I do? Maybe it was police coming to tell
me that Frank's dismembered remains had been found
stuffed in the laundry shaft.

Two knocks. Ack. Conner probably wouldn't knock,
just use the master key he certainly had possession of.
Maybe it was Stan, who'd found out where I was and had
come to strangle me.

I heard rustling now outside the door. I was done for. I
looked for a place to hide. The closets and the shower were
the first places bad guys in the movies looked. I scuttled
under the desk and pulled the chair up to hide me.

The door opened and I heard something being rolled
into the room. They were bringing Frank's body back in to
make it look like a suicide!

I heard two pair of footfalls, one going into each bedroom. They were looking for me now, maybe planning how
they were going to set Frank out. One went to the bar and
opened the cabinet, opened the refrigerator. Maybe they

were going to pour liquor down his throat and make it look like he drank himself to death.

It seemed like ages, but was probably only a minute before I heard a third pair of footsteps, these faster, walking in from out in the hall. "*Lo siento, senor,*" I heard a woman's voice say.

"We can go if you need your room sir," another women's voice said.

"Have you seen a woman here?" Frank asked.

I was so relieved, I couldn't move or speak for a moment as I heard Frank jogging to my bedroom. "No," the maids said.

He ran to the desk, and riffled through papers looking for a note. I was trying to untangle my legs and my tongue, when he pulled out the chair and sat down. His feet went into my crotch. He looked down in surprise.

"Shall we go, sir?"

Frank smiled down at me. "Yes, I think you'd better go. Thank you."

I put my hands on his knees to brace myself and pulled myself up between his thighs. He wasn't moving out of my way too fast. His eyes were simmering. "Why were you hiding from the maids?"

"I didn't know it was the maids and you weren't here and I was worried you were dead and—"

He cupped my jaw with his hand and leaned down and kissed me. Another one of those long, excruciatingly toe tingling kisses. He smelled like hot Dove, really hot Dove. I braced my hands on his thighs; he dragged me up in his lap. Suddenly my hands were everywhere, molding his chest, running through his hair, scraping across his razor stubble. He moved much slower and more torturously, shaking my hair loose and running his fingers through it. His hands barely skirted my sides. I shivered in the wake of spider webs of sensation and shifted on top of him. He groaned.

I tried to pull his shirt tail out of his jeans and his hands went to still mine. I opened my eyes and looked at him in question.

"I just thought you were dead and I was sorry we hadn't done this yet."

"Right idea. Wrong time."

"Oh."

"Honey Bee, I don't want you to want me because you are driven by the specter of death. I want you to want me just for me."

"What about you wanting me?"

"I already proved that the other night."

"Oh, well, that doesn't count because you were under the influence."

He grinned and helped me rise to me feet as he pushed his chair back. "Yeah, under the influence of *you*: The way your hair smells, the way your skin feels, the way you look at me . . . But correct me if I'm wrong, you're the one who put the brakes on it that night—you basically told me 'wrong time'."

I smiled back. "Touché."

"There'll be a right time. One day."

"Sure, as long as we both stay alive," I added.

Eighteen
♦ ♣ ♥ ♠

"**B**en isn't at Conner's house," Frank reported after hanging up with "his man" Joe NLN (my new acronym for no last name, which was common with Frank's associates and crooked poker champions).

"How does Joe know?" I asked as I slipped a Cynthia Rowley charcoal satin cropped jacket over a silver lace camisole.

"We have ways of knowing."

I gave him a hard look. "Are you some kind of commando?"

"Am I going commando?" Frank pretended to be affronted. "I thought we agreed to put all that suggestive talk on hold."

He wasn't going to answer anyway, so I played along. "Nobody said anything about not *talking* about it."

"You are a tease, Honey Bee."

"I've never been known to be. I guess you bring it out in me."

I would be first off the elevator. Frank arranged it by edging people out of the way, then dropping back to the rear of the car himself, so he could shadow me without looking like we were together. I exited and turned the corner of the hallway leading to the ballroom and saw a bigger crowd than the night before waiting for players.

A smattering of applause began and rose as I approached. I suppose it could have to do with the fact that, since only five percent of women play poker, it was a small miracle that I had made it this far. Maybe they had me confused with Jennifer Tilley, who Ben had told me was a poker whiz. I hadn't seen her playing in this tournament but I guess our hair looked somewhat similar.

I smiled at the crowd and that's when I saw Ringo holding a "Bee Cool Cooley" sign. At the same moment, I saw Daniel Conner step out of the shadows. He openly glared at me. Ringo reached over—I thought to shake my hand— but instead slipped me a pair of Gargoyles. I looked down at the sunglasses. "You gotta have some, Bee. Stakes are higher tonight. Every blink counts." I gave him a quick hug, which he returned with a thumbs up.

Amy handed me her lucky cloth cocktail napkin. A trio of women held a "Poker Babes for Bee Cool Cooley" banner. A half dozen other people hollered a bit of advice here and there. I thanked them all and waved again. They cheered louder. Conner growled at them to quiet down.

While he was otherwise occupied, I hurried to the check-in table, selected my seat assignment and strode quickly into the ballroom. It seemed strangely empty and quiet compared to the previous night. What had been nearly two thousand people then, tonight had been reduced to 197 people, twenty-three tables of nine players. The winner of each table would advance to the next semi-final round to be played the same night, in which Stan would actually join a table and play, making it four tables of six players each. The last four players would face off in the final round to be played the next night, televised live on ESPN.

I felt a hand on my elbow and jumped. A petite young blond woman smiled shyly. "I'm sorry I didn't mean to distract you. I guess you were getting into your game already."

I'd actually been thinking of ways to keep away from Conner until play began. But I nodded vaguely.

"My name is Beth Watson. I write for *All In Magazine* and wondered if I could interview you for a story?"

Oh my gosh, what did I have to say? If she were a gambling reporter, I bet she knew a few things about Steely Stan. "I tell you what—if I make it to the finals, I will give you an exclusive interview if you give me some information about Steely Stan in exchange."

Her eyes lit up as she handed me her card. "That's a deal. See you later."

"If my luck holds," I muttered.

I felt eyes on me and half-turned to see Conner enter the ballroom. I suppressed a shiver. Players had started taking their seats, so I made my way to table six. Conner moved toward me. I saw Frank come through a side door of the ballroom. His gaze found me at once. He saw Conner, frowned and walked quickly toward him, not reaching him before Conner made it through the boundary tape. I paused at my waitress from the night before and she gave me a thumbs up before I could say anything. Sliding on my Gargoyles to get the feel of them, I was just easing into my seat when I felt a presence next to me.

Conner leaned down to whisper in my left ear. "Miss Cooley, it seems you've garnered quite a fan club. The casino has been getting requests for interviews and the like. We wondered where we should direct these messages?"

"To my room on the twentieth floor, please." I nodded at the man who sat down at my right and, glad my eyes were hidden, tried not to show how grateful I was for the company.

"But you aren't staying in your room, are you?" Conner dropped his voice.

"Now how would you know if I was or wasn't staying in my room, Detective?" I turned to my fellow player, asking him loudly, "Do you think the casino has us under surveillance?"

Conner drew back. "Of course not, Miz Cooley. You misunderstood. We will make sure you get your messages."

He spun on his heel and marched away. Frank's shoulders visibly sagged in relief. My seatmate leaned toward me. He was in his fifties but trying to look like he was in his thirties, with gelled hair and a hoop earring. Time to start playing, I thought as he said, "He didn't even wish you luck."

I pushed back from the table just slightly and crossed my legs slowly, letting my leather mini skirt inch up a little too far. I peeked at him over the tops of my lenses and decided I liked the sunglasses. They were a new tool. "I guess he didn't want to play favorites," I purred. I usually didn't like to play these sexual games. I had never been good at it. But somehow knowing this flirting would play into my poker hand later properly motivated me. He dropped his eyes, tried not to drool, then put out his hand.

"I'm Tom."

"Pleasure to share a table with you, Tom." I smiled slowly as I shook his hand. "I'm Belinda."

Tom took a second to inspect my cleavage as he released my hand. "So, how long have you been playing Hold 'Em, Belinda?"

"Not very long. I think I just got lucky last night." I giggled and tried not to gag.

Tom's eyes lit. He'd already eliminated me from the table but not from his fantasies. "Well, if luck isn't your lady tonight, maybe we can meet for a drink later."

"Maybe, Tom." I giggled again.

The rest of the table had filled in while we talked, so I didn't have to repeat anything. The other seven men playing with me had pretty much decided I was out of there, except for one young algebra teacher type who looked immune to anything but numbers. That was okay, he could probably be beat with a well-timed bluff.

Out of the corner of my eye, I'd watched Conner stalk past our table, probably trying to intimidate me. It was working but I refused to show it.

"Did y'all see the news this morning?" I asked the table.
"They found a body all chopped up in a dumpster behind a
casino! What would make someone do that?" While the
table speculated about that a bit, Conner paused a step and
tensed. Frank shot me a warning glance. I might be pushing Conner too far, but all I had were hunches and intuition.

And luck.

She was my lady again. Three hours later, I was heads
up with the math junkie (whose name was Harold) when he
folded in fear when an ace fell on Fourth Street next to a
Flop of a suited trio of ace, deuce and four of hearts. I had
suddenly gone from folding several hands and calling this
hand to raising a hundred. He thought I either had a flush
or a straight or pocket aces, when all I had was a pair of
sevens, neither a heart.

But he didn't know that and no one else did, either. Still
no one could categorize me. Tomorrow night ESPN would
have commentators delivering the game to a television audience but by then it would be too late for the players to
benefit from any expert's categorization. Of course, I still
might not make it that far.

I shook Harold's hand and I had to laugh when he
leaned in and whispered, "Don't think Tom wants to meet
you for a drink anymore."

Tom had stormed off after calling what he thought was
my bluff but was really four Queens. "I don't think things
worked out the way he expected."

"They didn't for me either, but I have to appreciate
someone with such a natural flair for the game. Tell me, do
you figure odds and probabilities?"

I nodded, "In my head, like I balance my checkbook.
And sometimes what I come up with takes a backseat to
body language."

"Good for you. That's why I won't ever be a pro, I can't
let the numbers go. Not ever."

"I bet you stay on the winning side, over time, though,
don't you?"

He nodded and patted me on the shoulder as Conner accompanied a tournament official over to our table. For a moment I thought Conner had squealed that I'd taken Ben's place, but the official was smiling. "Congratulations, Miss Cooley. You advance with a sizeable check." He handed it to me. I tucked it in my clutch without looking. The numbers would distract me for sure. "Now, draw your table for the next round."

Just as I drew, I heard excited murmurs and applause break out in the ballroom. Steely Stan had finally appeared to play in the semis. Tonight he had his pet size Es on each arm and wore a cheetah fur coat, a copper silk shirt, black jeans, snakeskin boots, and thirty pounds of gold. He looked like a pimp.

While everyone was ogling Stan, Conner leaned down and whispered, "You know everyone's luck runs out some-time Miss Cooley. I plan to be there when yours does."

I narrowed my eyes at him. "Where is my brother?"

His thin lips spread in a mirthless smile and I wondered why I ever thought him attractive. He was as cold as a copperhead. "Your brother is going to be a star."

The tournament official, who'd run over to shake Stan's hand, now beckoned Conner. He walked away without a backward glance. Frank was pacing behind the boundary cord, not taking his eyes off me. I smiled reassuringly, but inside I felt like I was going to explode.

Ben is going to be a star? Does that mean Conner was going to kill him? That his body was going to be on TV in parts like Pete? Did it mean he already killed him?

I wanted to brainstorm with Frank, but it would have to wait. I looked at the number in my hand and then at the table where the tournament official was escorting Stan. Could it be my luck had chosen now to run out?

Stan and I didn't sit at the same table for the semis after all. The official walked past my table and onto table number one where Stan took the first seat. I took the third seat at table three. I found that portentous, since three is my lucky number.

Frank warned me it would be a different game starting with six players that I hadn't read yet. Sure enough, he was right—the cards fell differently and I had to play a bit tighter. I didn't like waiting for the ten best hands to bet, but this time I did. My patience paid off and I ended up heads up again with a pro from Paris, Phillippe. He was rude and demeaning but I continued to flirt. I'd been letting him catch calculated looks over the tops of my lenses. I intended to use that to my advantage now.

I had pocket Queens, both black, and let Phillippe see a worried look over my Gargoyles. He knew by now that I was only betting on decent hands, although I had played loose enough a couple of times to leave a bit of doubt in his mind. I called the blind. That, plus the worried look, should have told him I had a playable hand but not a great one. The Flop was a ten/clubs, three/clubs and an ace/hearts. He raised a thousand. I thought he had something, maybe an ace. He'd played like a bit of a Maniac. I didn't think he'd have stayed in the game this long except he'd had incredible luck with the cards.

I waited as long as the dealer would let me to bet. I even let him give me a verbal nudge. I called the thousand. An ace/clubs fell on Fourth Street. If he had a pocket ace I might be sunk, except I was a card away from flush. I calculated the probability, pushed the chair back and crossed my legs. He looked down while I let my stiletto sandaled foot bounce nervously. He went all in. I called.

The dealer nudged Phillippe to turn over his cards. Instead, he smiled smugly, enjoying what he was certain was a win.

A deuce of clubs fell on The River.

So, I turned over my pocket cards, showing a flush. He flung his cards at the dealer and mumbled what I was sure was an invective in French. He'd had a pair of tens. I'd talked him into the bet!

I hadn't noticed, but we'd been the last table to finish, so when he threw his cards down, everyone watching cheered, some chanting, "Bee Cool, Bee Cool."

I'd gotten lucky again. But I'd take it. I shook the official's hand and took another check. "We look forward to seeing you tomorrow night, Miss Cooley," he said.

Stan had won his table but hadn't hung around. Conner glared from the ballroom doorway. Cocking his head, Frank was throwing me a heavy look that said "Get your ass over here."

I waved at the well wishers and gave Ringo another squeeze. "The Gargoyles made the difference," I told him. He grinned. I rubbed his bald head as I headed toward the elevator, with a couple of Conner's goons escorting me.

Frank and I had agreed to meet in the room, but he would follow me to make sure no one tracked me. Of course that was ridiculous because I was being followed by dozens of fans, not to mention Conner's men. I suppose all the attention would keep Conner and Stan off me better than even Frank would.

Which was a good thing, because Frank had disappeared. I was waiting for the elevator and wondering how I was going to get to Frank's room undetected, when a bellman handed me a note.

Meet at the yellow bomb out front.

It could have been a setup, except I knew Frank's handwriting.

I made it to the lobby, after being stopped only three times, once by a local reporter and twice by women who wanted to know how I stayed so cool when I was being bullied by the male players.

I thought about telling them the truth—have the pro kidnap your brother and you will have real motivation to be cool. But instead I just said, "You've got to believe you have as big a right as they do to be sitting at that table."

I pushed my way out the doors and the yellow Hummer pulled up. I jumped in and Frank sped off. "Joe called.

There's a Fresh Foods truck out back of the Galaxy and he saw the driver and another man he tagged as casino security arguing about what to do with 'the extra baggage.' Then the man in the suit got a suitcase, unzipped it and showed the driver some money. We'll follow the truck. Maybe we'll find Ben."

Nineteen

♦ ♣ ♥ ♠

We got to the Galaxy in time to see the Fresh Foods truck turning south and heading toward us on Las Vegas Boulevard. Frank pulled into the casino's circular drive and negotiated around tourists toting luggage out of vehicles. Soon, we were behind the truck, headed south. At Tropicana, the truck turned left. Frank hung back to keep about a half dozen cars between us and followed.

"Why isn't Joe following the truck?"

"I sent him to see if he can shadow Stan."

"But Stan was at the Lanai," I pointed out. "What if the limo swoops in and takes him off before Joe gets a tail on him?"

"That won't happen any time soon," Frank said. "I happened to see the limo in the garage and I slit a hole in the tire while the driver was making time with one of Stan's girls."

"Smooth."

"So, you won." Frank finally acknowledged. "Congratulations. Although I'm not sure I want you to go through with the final round."

"What?" I sat bolt upright and screamed.

"I think this might be getting too dangerous. Conner knows who you are, Stan knows who you are. Maybe you should just fade out of sight and we'll try to find Ben in ways like this."

We'd reached Highway 95 and the truck turned south. It was three o'clock in the morning so there wasn't much traffic to disguise the big yellow Hummer. I just hoped the driver didn't expect to be followed.

"I'm not quitting. I'm just getting to the point where the pressure is paying off. Conner told me tonight that Ben 'was going to be a star'."

"What does that mean?"

"I assumed that was his way of telling me he's planning on killing him." I swallowed. "Or already has."

"Don't think that way, Bee," Frank assured me, following the truck onto the Highway 93 east exit toward the Hoover Dam.

I looked out at the desert, which seemed so much more desolate and desperate in the moonlight, wondering where my brother was and how I was letting him down by not being able to find him. We crossed over the Hoover Dam, its power and beauty electrified at night. Once we crossed over into Arizona and Lake Mead was behind us, there wasn't much to see in the dark. The excitement of the night and the rhythm of the road caught up with me. I drifted off to sleep.

I wasn't sure how much time passed before I felt Frank jog my shoulder. I blinked up at his face. His eyes were urgent in the dark. "Bee, wake up. Quick."

Yawning, I lifted my head out of his lap. We weren't moving. It was blacker than night. Even the interior lights, including the speedometer were off. Looking out the window, I gauged we were pulled off at a rest stop. A truck I recognized as the Fresh Foods' one we'd been chasing was about a hundred yards in front of us. The passing lights of the vehicles on the highway gave me a snapshot view of the rest. A dark, late model sedan was next to it, and I could see two figures between the vehicles. I was so tired, I felt like the produce truck had run over me, several times.

"What's going on?" I asked, my voice groggy.

"I'm not sure, but it's tense," Frank answered, his eyes focused on the scene before us.

"Where are we?"

"In northern Arizona, somewhere, maybe near Chloride. You really weren't asleep that long. About an hour."

One man got in the truck; the other in the driver's seat of the sedan. The produce truck moved off. The sedan didn't. After about thirty seconds, Frank started the Hummer and drove on too. We couldn't see in the tinted windows of the sedan when we passed, but it remained motionless.

We'd driven another ten miles before we heard it. A zing. A ting. A cracked rear window.

"What's going on?" I thought I knew, but I hoped I was wrong.

"We're the target and someone has a gun," Frank answered, his jaw flexed. He wrenched the wheel and tried to run the car next to us off the road. I'd bet anything it was the dark sedan from the truck stop, but it didn't take an Einstein to figure that one out. Frank let the sedan get ahead of us. He gunned the massive engine to try to ram our enemy, but instead the driver's accomplice shot our right headlight out.

"Damn," Frank spit out. "Where is the truck?"

I couldn't see it anymore. It must have taken a side road or doubled back to the rest stop or who knows what. Frank was steamed. He cranked the wheel and we did a fishtailing U-turn in the middle of the highway, turning us back to Las Vegas. We had just enough time to catch our breath before the sedan pulled even again. "So they just don't want us off their tail, they want us dead." I pointed out, ever observantly.

The sedan dodged just inches in front of our right bumper. Frank whipped the wheel to the left and struggled to keep the Hummer on the road, swearing under his breath as an oncoming car swerved and honked. "We're going to kill someone."

"I'm not as worried about them as I am about us right now."

Frank's mouth tightened. He angled the Hummer ahead of the sedan and floored the accelerator. We were going a hundred miles an hour. Cars pulled off the side of the road to get out of our way. Smart idea. The sedan was coming after us, but dropping back. I guess those Caddies don't have the engine the Hummer's do.

We were a quarter mile ahead of the sedan when Frank spoke again. "We can't do this all the way back to Vegas. Here's what is going to happen. You are going to crawl over here and take the wheel. Stay in this lane. Drop the speed about ten miles an hour, gradually, so they slowly catch up. Once they are about a hundred yards away, I'll tell you when, slam on the brakes."

"Ninety to zero in five point two seconds?" I asked.

"Less than that," he answered tightly.

The worst part of the whole thing was trying to get in the driver's seat. I was rubbing up against him and he was rubbing up against me, but we were going a hundred miles an hour and someone had to keep a hand on the wheel. Once I'd finally taken over everything, including the gas, I followed his instructions. They gained on us. My heart pounded. Frank crawled to the back seat on the passenger side.

"Now!"

I slammed on the brakes. I felt like the Hummer was going to do a somersault, but instinct helped me keep all four wheels on the asphalt.

"Get down," Frank yelled. I dove my head under the dashboard. I heard five loud pops.

When I peeked out Frank was on the floorboard, with a gun in his hand pointed out the window. "Where'd *that* come from?"

"Move, Bee, move." He yelled.

"I can't see." I argued. Ping. Crack. They got my windshield, dammit.

"Gun the gas, I don't care where we go right now, just move."

I moved my foot off the brake, and pressed the gas. We bounced off the road. I hoped my luck held and it was flat desert, not canyon territory. Frank was still focused on the sedan, gun drawn. I thought someone ought to look where we were going, so I lifted my head just barely above the dash.

The sand was dropping off right in front of us into a black hole! I cranked the wheel and threw Frank off balance. He swore. Zing. Crack. Ping. "What are you doing?" he demanded, crawling back to his window and sending off a round of shots toward the sedan.

"Unless this Hummer is really the Batmobile, I think we ought to avoid canyons."

"Huh," Frank said, "I'll cover you. Get up where you can really go and drive. Fast. Now."

He fired off another volley of shots and I gunned it, four wheeling it to the road, out of gunfire range and back toward Vegas. I looked in the rearview mirror. "Why aren't they following us? Did you kill someone?"

"No, Bee, I just shot out their tires."

"But you fired five shots the first time."

"I wish you weren't so observant sometimes. I missed one, okay?"

With one last look back at the crippled sedan, Frank crawled back up front in the passenger seat. "You want me to drive?"

I'd started to tremble with the aftermath of the adrenaline rush. "No, I think it will help me to have something to do."

Frank nodded and pushed his jeans leg up and slipped his gun back into his boot.

"Why do you have a gun?"

"It comes in handy in the—"

"Security business." I finished for him.

"Uh-huh," Frank agreed.

"When are you going to tell me what you really do for a living? Where you really live?"

"One day, Honey Bee, one day."

"And when are you going to tell me how I'm going to

repay you for doing all this to help me? I think the rent-a-Hummer is trashed." I paused to swallow the lump in my throat and was horrified when my breath caught on a sniffly sob.

"Don't worry about the Hummer. I think we need a new ride anyway. The yellow is a little obvious." Frank paused and pulled my hair out of its hasty bun. His fingers shook the strands loose to cascade around my shoulders. "As for repayment, I've thought of dozens and dozens of ways you can do that."

I blinked away a tear. I squirmed in my seat. "Hmm, you have?"

"You bet. I love homemade cookies. Oatmeal, chocolate chip, peanut butter . . ."

We got back to the Lanai at dawn, having left the poor Hummer behind an abandoned warehouse in Boulder City and calling a cab. I was going to miss it. I'd talked to Mom again, who hadn't heard from Ben, "the little rascal," but had heard from Pauline at the dentist's office that a woman's chances of getting pregnant drop from something like eighty percent to two-point-five pecent after she turns forty so Mom decided to make a moral exception and let me and Frank have a baby before the wedding so it wouldn't be too late.

Okay, Mom.

"What did she say?" Frank asked as we walked to the elevator.

"That she hadn't talked to Ben."

"Long conversation just to say that."

"Uh-huh."

We waited for an empty elevator because Frank had decided he couldn't afford to leave me alone. He'd just disable the security cameras along the way to our room, along with those on random floors along the way to throw Conner off track. It seemed to take hours to get to our room. I was so exhausted I almost didn't care if Conner was waiting for us on the twenty-fifth floor with instruments of torture. I just had to get to sleep.

Joe called as Frank was sliding the keycard in. I wanted to wait to see what he said, but when I saw the disappointment and frustration in Frank's face I knew it probably wasn't anything I wanted to hear. Frank swept the bedroom for bad guys and okayed me to go in as he listened. I threw off my clothes and crawled into bed.

Twenty

"**B**ee?"

I snuggled deeper under the covers. Frank's voice was just playing into my dreams, which included doing X-rated things at one hundred miles an hour.

"Do you always sleep this way?"

"Hmm?"

"I said, do you always sleep this way?"

I cracked open an eye and saw Frank's right eyebrow hitched in question. Uh-oh. Real life was coming back to me. I was naked. I grappled for the covers. I was on my side, covers tangled around my middle, bare leg over a spare pillow. I think the important parts had been covered, but unless Frank thought I wore a strapless thong nightie, he probably figured out the answer to his question.

This wasn't the way I'd planned him to be viewing my forty-year-old body, with the afternoon light streaming in, highlighting every imperfection. I sighed. Oh well, all he wanted was cookies anyway.

"I was wondering if you sleep walk, because I think I want to be your roommate a little longer."

"Very funny," I told his mile wide grin.

He sat down on the edge of the bed. "Stan went to one of his babes' hotel rooms last night. Joe checked after he left—no Ben. Then he went to the Galaxy and Joe lost him."

"So we don't know any more than we did yesterday, except Fresh Foods is up to something so no good they will kill to protect it. We have to connect Stan, Conner and Ben to the Galaxy, Fresh Foods, Mexico and snuff films."

"And one more thing," Frank said. "Joe went back to the loading dock at the Galaxy and snooped around a bit. Remember me saying the two men wrestled with the trunk and the top came unlatched? Apparently something fell out. Joe found a Ziploc full of pills."

"Drugs?"

"We don't know yet. Joe had to drive them to a friendly lab we've worked with in California for testing. So he's out of pocket for a while."

"Maybe it is that date rape drug. Maybe they use it on the girls they kidnap for the snuff videos."

Frank's eyebrows rose. "Good thinking, Nancy Drew."

The cell phone in Frank's pocket rang. He answered and I shooed him out of the room so I could shower and dress. It was three o'clock in the afternoon. I felt like my days and nights had been turned upside down here in Vegas. I was going to have more than jet lag when I got home. Whenever that might be.

I lingered in the shower until I heard the bedroom door open. Uh-oh. I stepped behind the towel hanging over the clear Plexiglas, realizing with horror that it only covered my top half. A wet naked me was probably worse looking than a sleepy naked me. After all, things are less likely to sag when a body is horizontal.

"I'm not finished," I called, hoping the panic didn't come through in my voice.

"No kidding? Can I join you?" Frank teased.

Hmm. I needed to turn the hot water down. I was starting to tingle all over.

I looked down. Cellulite looked up. "That's probably not a good idea."

"Spoilsport!" Frank called.

"Cretin," I shouted back.

"Then this is fair warning. You have five minutes to get out of there or I will let my fantasies take control."

Hmm. I could always say the fantasies made me do it. I sighed and rinsed the conditioner out of my hair. In only four minutes I was out, dry, wearing the plush hotel robe and surveying my frightening wardrobe. What was I going to wear on national television tonight? The only good thing was I would only be taped from the waist up. Maybe viewers wouldn't know I was mixing labels. I needed something powerful, something sexy—something that would match my silver Gargoyles. I'd wear my crimson suede jacket, pewter satin camisole that dipped just a little too low in the middle, my Ziamond teardrop dangle earrings. I'd have to rewear my black satin pants and spangle stiletto sandals.

After the outfit was laid out on my bed, I wandered into the living room.

Frank looked up from his computer. "Why aren't you dressed?"

"What's the hurry? The finals don't start for hours."

"We're going to go to the Cook County lockup."

"I'm sorry Frank, but we don't have time to go to jail today."

He glared. "Bee, I'm serious. Deidre called. One of the girls she dances with got to talking and said her boyfriend was just released from jail. While he was inside he was cellmates with a guy from Nogales, on the Arizona/Mexico border, who told him he works for Fresh Foods."

"So maybe he can tell us where the Fresh Foods warehouse is," I said, excited at the break.

"More than that. Maybe he can tell us what Fresh Foods is up to."

"We can't get our hopes up. I'm sure most of the employees don't know what's going on."

"This guy does. He indicated to his cellmate that he did a lot more than just move lettuce. He told them he didn't like what they wanted him to do, next thing he knows he's thrown in a patrol car and behind bars on what he claims is a trumped up charge."

"But he didn't mention Conner or Stan?"

"Not that I know of. But the day after he told the guy this he was attacked by another inmate and was lucky to survive."

"Coincidence?"

"Maybe, but I doubt it. We need to hurry, Bee. I'm not sure how long this guy can hang on."

I hurried into my bedroom and threw on the clothes I'd gotten ready for that night. Frank had rented another car that was waiting for us outside the front door, a black Lincoln sedan with tinted windows similar to the one we'd left crippled on Highway 93.

"If you can't beat 'em, join 'em?" I asked as he held my door for me and tipped the delivery driver.

Frank shrugged. "At least it will be less conspicuous."

"Actually, I think you should have rented an armored tank." I pointed out as he slid into the driver's seat.

"I don't plan on having a chase today."

"Good because I didn't wear my running shoes."

"I bet you don't own running shoes," Frank said dryly as he pulled away from the curb.

"I consider other things better exercise."

Shooting me a sidelong look full of innuendo, Frank hitched his right eyebrow. "And what would those 'other things' that get your blood racing and heart pumping be?"

Wicked man. "Shopping."

"So, do you like window shopping or really *doing it*?"

I looked him up and down, slowly, appraisingly taking in the swell of bicep below his charcoal knit polo shirt, the press of his quadricep against his Levi's, the size of those black Roper boots on the accelerator. Hmm. "Depends if I like what's in the window."

Frank chuckled, deep and low. "You're dangerous, Honey Bee."

"Nobody's ever told me that before."

"Maybe nobody's ever really known you before."

I had to leave that one alone because, as usual, he said exactly the right thing and left me so overwhelmed that I was touched, tongue-tied and afraid.

We actually didn't have to go to jail after all. The deputy on duty told us over the phone that Rudy De La Rosa was at Las Vegas General Hospital in serious condition. He wasn't sure he was allowed to have visitors, but we could try.

Once we'd made it through the metal detectors (with me holding my breath because of Frank's gun that he'd apparently removed), Frank leaned down to me. "This is going to be your starring role, Bee. Good practice for tonight."

"What do you mean?"

"I mean, if they allow anyone it will be only family. I look gringo, I sound gringo and I am male. You, on the other hand, put on your shades, take down that hair and push up that bra and you can be anything you want to be to the cops on duty."

"What about the nurses?"

"That's where your Spanish comes in: fast and loud as you can and the same for the crying. I know you can cry."

I shot him a loaded glare. He smiled. "Come on, you can jerk out a tear or two for your—"

"Mi esposo?" I sniffed.

Frank pulled a handkerchief out of his pocket. It was warm and smelled like Dove. Did he eat the stuff? Did it exude from his pores? I breathed it in.

He watched me and cocked his head. "You're supposed to blow on it, silly, not inhale it."

Oops. I slid my Gargoyles onto my face.

He grabbed my elbow protectively and led me forward.

We turned the corner and saw a uniformed guard sitting outside a door. "Excuse me," Frank said. "Is this Rudy De La Rosa's room?"

The obvious rookie stiffened then stood. "Who told you?"

"A carcel," I said, cocking my chin toward the door. *"Déjeme entrar. Soy su esposa."*

He drew his eyebrows together and shook his head. "Is this the wife? Did she say she wants to go in?"

Blinking apologetically, Frank nodded.

The deputy shook his head. "No visitors."

Pushing my size Ds together strategically with my upper arms, I let off a rapid fire litany in Spanish. The poor guy stared for a moment at my cleavage and then looked at Frank in dismay, holding up his hand. "Tell her to stop."

Out of the corner of my eye I saw a nurse look around the corner and put her finger to her lips. The deputy nodded desperately. I raised my volume a tick or two and went on about how my poor kids at home might not have a father and how were we going to live? Besides, I had to find out where his *sancha* lived, because that is where most of his money went, when the babies went hungry. More nurses joined the first. One walked up to us.

"What's the problem?"

"She wants to visit her husband, but—"

"Oh just let her in," the nurse snapped. I think she could relate to the *sancha* thing. "She is disturbing the whole floor. We can't have that."

"But I'm sure the doctor—"

"This guy isn't going to lose any more blood talking to his wife than's already flowed out of him from that knife wound. Chill, Junior."

The deputy sighed and gestured for me to go in. I blew my nose, scurried in, giving Junior a nice eyeful of cleavage to think about while Frank slipped by. It wasn't what it used to be, apparently—he stopped Frank with a hand to his chest. "Only family."

Uh-oh. I was on my own.

Rudy had been listening to the ruckus, because he watched me come in the door with a wide smile. "*Eres mi esposa? Que buena suerte tengo!*"

"Aren't you kind," I told the pale, thin boy with angel eyes who couldn't be more than eighteen.

"No, you are beautiful. Who are you?" he asked curiously.

"My name's Belinda. It's a long story," I began saying, sinking down into the chair next to his bed. I slid my glasses to the top of my head. "But I don't have much time, so I will just have to tell you the important parts. My brother is missing and I think the people you work for might have kidnapped him and hurt him."

His eyes closed for a moment, then opened with fiery hate. "They put me in jail, they hurt me."

"What happened?"

"I work in Nogales, packing fruits to bring here. I work for two years. Now someone doesn't come to work one day and they tell me I have to drive the truck to Las Vegas. They say the drivers make a lot of money. So I go. They give me a cell phone and tell me they might call to check on me. But they call and tell me where to stop. A rest stop on a highway. A man who says he is an inspector for the company gets out and tells me he needs to check something inside. He is inside the truck for about twenty minutes then he leaves.

"I don't like it. I go into the truck and check myself. I opened a couple of boxes and everything was okay. I checked another box and saw a mango that looked strange. I pulled on the stem and the top came off, it had no inside, no pit. It was just an empty hole. I tried to check the rest of the boxes but only found two more mangoes like that. Then my bosses were calling because I was late. They were suspicious."

"What did the inspector look like?"

"Big, two hundred fifty pounds, big hat, big mustache, big everything except mean little eyes." It could easily be Steely Stan.

"When I went to go back to Nogales, the same thing happened. They called me and told me to stop, a different place this time."

"But I thought you only exported fruits. You import them into Mexico too?"

"Apples, from Washington we take to Mexico. And this time more inspector men came on the truck and when they left I drove on for a while before I stopped and checked. I didn't see anything at first, but then the middle of one looked wrong and I pulled the stem and the top came off. No core inside just a space with a bag full of pills. Drugs."

"What happened?"

"I didn't want to go across the border with that. I turned around and came back and told them the truck was acting wrong, that it needed work. I don't think they believed me. When they told me to drive a different one, I told them I quit. A police man picked me up when I was waiting for my bus and arrested me for stealing from a convenience store. I didn't even go into a convenience store here in Las Vegas."

"What did the policeman look like?"

Tall, over six feet. Dark hair, dark heart. *Ojos muy azul.* Daniel Conner.

"Why didn't you tell anyone about this?"

"The man who stabbed me in jail? He told me if I said anything that they would take my sister and do bad, bad things to her."

I tried to hang on to my temper. I felt like taking Frank's gun out of his boot and blowing Conner's brains out. "Tell me where the warehouse is here in Las Vegas."

"It is on Goodwin Street on the north side of the city."

The door swung open and a nurse bustled in. End of interrogation. "Time to take your vital signs, sir."

Good thing she wasn't going to take mine. They'd be off the chart.

Twenty-One

♦ ♣ ♥ ♠

I tried to relay as much as I could to Frank in a frantic whisper on our way back to the parking lot but we were interrupted when Joe called on his cell phone. While they talked, I tried to enjoy the desert sunset—I don't think there is a richer orange in the world. I also tried to focus on my strategy for the final round of the Hold 'Em tournament, but my mind was buzzing from what I'd learned from Rudy and what it meant when combined with what we already knew.

Later I wished I hadn't been so distracted. I might have figured out we were being followed.

As Frank held the passenger door open for me, he hung up with Joe. He looked at me, "You'll never guess who owns Fresh Foods."

"You're right. I'll never guess because my brain is already overloaded from trying to connect the dots on the rest of the puzzle."

Frank looked at the digital clock on the dashboard as he turned the key. It was already six o'clock. "I've got to get you back and get you some dinner before your tournament."

"So, who owns Fresh Foods?"

"His name is Ranocy, Joseph Ranocy."

"Do we know him?"

"Listen closer, Bee," Frank said. "To the last name."

"Cyrano with the letters scrambled," I paused as Frank nodded. "Well, that explains his wealth, I suppose. It explains why he seemed to be more a CEO with a sick hobby than your garden variety pervert."

"Of course it doesn't explain why his company is sponsoring Stan, who may be producing and smuggling snuff films that Cyrano clearly did not approve of."

"Do you remember how weird he got when we said we'd heard Fresh Foods wouldn't be sponsoring Stan anymore?"

Frank shrugged, keeping too close a watch on his rearview mirror for my taste. "Maybe Cyrano found out about what Stan and Conner were doing and wants to shut it down."

"But that doesn't explain why he wanted to sponsor him in the first place," I mused.

Suddenly, Frank made a hard right onto a side street and gunned the engine. I grabbed for the dashboard to keep from flying into his lap. "Miss your turn?" I asked as my head bounced off his shoulder.

Frank's mouth was a tight line. "Our friend in the sedan got his tires fixed and is behind us."

I looked back and saw the car gaining on us like a long black shark. Frank hooked a sharp left down an alley between two buildings and landed us south on Paradise Road. We were parallel with The Strip now, the darkening sky illuminated by the neon to our right. I could see our hotel in the distance, the oversize motorized palm trees on the roof swaying. Frank whipped in and out of traffic and headed right toward an oncoming Clark County Sheriff's Department cruiser. It did a wild U-turn after us, ending up behind our pursuer.

"What are you doing?" I asked.

"As much as I don't like the cops here, I think they might

ask questions first and shoot later. The guy chasing is going to shoot. Questions won't be involved." Frank cranked the wheel to the left then right, barely avoiding a slow moving Volkswagen Bug. As Frank spun right down Spring Mountain Road, I looked back to see the police car going straight on Paradise. The black sedan was still gaining on us.

"What's going on?" I breathed.

Frank whistled under his breath. "Conner called the squad car off. He's got major pull."

"How do you know the black car is Conner?"

"He's the only one who could call the wolves off a high-speed chase."

We fishtailed onto Koval and almost made it back to The Strip before Frank slammed on the brakes. The black car zoomed past us before correcting and spinning in the middle of the road as we ducked into a side street behind the casinos. I thought for a minute we'd lost him as we flew past the backside of Bourbon Street. Frank slipped next to a dumpster behind Barbary Coast and we waited, engine idling, holding our breath as the seconds ticked by. Suddenly it appeared, headlights blinding us, heading for our back bumper. Frank stepped on the gas and we leaped ahead, bouncing off the curb, and finally through an alley and back onto Las Vegas Boulevard.

"Maybe he'll have a harder time being aggressive here," Frank said through clenched teeth.

But it didn't look like the traffic or the tourists had intimidated him as he rammed our bumper.

"Ouch," I said, "It looks like I'm not going to make enough in the tournament to replace all the cars we're going to lose."

"We just hope that's all we're going to lose."

As I mulled over that happy thought, Frank swerved into the Mirage parking garage, squealing across the smooth concrete.

"Bee," Frank said tensely as he wheeled around the turns, his knuckles white on the steering wheel. "As soon as I slam on my brakes, we are going to run for the stairs.

Don't wait for me, don't call for me, just run as fast as you can, into the casino. Conner doesn't have any pull in the Mirage, so hopefully he can't call the house goons to shackle us. We'll meet at the Hold 'Em tables. If we get separated and I'm not there in five minutes go back to the Lanai and get to the tournament. You'll be safe in the TV lights. Do not wait more than five minutes, you understand? The longer you are here, the more you risk getting caught. If you get caught, the odds of ever finding Ben will virtually disappear."

We were on the fourth floor now. Frank had risked hitting parked cars and bystanders to get us far enough ahead of Conner that he was out of sight. I yanked off my shoes and held them. We heard Conner's wheels squealing around the corner as we opened the doors and ran for the stairs. Frank had stopped so close I was only half a stride away. I was already half a flight down before I heard him screech to a stop. I heard a huge thump and a gunshot.

I paused on the stairwell. Frank wasn't behind me. Maybe he'd gotten a shot off at Conner. Then I remembered the hospital metal detector. He didn't have his gun.

I turned around.

Don't wait for me. Don't call for me.

I backtracked two steps, my heart at my throat, blood pounding, sweat trickling down my backbone.

Run as fast as you can. We'll meet at the Hold 'Em tables.

I raced the rest of the way down the stairs and wound my way through the tropical gardens toward the casino lights. I couldn't hear anything else definitive from the garage, no matter how hard I tried. I stepped on a rock and bit my tongue to keep from yelping. A man was holding the casino door for his wife and I slowed to keep from alarming them. He gave me a strange look but nodded me through. I thanked him quietly and hotfooted it past the gift shops toward the sound of slot machines.

Once I reached the casino floor, I paused, sucking in a deep breath and willing my adrenaline under control. I had to find the Hold 'Em tables. I glanced at my watch. It had only been two and a half minute, but it seemed like a week.

Just as I located the poker tables, I felt a hand on my shoulder and looked to my right to see a casino security goon looking down at me. He had to be six foot five. Even my famous heel kick wouldn't catch his crotch. I was devising other ways to get free before he dragged me to Conner when he said, "Ma'am, we have a no shirt, no shoes policy here."

My hands flew to my chest. Had I been breathing so hard, I'd ripped my blouse?

My shoes knocked into my right breast and I remembered I was still barefoot. I forced a laugh that hopefully covered my sigh of relief. "Oh, these shoes have been killing me all day. I'm sorry. I forgot I'd taken them off. No wonder my feet didn't hurt."

He gave me a nutty broad look and watched me strap the sandals back on before he wandered off.

I had one minute to meet Frank at the Hold 'Em tables. I didn't see him, but I'm sure he hid better than I did. I scanned the backs of the heads of the players. From here I identified two potential heads. I figured he'd have found another way down, maybe the elevator or through the tropical forest instead of on the pathway, which was why I hadn't seen him. I got as far as they would let me get without playing.

"You want a seat?" the pit boss asked.

"Maybe in a minute," I answered, on closer inspection discounting both players I thought might be Frank. "I'm supposed to meet someone here. We probably want to sit together."

She nodded and left me alone. The last minute ticked by with excruciating sloth. No Frank. I scanned the other tables, craps, roulette, blackjack. No Frank. I waited another minute. Every dirty blond male head with his back to me made my heart race. No Frank.

Do not wait more than five minutes, you understand?

Another minute passed. I couldn't swallow. My imagination drew all sorts of undesirable conclusions, from Conner running Frank down with the black sedan to Conner knocking Frank out and kidnapping him to Conner shooting Frank and leaving him to bleed to death on the slick concrete of the parking garage. The last image made me backtrack through the casino until I got to the hallway leading to the gardens. Frank would kill me for doing this. I wouldn't mind him killing me if he lived. But if he was kidnapped and I went back, was caught by one of Conner's lackeys and then couldn't get help for Frank, we'd be in worse shape than we were in now. At least I was free; at least I could call in reinforcements. I could find Joe—by some miracle since I didn't know anything about him, including his last name—and ride to Frank's rescue.

Maybe Frank had just taken longer than he expected to pulverize Conner and headed back to our hotel. Maybe he was now twiddling his thumbs at the Lanai, waiting for me outside the tournament ballroom and nervously envisioning my demise because I was taking longer than we'd planned to return.

I had to hang onto that possibility to propel myself out of the Mirage and onto The Strip. I racewalked past Caesars Palace, trying not to remember my last hours with Ben. Getting mushy now wouldn't do anyone any good.

I might be the only one able to ride to Frank and Ben's rescue. Time to gather my resources and come up with a strategy.

Resource number one: I was free.

I walked through the front doors of the Lanai.

Resource number two: I had incriminating information.

I saw the posters advertising the final round of the Lanai Pro-Am Texas Hold 'Em Tournament "Live on ESPN!"

And that gave me resource number three: I had the media's attention. By the end of the evening I'd have a microphone at the end of my lips.

Twenty-Two

♦ ♣ ♥ ♠

I had eyes only for the television crews. The ESPN cameras were already inside the ballroom, focused on the final tables. If I could just make it to the local news reporters lined up interviewing tournament officials and fans, I could tell them—

A hand grabbed my upper arm. "Miss Cooley, the casino and the tournament have been looking everywhere for you. We were getting quite desperate."

I recognized one of Conner's security cohorts. He was squeezing a bit too hard and I tried to wrench my arm away. He squeezed tighter.

"I just need to go . . ." I drifted toward the news cameras. He directed me back toward the ballroom door.

"Sorry, Miss Cooley, there's no time to powder your nose right now. That will have to wait for a commercial break."

With that, he ushered me into the ballroom where the cameras started whirring and flashes popped. Microphones were under the reporters' mouths, not mine. Go figure. I should have written the message across my forehead, my cleavage or my rump since that is where the cameras seemed to be focusing.

I scanned the crowd. Amy was there with Junior waving a "Buzz 'em Bee Cool!" banner. The Poker Babes were back in larger force. Ringo was there with a "Hold 'Em Dudes for Bee Cool" sign and a horde of his fellow nerds. About a dozen women in silver mirrored Gargoyles just like mine were wearing matching gold spangled halter tops and lipstick in the same Crimson Desire shade I favored. "Hold 'Em's new Mae West" one hand lettered sign read. Spring peeked out from behind it along with all the folks I'd played with in the room. They all waved and hollered. I waved back and tried not to look as disappointed as I felt when Frank's face didn't pop up in their midst. I looked at a group of unusually tall women in business suits holding a "Bee Cool for President" sign. I peered closer. It was Carey and friends. She nodded and waved. I grinned back and winked.

The tournament president leaned into me, whispering, "What a grand entrance. Wily of you I have to say, and good for the game, but it about gave me a heart attack." Then he pulled back and smiled, shaking my hand for the cameras. "Thank you for joining us, Miss Cooley, for the final round of the first annual Lanai Pro-Am Tournament. Please draw your seat."

It seemed silly, since my seat was obviously the only open seat left. Although I'd been hoping to sit next to Steely Stan from the get-go, I wasn't even at his table. I reached in and handed the official the only slip of paper left. He read, "Table two, seat one".

My only piece of good luck today: I would have the dealer button first.

I could feel Stan glaring at me through his Oakleys. He was probably pissed I'd stolen his thunder by arriving last. Too damn bad. I pulled my Gargoyles out of my pocket. I was more pissed than he was, and I was going to have his cojones by the end of the night. That was the only way I was going to have my say on camera.

My only chance to find Ben and save Frank.
I had to win.

*T*he cards had been good to me so far. I was intensely focused. The man sitting next to me joked that he'd
heard he'd at least get kissed before I screwed him over for
first at the table. When he was eliminated, he said he hadn't
even gotten a giggle or a smile, much less a kiss.

Still I didn't smile.

I had psyched out the table. My tension was infectious,
although they must have perceived it as emanating from
the game of poker when in fact it emanated from the game
of life and death.

I could feel Stan's stare every now and then, but I never
wavered. Conner hadn't showed up, and I noticed that
caused a bit of consternation among his troops. They fid-
geted, whispered and checked their beepers more often
than usual. Casino security chief Cedillo paced around the
room, obviously not as well versed on the security plan as
he needed to be. One of the local news reporters read the
loophole and inched over toward our table, swooping in
when she saw a security goon's back turned and swinging
a mic in front of my face.

"Josey Micky KWOP news. How do you feel about
usurping the role of crowd favorite from Steely Stan, Miss
Cooley?"

"I'd feel better about it if my brother and boyfriend
weren't missing," I began saying.

The little strawberry blonde gasped, her blue eyes wide.
"Do you think it has something to do with the tournament?"

Apparently the security force wised up, because the reporter suddenly squealed and was yanked back out of
earshot before I could answer. The tournament officials
evicted her from the room. I watched her go with a sinking
spirit. Maybe that was enough to raise questions, maybe it
was enough to bring police. Maybe it was enough for Conner to let Ben and Frank go.

If they were still alive.

In the first hand heads up with the button against the pro from Florence, I peeked at my pocket: three/club, three/heart. I could call the big blind, which would be safest. I could raise, which would be semidaring. But since I had probably a couple thousand dollars in front of me, I could go all in, lose and still stay in the game because I had more chips than the Italian did. I remembered how the cards fell when Frank and I had played heads up and when I'd ended up heads up before. Italians were known for being loose players. It didn't seem that risky after all.

I went all in.

He went all in.

The Flop was a bunch of blanks to me: nine/spade, five/club, Queen/spade.

He had a King/heart, ten/spade in his pocket.

We all held our breaths as an ace/heart fell on Fourth Street and deuce/spade fell on The River.

I'd won.

The Italian shook my hand and pinched my ass behind the TV cameras. "I think you're pretty hot, Bee Cool."

Dismissing him with a skeptical look, I looked toward the last table where the other five waited, since our table had taken the longest to finish. Stan, of course, had made it. He had an empty chair to his left.

I smiled. Stan glowered. Not only could I rattle him with what I had to tell him, I got to see all his bets before I bet myself. I couldn't be in a better position.

The tournament president appeared at my elbow with his fishbowl. "Your last draw of the tournament, Miss Cooley. Good luck."

I handed the slip to him without looking at it, and headed straight for the seat next to Stan. I could hear the ESPN commentator rattling on in excitement from his seat behind the barricade, "This could prove to be one of the matchups to remember in Hold 'Em history. 'Steely Stan' has proven himself unbeatable for the last year, winning not only the World Series of Poker but every other major Hold 'Em tournament. Belinda 'Bee Cool' Cooley, who's become a crowd favorite here at the new Vegas casino, the Lanai, has come virtually from nowhere to sit at this final table as the only woman and the only amateur among five pros."

"There is no virtually about it." A female commentator cut in. "From what we understand, Belinda Cooley hadn't played poker until a few days ago. I find this hard to believe, and likely some sort of stretch of the truth. But she doesn't have any tournament experience—that much is true. I suppose we could say she is a poster child for the part luck and innate skill plays in this game."

I glanced at my watch. It was time for the eleven o'clock news. I could see the reporters from the three local stations outside the ballroom door, broadcasting live. As the tournament president signaled the dealer to begin and a hush spread through the room, I prayed Josey from KWOP would play my soundbite and that it would break the case wide open.

Twenty-Three

♦ ♣ ♥ ♠

"**Y**ou think you're real hot, don't you?" Stan hissed as he brought his highball to his lips to swig whatever clear liquid he was drinking. The tournament had decided to even the odds a bit in the last round by letting us put in secret drink orders. It took away an element of one of the weapons I'd used thus far with success.

But if I had to guess, I'd say Stan was drinking vodka. His movements were more studied and careful than I had seen him make so far. Perhaps I could get him to say, or better, do something he would regret.

But he threw me off balance first.

"So, Bee Cool, I hear your boyfriend is drinking again. That's too bad. I know you must be worried, having to sit here while he's getting soused. It's pretty easy to die of alcohol poisoning, you know. And drunks fall off high places all the time."

I stiffened. He knew about Frank. He knew Frank drank. They had Frank. They were pouring alcohol down his throat and were about to push him off the top of the Mirage parking garage. "I wouldn't know, actually," I said, trying to infuse my tone with scorn instead of the panic I was feeling. I dropped my gaze to his glass and hoped it burned through my Gargoyles. "But I guess *you* would."

His neck reddened. His knuckles whitened.

I peeked at the cards in front of me, willing my hand not to shake—Ace/spade and King/heart. Good thing the cards were falling for me, because nothing else seemed to be. I waited for Stan to call the big blind and I raised. Everyone else at the table folded. Stan called my raise.

The flop was a five/club, six/heart and King/diamond. Two blanks and one semipossibility for me. He could have a straight working or two pair or who knows what.

Where was Frank?

Stan bet ten thousand. I called.

The turn was a seven/club.

Where was Ben?

Stan bet another ten. I called.

The River was a three/diamond.

Stan bet another ten. I called.

I heard the ESPN commentator say something about "calling station."

His pockets were a four/club and King/heart. He double beat me. I decided right then and there that I had to change everything. Whatever he said had made me emotional and I couldn't get that way in a game. I was distracted, too busy thinking about Ben and Frank to read any of his body language. From now on, I told myself, I would play two games simultaneously. Hold 'Em and save 'Em.

I would save them by psyching Stan out of his mind.

It wasn't hard to win the next couple of half-decent hands I had, because everyone at the table had immediately underestimated me after the way I played the first hand so badly. Now I had them confused.

That was exactly where I wanted them, especially Stan.

I'd refrained from any talk until I got my mind squarely back into the card game, but now that I felt more secure, I could start shaking Stan's tree.

"I hear you are a supporter of third world cinema," I said low but loud enough that the microphones might pick it up. "Of Mexico, especially."

His head snapped toward mine. I smiled. Slowly.

"I think Sundance is great," he answered. His head snapped back to the front of the table. His fingers moved stiffly to flip up his pocket cards like the tin man.

I had a pocket pair of tens. I played through against three of the other pros. Stan folded early on. No telling what he had, but he did drain another glass of whatever. He flashed a number two to the waitress. We were given the choice of two drinks, with one being water. I wondered if he were ordering another vodka or if he was switching to water. I won about thirty thousand dollars on that hand, but infinitely more in the psychological war with Stan.

My advantage didn't last long, though, because two hands later he pretended to drop his cocktail napkin and leaned down next to me.

"Your brother is a very good actor," he whispered.

I couldn't suppress my shiver. Nausea rose in my throat. I grabbed my glass and took a gulp to wash it down. The other players watched me curiously, waiting for my bet.

I suddenly couldn't remember my pocket cards. I folded.

"**P**sst. Bee?"

In my stall, I tried to ignore the woman next to me. We'd been given a fifteen minute restroom break while ESPN ran commercials and a background story on each of the players. One of the pros at the table told me they'd interviewed his family. I wondered who they'd found to yak about me. If it was my mother, it was going to be scary.

Since they'd sent me with one of Conner's goons who was posted outside the door, the odds of me getting to a pay phone to try to find Frank were nil, unless I could give him one of my famous heels to the groin. . . .

"Bee?" my would-be fan persisted. This restroom had been locked since noon, I was told. And the goon with me cleared the bathroom before I went in.

"Yes?" I sighed as I opened the door.

She grappled with her lock and shoved the door open, falling through. I recognized her but I couldn't remember from where.

"Beth Watson," she held out her hand. We shook as she continued, "I've been waiting in here, standing on the toilet seat, since noon to talk to you. Thank goodness you needed to pee."

"You win the award for persistence," I commented.

"Well, you promised me the exclusive," she said.

"I remember. I would've given you the interview without a twelve hour wait in the loo."

"I believe you," Beth said, breathless, grabbing my forearm. "But I had to tell you what I found out about Steely Stan as soon as I could. I left you a message at your hotel room, but when you didn't call me back, I knew this was probably the most guaranteed way to catch you before the end of the tournament."

Damn, we'd been so busy I hadn't checked the room messages since yesterday. "What?"

"You know they call the girls that hang with Stan his Squeezes, right?" I nodded and she went on. "Three of the girls known to hang out with Stan have each been listed as missing with their hometown police departments over the past couple of years. Shari Reichardt, Marianna Gomez and Lisa Aaron. The detectives I talked to each said that they contacted this county's sheriff's department to check out Stan. They were assured by the detective he'd cleared an interview but they would keep an eye on him."

I felt my hands going clammy. My heart raced. I couldn't breathe for a moment. Finally I swallowed and asked, "Did they give you the name of the detective?"

"Daniel Conner."

* * *

Struggling to maintain my composure, I walked slowly back to the Hold 'Em table. I now had the only proof that Conner and Stan were connected. Had Conner forced Stan to give him a cut of the Fresh Foods smuggling deal in exchange for keeping quiet about the disappearances? Had they cooked up a bigger plan once they found themselves kindred evil spirits, or had they been in it together before? Did Conner get himself assigned to the cases just to cover them up?

And what had happened to those girls?

The same thing that was happening to Ben?

I stopped my thoughts from traveling in that direction. I had to compartmentalize. I had to play my two games and win. I had a new weapon. Now I had to decide how to use it.

Twenty-Four

♦ ♣ ♥ ♠

By the time I eased into my seat, I was deep in my best zone for playing Hold 'Em. My focus was sharp. I could feel the players around me and nothing beyond the table. I couldn't hear the commentators anymore; I couldn't hear the crowds' calls of encouragement, either. I needed to win as soon as possible so I could get on with finding Frank and Ben before it was too late.

My new cohort and budding investigative journalist Beth was busy trying to track down a guy named Joe who worked for a security guy named Frank Gilbert. Once she'd exhausted all avenues there, she was going to look up the Hold 'Em dealer that had started to tell me about Stan's "other job." That's all I could really afford to let her do. There was no way I was going to let anyone else die or get hurt because of me.

I ignored Stan as I peered at my pocket cards—muck. I folded. Stan's chest puffed up. I folded the next three hands, playing a waiting game, hoping to make Stan over-confident and letting him knock out the competition. It worked. He narrowed the field to three in less than an hour with big bets and reraises.

Five hands later, I had a pair of Kings in my pocket and decided to call the big blind. Stan said almost inaudibly behind his big mustache, "Bet you'd make a great actress. Bet you make lots of noise. Bet you have one killer scream."

"I bet they give gringos life in prison for murder in Mexico. I bet life expectancies aren't too long behind bars south of the border either, Donald."

Stan paled.

The flop was a Queen/spade and two blanks—three/diamond, ten/club.

I raised fifty thousand. The only other player left was a middle-aged pro from Atlantic City. He was a huge chauvanist and had spent most of his game staring at my chest behind his Oakleys and snorting at my bets. I know he was still deciding whether I was a rock or a Maniac. Either way he had no respect for me. He raised fifty and Stan called.

Fourth Street was a Queen/heart. I went all in.

Stan, still pale, folded. The Atlantic City chauvinist went all in, having decided I couldn't read my cards, I guess.

The River was a ten/diamond. A.C. Chauvinist ooched around in his chair. Guess he had a pocket ten.

We showed our cards and he said a word that had to be bleeped from live television. Out of the corner of my eye, I saw Beth elbow her way to the front of the boundary and give me a thumbs up. Whatever that meant. She found Joe? She'd found Frank? She'd been hired by the *Washington Post*?

I'd have to wait to find out.

The dealer asked if we needed a break before the first heads-up hand. Stan had recovered his composure and was looking to hurt me again. He'd acted like a rattlesnake every time he'd been hit. He'd coil and strike again.

"I'm ready," Stan said authoritatively and the crowd ooed. "But this is Miz Cooley's first big tournament. Oh, sorry, her *only* tournament. So if she needs more time, I certainly understand."

Sure he did. Actually, I wanted to take more time. But since I wouldn't be able to do what I wanted with that time—like try to find Frank and contact Joe—I eschewed the offer in favor of keeping Stan off balance. "Thank you so much for your consideration, Stan, but I'm ready," I announced. My fans roared.

Stan frowned. Obviously this wasn't playing into his expected hand. I hoped the cards wouldn't either.

I drew the dealer button for the first hand. ESPN would be showing our pocket cards to the viewing audience at home. I doubted this would affect my play. After all, I pretty much didn't know what I was doing, so looking stupid to couch potato poker experts was a foregone conclusion for me. Stan, however, had a reputation to uphold. He was the winningest Maniac in the history of the game, according to Ben. He might take some risks just to dazzle the viewers. I was counting on that.

As the dealer began to shuffle, a hush fell over the crowd. I did some quick math on the chips in front of us and decided Stan had a forty thousand dollar advantage. That was a good thing. He would play a little looser.

An hour later I hadn't made much headway. I wasn't getting cards and was doing a lot of folding. TVs across America were changing channels because this game had to be more boring than watching paint dry. I refused to lose, though. I knew if I waited long enough for the right cards, it would be time to really play. The tournament president was pacing, sweat popping out on his forehead. The PR flack for the casino was wringing her hands. I know they all wanted to slap me around.

"Bad case of nerves?" The dealer asked quietly during a commercial break as Stan chatted with one of the ESPN commentators. I could hear him say that it might take all night but he'd win by the blinds.

I smiled, winking behind my Gargoyles. "Nerves. Exactly." Exactly what I want Stan to think.

The tournament president wandered by. "We would love to see some action."

I smiled. "So would I." I motioned to the dealer and joked, "Talk to him."

When we were back on the air, the dealer gave us our pocket cards. I placed the marker on mine and prayed for a miracle. I peeled up the edges and let them slap back down. Finally. My luck was turning. Queen/heart, King/spade.

I called the big blind. Stan was so taken aback that I'd placed a bet that he paused, then raised fifty thousand. I called.

The Flop was nine/heart, deuce/heart and nine/spade.

I bet a hundred thousand. Stan raised fifty. I called.

The Turn was a nine/diamond. I checked. Stan bet fifty. I called and guessed he was trying to play the board with a big kicker. As long as I kept calling, I would keep him from getting suspicious of my hand. The way he kept nodding smugly, I knew he thought I'd been shamed into betting by the dealer's and official's comments. If I didn't get a King I would have to play the board too, with a King kicker. I prayed he didn't have an ace.

The fourth nine fell on The River.

Stan grinned and bet another fifty. I called. We showed our cards and he had a blank and a Queen kicker.

My fans howled. I guess they hadn't had much to cheer about up to now. I'd gotten lucky, and I was counting on a lot more of that.

"At least that woke everyone up," Stan muttered, as if he'd lost as a favor to the fans.

"Marianna, Shari and—hope so," I said as I brought my glass to my lips.

Stan went eerily still. Slowly, he turned his Bolles on me. The air around us dropped temperature. I suppressed a shiver and grinned, even more slowly, right back at him. I hoped Frank had made it through, because if he didn't and I didn't find a clean cop once this game was over, Stan was surely going to find a way to kill me before I found Ben.

I could hear the commentators chuckling along about "bad blood" and "anti-fish." "Steely Stan tapped on the aquarium and a shark popped out," one of them chortled.

I wanted to tell them it was just one hand, guys, but I was grateful for the distraction. Stan could hear what they were saying too and I knew it would keep him from plotting exactly how to dismember me. I looked through the crowd and saw my very own Lois Lane bouncing on the balls of her feet. Beth saw me look at her, snatched a "Bee a Cool Poker Babe" sign, turned it over and scribbled something, flashing it at me. *Found Joe, phone, no Frank, bloody Lincoln,* I read before one of the security goons grabbed her by the arm and kicked her out of the ballroom. That was the last of her I'd see for a while. No one was allowed in after the round had started and everyone had to turn their cellphones in when they'd come through the doors.

Stan must have read the sign too, because he turned to me and spread his lips in an evil grin. "All alone, now, I see."

"With nothing to lose." I added under my breath. I forced myself to shut off the emotions that threatened to overwhelm my intellect.

"Except a game of cards and your life," Stan reminded me as the dealer dished out our new pockets. "In that order."

Twenty-Five

♦ ♣ ♥ ♠

Frank might have ditched the car (after all, we'd done that once before with good reason), but I knew he would never purposely leave his phone. That's when I knew where Conner was, hacking Frank into little pieces and throwing him in the dumpster behind the Mirage. Or maybe driving him out to the desert and leaving him for the vultures. Or maybe he'd already pushed him into one of the palm trees at the Mirage and he wouldn't be found for days. Ben had a worse fate before him.

When Stan had said that creepy thing about my brother being a good actor.

It all fell into place.

They were keeping Ben to act in one of the snuff films. That's how they were going to kill him. Opportunists that they were, they'd make money on him while disposing of him. How handy. I doubted they'd waste their time with Frank—he knew too much and every second he was alive was a second they put their operation in jeopardy. Ditto with me.

Except now, thanks to Beth, I knew more than Frank

did. And I was about to have the spotlight. If I could just get the cards and keep my cool long enough to talk Stan into going all in.

It took three more hands which depleted my chip store to a nerve wracking level. I had only enough chips to cover maybe four more hands worth of blinds. My fans were holding their signs more limply. The tournament president held his head in his hands. The Lanai PR flack had resorted to drinking tequila shots.

The back of my pocket cards mocked me. Stan sighed heavily and drummed his fingers on the table. The dealer shot me a sympathetic look that also meant hurry it up. The commentators were practicing their eulogy. I peeked at my cards.

Ten/heart, Queen/heart.

I calculated the odds of a flush, and a royal flush, in heads up play. I didn't really like any of them, but knew that I had to play this hand. I called the big blind. Stan raised fifty thousand. I called. He had something in his pocket for sure.

The Flop was a King/heart, eight/diamond, Jack/heart.

I could make it with a number of cards: a heart would give me a flush, the ace a royal flush, the nine a straight flush. Five different cards would give me a simple pair. Stan could have a flush working with ace high to beat me or three of a kind.

We both checked.

Fourth street was an ace/spade. I felt the energy zap through Stan even though he remained motionless. He had pocket aces. I was sunk unless I got exceptionally lucky. He went all in. My fans dropped their heads.

I could limp off or I could stay and fight.

"All in," I said clearly, pushing my chips forward on the table. My fans cheered.

"Decided to put everyone out of their misery a little quicker, huh?" Stan snorted.

The River was an ace/heart.

The roar from outside where the crowd watched the

game on TV monitors in a closed circuit telecast shook the ballroom wall. My fans inside were dead quiet. Stan's fans clapped. With his Bolles on me, Stan rose as he turned his cards over, ready to accept the congratulations from the crowd as he put his fist in the air for victory.

I waited a beat. Then quietly and slowly turned my pocket cards up. The roar from outside quieted like it had been turned off with a switch. All the fans, mine and his, inside the ballroom, blinked blankly, stunned.

"Royal flush wins!" The ESPN commentator declared belatedly, finally finding his voice. "Belinda 'Bee Cool' Cooley has done it. She's won the first annual Lanai Hold 'Em Pro-Am, beating the great Steely Stan!"

All at once, my fans started screeching and clapping and shouting, jumping up and down on top of each other. It was bedlam outside the boundary tape. A group of Stan's fans all wearing fake mustaches grabbed a "BEE COOL" sign from one of the Poker Babes and started dancing around with it.

"Guess I didn't lose everything, did I?" I asked Stan quietly.

He took a step toward me. "That's just a game. It's your life I'm interested in."

As I backed away from Stan, I felt a hand at the small of my back. Expecting the tournament president to be ready to guide me to the media, I gratefully let him push me away from Stan, who gave him a heavy look, through the boundary tape and the madding crowd. Ringo gave me a noogie as I passed. I tickled Junior's adorable belly and gave Amy a cheek for a kiss. Carey shook both my hands, with tears in her eyes.

Grateful as I was for all this support, all I could think of was Frank and Ben. I tried to push the sudden wave of sadness away. I blinked away a tear.

Carey stopped us. "Where are you taking Bee? We want to celebrate!"

Just then I smelled a waft of Iceberg Effusion.

"She has to get ready for her media interviews," a familiar voice said, confirming my worst fear.

I started to twist out of his grasp, but Conner was too quick. His hand held my arm in a vice grip.

"Hey, mister," Carey said, her brow furrowed in concern and confusion. "Did you know your head is bleeding?"

"It's a rough world out there, you he-she," he threw over his shoulder as he pushed me ahead.

"Carey, hel—" The click and cold metal pressing against the flesh under my jacket cut off my plea. Conner leaned down to whisper in my ear. "Keep walking and keep quiet or I will blow straight through your belly."

"Isn't slicing and dicing more your style?" I asked.

"Shut up," he hissed. "Nobody can tie me to that."

"Want to bet?"

Carey, who apparently hadn't bought Conner's insensitive blow off, began nudging her companions and gesturing toward us. I threw them a desperate look.

Looking back the way we'd come, I could see Stan sidling over to an exit door.

"Your partner gets a free ride out of here, huh?" I asked, deciding if anyone had any incentive to stop Stan it would be Conner.

Conner looked over his shoulder at Stan, paused and swore under his breath. Before he could decide whether to ditch me in favor of going after that partner, the doors Stan had been heading for flew open. Frank strode through with a phalanx of uniformed sheriff's deputies behind him.

"Conner!" I heard the tournament president call over the crowd. Conner paused as the president continued, "Where have you been?"

Frank, his T-shirt torn, jeans bloody and face swollen and battered, tried to locate us through the crowd. Conner pushed the gun deeper into my kidney. We were a step away from an exit when I heard Frank yell, "Let her go!"

"Go to hell," Conner shouted back, spinning around, dragging me in front of him, drawing the gun out from under my jacket and holding it to my temple. The fans, who'd gone into an uneasy, confused quiet, now screamed and scattered at the sight of the slick black semiautomatic. Stan was taking advantage of the chaos and inching his way to a different exit, trying to shake loose of one of his "Squeezes." The camera operators couldn't keep up with the action. I saw the red lights flashing on their cameras and figured we were still on live TV. Guess the folks who went to the bathroom when I folded that second to the last hand would be sorry.

"Daniel Conner, you are under arrest," a plainclothes policeman yelled. "Let your hostage go, drop your gun and put your hands in the air. We just want to talk to you about a few things. What might be no more than a misunderstanding is turning into a felony, Conner. Think about it."

Out of the corner of my eye I could see Carey and her castmates behind us. Instead of stampeding toward the nearest exit along with everyone else, they'd gathered in a huddle with their heads together, whispering. They looked like they were planning to march at the ticker tape parade.

"There goes your buddy," I told Conner. Stan was only about twenty feet from the door on the wall adjacent to us, having shoved his girlfriend into a table that collapsed under her. What a gallant fellow.

"You'd better stop right there, Stan my man," Conner called as Stan put his hand on the doorknob.

A man with his back to us stepped forward and blocked the exit. Stan paused, indecisive.

Frank took a step forward.

Conner tightened his arm across my throat in a wrestler grip. "I'll pull the trigger, if anyone comes any closer."

"What good will that do, Conner?" the cop asked. "We'll just smoke you anyway."

"I refuse to die alone."

Just then what felt like a ton of bricks hit us.

I hit the floor hard.

I heard a gunshot.

I braced for the blood to start flowing.

Twenty-Six

♦ ♣ ♥ ♠

I was in excruciating pain.

I pushed on the body above me. My left breast was pinned to the casino floor by a knobby male knee in pantyhose. The tangle of arms and legs on top of me wriggled and shifted. A hand reached into the fray and pulled me through the women's suits and briefcases and stodgy pumps. I was face to face with Carey.

"What happened?" I breathed.

"The Wall Street Women came to your rescue, girl!" She giggled.

"Thanks everybody. I can't believe you'd risk your lives for me." The group, half still in disarray on the floor, gave me waves and thumbs up as they high-fived each other.

"Don't worry about it," Carey said, waving off my gratitude. "That guy pissed me off."

"Where *is* Conner?" I asked, looking left and right and only seeing police uniforms.

Carey pointed. He was handcuffed face down on the floor.

"Where's Stan?"

Carey pointed. He was lying face down in a bloody pool on the floor.

"Your cozy pal shot him through the head. One bullet square in the middle of his forehead. I bet he's taken some target practice."

"I guess he has." I shook off the shiver that ran down my spine when I remembered the cold feel of the gun against my skin and the empty sound of his voice when he said he wanted to kill me. And he wouldn't have had to aim. "He's a cop."

"Huh, he won't get along so well in the pokey, then." Carey flashed a sadistic grin.

The media were descending, red lights blinking, microphones at the ready. The uniformed officers were trying to hold them back, but they couldn't stop the onslaught of questions.

"Does this have to do with your mammoth win over the King of Hold 'Em?"

"How do you feel about being held hostage at gunpoint just seconds after winning the biggest pot in poker history?"

Really! What had I won? Frank never told me what the total pot was. I was thinking I'd won a chance at Frank and Ben's freedom, but maybe I'd won an extra week or two on my rent as well.

"Does this have anything to do with the disappearance of your boyfriend and brother?" my broadcast buddy Josey asked.

"Your boyfriend?" A voice asked behind me. I turned around. "Do I know him?" Frank smiled and wrapped me in a hug.

I pulled back and looked at him, gingerly touching the bruises and abrasions on his forehead and jaw. His nose was twice its normal size and looked like it was broken. "It was a spur of the moment thing," I started to explain, my tongue tripping over the rush of words. "She had a microphone there and I only had time for a sentence or two. I couldn't exactly say my brother and a guy-I-met-in-the-bar-who's-put-his-life-on-hold-to-help-me-learn-how-

to-play-Hold-'Em-so-I-could-get-in-thick-with-the-bad-guys
-who-probably-took-my-brother-so-we-can-find-him have
disappeared."

"Don't forget I fed you too." Frank pointed out, then
leaned in and whispered in my ear, "And maybe kissed you
once or twice."

I felt a blush creeping up my neck at a most inappropri-
ate time, on live TV to boot. Thankfully, the plainclothes
cop who'd done the negotiating with Conner chose that
moment to interrupt, holding out his hand between us for
me to shake. "Miss Cooley? I'm chief of detectives Lou
Patterson. Are you okay?"

Frank cleared his throat and stepped back.

I didn't know if this was a good cop or a bad cop, but
since I wasn't dead and he might be the one to thank (besides the Wall Street Women of course), I was going to go
with good. "I'm fine."

"First I want to apologize that one of our men is respon-
sible for the trauma you've withstood over the last couple
of days. I wish you'd come to us right away, but I can understand why you didn't. Mr. Gilbert has had dealings with
us in the past and perhaps was justified in his portrayal of
the force. I just took over the department six months ago
and we are trying to clear out the bad element. It seems I
hadn't rooted out Conner yet." He clicked his tongue in
dismay, then looked at me again. "Now, we have a lot of
questions to ask, if you can follow us—"

"Forgive me, but can we do questions *after* we find my
brother?"

A uniformed officer tapped Patterson on the shoulder
and whispered in his ear. "We just got a tip on your brother.
A maid at the Galaxy called, she thinks he may be in a
room on the twelfth floor. She accidentally went in despite
the 'Do Not Disturb' sign yesterday. She thought the occu-
pant was just hungover, or maybe sick, but now that she's
seen you on TV news, she thinks that it's your brother, possibly drugged."

"Dead end. My brother and I don't look anything alike."

"Miz Cooley, you are probably right, most tips we get don't pan out. But the rare times they do makes this one worth checking out. Conner isn't talking, he's undoubtedly going to lawyer up. Stan is not an option, obviously. We want to find your brother before it's too late."

"He's right, Bee," Frank said, putting his hand on my shoulder.

Part of me was afraid of what I'd find. We'd put a lot of pressure on Stan and Conner in the last thirty-six hours. It doesn't take long to kill someone and stuff their body parts in a dumpster. Or hold a pillow on their face and walk away. Or worse . . .

"Are you okay?" Frank whispered.

I nodded and tried to smile. "I'm just trying not to get my hopes up."

Patterson, a trio of uniformed officers and two of his detectives accompanied us to the Galaxy. Frank and I rode in a squad car, Frank filling me in on what I missed while I was winning the tournament.

"Conner blocked the Lincoln in when he stopped, then got out, waving his Glock around, and trying to force me into his car. I got lucky, because another car drove past and Conner had to hide his gun. I took the opportunity to knock him to the ground. His gun went flying. I lost my phone somehow. We both got some good licks in."

"I think you got more than you gave," I teased, looking at his fat nose.

"Very funny. Anyhow I managed to knock him out. I should have tied him up too, apparently. It never occurred to me he was desperate enough to come after you here." Frank paused and looked out the window at The Strip, frowning. I knew he was seeing what could have happened if Conner had gotten me out of the ballroom. I had no doubt he planned to kill me. Apparently Frank didn't either.

I put my hand on his knee. Frank looked at me with eyes so dark they drew me in. Neither one of us spoke for a few seconds, but we were saying volumes. I guess he really cared.

"Look at it this way, Frank," I said, finally breaking the silence and trying to lighten the mood. "If you hadn't helped me, I might have been dead a long time ago."

"If you hadn't come to Vegas in the first place you wouldn't have been in danger." Frank added with some added dimension of anger I couldn't really figure.

"And if I had never been born, I couldn't die." I continued, trying to point out the futility of what-ifs.

Shaking his head, perhaps shaking off the thoughts that filled it, Frank continued with his story. "With Conner out of commission, I took his car. I wanted to search it, plus I wanted to find the Fresh Foods warehouse. I figured if anyone saw me, they'd recognize this as Conner's car."

"So you didn't worry about me at all," I teased.

"As a matter of fact, I drove first to the Lanai and made sure you got there. You were in the process of reraising that man next to you at the first table right out of the game. I can't believe you did that with an ace kicker."

I grinned. "You shouldn't have come looking for me. You should have been looking for Ben."

"But you just said . . ." Frank shook his head, bemused.

"Women." The officer put in.

"Speaking of women." Frank pulled his phone out of his pocket. "You *have* to call your mother."

"She can wait." I waved off the suggestion.

"No, she can't," Frank said. "She started calling me while I was breaking into the warehouse and has called a half dozen more times since. She saw you on ESPN. She's mad at you for not telling her about your 'secret' hobby and that you were going to be famous. She wanted to be here . . . there's more. I think you forgot to tell me you might be trying to get pregnant?"

"Huh?"

"Well, your mom asked if you were pregnant yet."

I groaned and held my head to stave off the mom headache. Frank looked amused. "The good news is I think she missed the end with all the shooting because she didn't sound frantic, just peeved."

I tried not to smile. "I *told* you not to give her your phone number."

"Women," the officer repeated.

Frank did deep breathing exercises while I talked quickly to Mom, leaving out the part about Ben being missing and me almost getting killed. I ignored the pregnancy question.

"Go on with your story," I urged as I handed him back his phone.

"In Conner's unmarked were a set of keys and a briefcase containing, among other things, a computer chip vacuum sealed in plastic, a logistic chart and a map showing those two rest stops. I turned them over to Patterson and the cop computer geek has already picked up the chip to ID, but the briefcase itself appears to be Stan's. Since Stan is dead, I guess it will be easy for Conner to plead ignorance as to what's inside."

"Conner tied himself to both Ben's kidnapping and Pete's murder when he had me by the throat," I said.

Frank shrugged. "Hearsay. We need hard evidence, Bee."

I hadn't told him about what Beth found out about Stan's missing women. He listened intently and I noticed the officer in the front seat did too. "I wonder where those girls are," Frank said quietly. "That's evidence. Especially if we find the paperwork."

"Or the bodies." The officer pointed out.

Frank nodded grimly. "Bee, we've opened up one ugly can of worms."

Twenty-Seven

♦ ♣ ♥ ♠

*F*rank was just beginning to describe what he'd found at the Fresh Foods warehouse when we pulled up in front of the Galaxy. After he'd determined Ben wasn't being held there, he'd opened box after box of produce until he finally found one that had the middles cut out of the apples as Rudy had described. Nothing was inside, but we'd already decided that the rest stops were where the actual items were placed inside or removed.

Patterson's detectives were in the process of securing a search warrant for the warehouse, hoping to get there before it was too late and that evidence was gone.

A sign outside the door welcomed members of the "Space: 2006" convention and dozens in "I Love Aliens /Welcome to Earth" T-shirts filled the lobby as we weaved our way through the simulated planets, space shuttles and aliens to get to the elevator. I jumped when my arm brushed a fake E.T. I was never going to feel the same way about wax figures again.

The hotel security officer joined us. There were three "Do Not Disturb" signs on doors on the twelfth floor. The maid had said she couldn't precisely remember which one contained the man in question so the cops had to knock on doors. The first couple were on their honeymoon. Still, on Patterson's orders, the uniforms searched the suite and returned a little red faced. The second door didn't answer the knock or the "Security, open up!" Patterson slid the master key in, made me and Frank step back against the hall wall, and he and the uniforms entered, with guns ready.

Nothing happened. Seconds ticked by. I didn't realize I was holding my breath until I started to feel lightheaded.

A grim looking Patterson peeked his head around the door frame and motioned us in. "Come tell me if this is your brother, Miss Cooley."

Uh-oh. I looked at Frank, wide-eyed. Frank was in cop mode, his face unreadable. He cocked his head at the open door and put his arm across my shoulders to lead me there.

The uniforms were standing in the doorway on the other side of the living area, staring in the bedroom. I couldn't see their faces.

What was I going to tell Mom?

I walked on legs I couldn't feel to the doorway. The uniforms parted and I looked at the bed. Ben lay there, fishbelly pale under a new beard, thinner than I'd ever seen him, eyes closed. Patterson was holding his wrist and looking at his watch, which I might have thought was a good sign, if I'd been thinking instead of feeling.

"Oh!" I clapped my hand over my mouth to keep from wailing.

Ben's eyes fluttered open, his pupils dilated. "Bee?"

I ran to the bed and pulled him upright. He was weak and, boy, did he smell. I coughed as I hugged him.

"Is that a new perfume, BeeBee?" he asked in a froggy voice. "It's nasty."

I pulled back to look at him. "You're the nasty one, stupid. I gather you haven't been showering, or," I paused to sniff, "using the facilities. And you've been drinking."

Ben's eyebrows came together. He squinted at the room. "Where the hell are we anyway? And who are these guys?"

I looked over my shoulder at the group. Patterson was on his radio calling in the crime scene techs. Frank was coming out of the bathroom with a prescription bottle half full of blue pills and an almost empty bottle of gin on a plastic tray. "Rohypnol. Roofies with a gin chaser. Bet he's been out of it since he got here. Conner was probably late to feed him his next dose."

"Frank, what are you doing here?" Ben demanded, his voice wavering but stronger. "Wherever *here* is."

I looked at Frank who looked at Ben. They held a silent conversation. Hmm.

"What's going on? How do you two know each other?" I demanded.

"Ooo, I feel faint." Ben flopped back of to his pillow, closing his eyes tight.

"Benjamin!" I warned. The wimp was ignoring me. Grr. I turned to Frank, who'd handed the tray to one of the uniforms. "Frank, you'd better start talking."

"It's complicated," Frank said.

"Uh-huh."

Patterson looked at Frank. "Go ahead and get this straightened out while I get my detectives dispatched and crime scene organized. We'll need to interview all of you. And paramedics need to check Ben out. They're on the way. You have until they get here."

Nodding, Frank sat down next to me on the bed. "A couple pharmaceutical companies have noticed some inexplicable decrease in their stocks of drugs. One of them is the maker of roofies, TruPharm."

"Ben's company."

"Ben was actually one of our suspects but, during our interview, he offered to help us get information about Stan. There were rumors of Stan smuggling something between here and Mexico but no one knew exactly what it was. Ben had heard on from an online chat that it might have to do with prescription drugs. We went with it because Ben was already registered for the tournament. We didn't think he'd try to act like James Bond, for God's sake."

"Hey," Ben said.

"Focus mode," I said.

"Anyway, the drug angle we had. The snuff films were a surprise. We now think that the operation is double sided. They smuggle out the snuff and smuggle in the prescription drugs.

"Why didn't you tell me you knew Ben?"

"It was stupid to bring you to Vegas," Frank said, glaring at Ben. "I couldn't figure out why he would have put you in danger. Your presence made it look like he might be in it with Stan and trying to throw us off the scent by offering to help."

"But why?"

"Well, you could pass for one of Stan's Squeezes."

"Yah, maybe twenty years ago."

"You could've fooled me, I told you that."

I tried not to blush. It would dilute my anger, and I wanted to stay mad. "So at the bar, you were trying to figure out if I was a bad guy or good guy?"

Frank nodded.

"When did you decide?"

"When you called me, I thought it might be a setup. But when I saw you, how sincerely upset you were, I knew it wasn't. Then I was worried because I knew that either Ben had gotten in over his head or he was in deep with the bad guys. Either way you were in danger. When you happened on Conner and Pete in the stairwell, it just made it worse."

"Why didn't you ever tell me?"

"I couldn't. Not only was the investigation classified, but the more you knew, the more danger you were in. And the more I got to know you, the more danger I was in, because I cared a little too much to work on this with the proper perspective."

There was no stopping the heat that slid up my neck, then other places down a little lower. Hmm. "You're just saying that."

Frank hitched that right eyebrow. "You think so?"

I was drawn into those deep dark eyes. Slowly I shook my head.

"Hey, you *cared* too much? What does that mean!" My wimp of a brother chimed in, suddenly feeling better. "What went on between you two, anyway? Did you take advantage of my sister, Frank? Am I going to have to clean your clock?"

Frank and I started laughing. It felt so good after the stress of the last few days that I almost couldn't stop. Behind us Ben had sat up in bed. "I wasn't kidding, you know. I can hurt you. My sister's already had her heart broken once this week."

I cocked my head at Ben. Not only did Frank outweigh Ben by fifty pounds right now, he also was ten times tougher. "Ah, Toby didn't really break my heart. Bruised it up a bit maybe. I don't think it would feel this good right now if it were broken."

Ben shook his head and flopped down in the bed. It was a bit too deep for the man who was the president of the Slam, Bam, Thank You, Ma'am Club.

"Why didn't they kill you, Ben?" Frank asked.

"Hell if I know," Ben croaked. "I followed Stan and heard him talking to this tall guy in a suit and short sweaty fatso about problems with 'the shipments' and a driver who got suspicious that they had to get rid of."

"Rudy," I breathed. Frank nodded.

"Then, I followed Stan back to the Hold 'Em tables, sat next to him and during our play, told him I worked for a drug company and wanted to find an outlet for some of the drugs I lifted. I gave him my room number."

Frank shook his head. "Smooth, Ben. Why didn't you just draw X's across your head and Bee's for them to use as target practice. Thank God she wasn't there when they came to get you, you fool."

Ben shrugged and looked ever so slightly sorry. "Hey I'm a sales guy, I was trying to sell him so I could turn him over to you. I didn't like being a suspect.

"Anyhow, the two dudes from earlier attacked me in the room, knocking me out. I remember coming to in another room and hearing Stan tell them that we had to find out how much I knew so they could figure out how much they would have to change before they offed me. I guess I didn't tell them enough when I was drugged. Or maybe they kept me drugged until they could question me."

"Stan told me they were going to make you a star," I said softly. "I think they'd planned to use you in one of the snuff films."

Ben paled even more. "You're kidding."

Frank shrugged. "Makes sense. They were the ultimate opportunists. That would kill two birds with one stone, so to speak."

Patterson walked in, sliding his cell phone back into a holder on his hip. "That was our computer geek. He says the computer chip you found in the briefcase had what appears to be an authentic snuff film. The girl is young, Mexican, possibly a sixteen-year-old who went missing from Nogales. The man is Caucasian. Unidentifiable. You never see his face. She is strangled to death."

Patterson paused and we all sat there in a brief silence, lost in our thoughts, mourning a girl we didn't know.

I suddenly remembered Rudy's sister and the threats against her. I told Patterson about them both. He spoke to one of the uniforms who left quickly.

"Patterson, you also need to get a hold of Deidre, to see if this is the film she saw, if not, there are others," Frank said, his face stony.

Patterson nodded. "The FBI and DEA are both on their way. This investigation is far from over. Suffice it to say that the three of you have uncovered a labyrinth of crime and I imagine we haven't even seen down most of its corridors."

Patterson's phone rang. "What?" he demanded of the caller so sharply, we all looked at him. He barked some orders into the phone and hung up saying "I'll be right back."

He looked at all of us. "Conner didn't shoot Stan. His

department issued bullet was found lodged in the wall behind Stan. Crime scene suspects from the blood splatter
that the bullet that killed Stan came from forty-five degrees
to the right of where Conner held you, Miss Cooley."

Twenty-Eight

♦ ♣ ♥ ♠

I didn't see Frank and Ben for another six hours. Investigators, federal and local, were interrogating Ben at the hospital while he was hooked up to an IV to treat his severe dehydration. Frank was locked in a room in the Cook County Sheriff's Department with the FBI and DEA. I wasn't even sure which agency was interviewing me, although I'd guess it was federal, since they seemed to have the upper hand. Patterson was cooperating, but clearly unhappily.

I hoped the law enforcement turf war didn't compromise the investigation. I knew there had to be others out there who knew enough about the operation to keep it going with a new smuggling venue. And, I had a sinking feeling that Stan was just a lackey himself. The real boss was still out there, somewhere. Maybe he was the one who'd pulled the trigger, killing the King of Hold 'Em.

"Feel free to wait for Frank, if you wish," Patterson told me, when I was finally released, dry mouthed from talking too long, thick headed from lack of sleep, yet jittery from too much coffee. "But they may keep him for the rest of the day."

Day? I looked out the tinted window in amazement. It had to be near noon already.

"If you decide to go back to your hotel, I will have an officer drive you and escort you through the media, which I'm sure is not only downstairs here but waiting for you at the Lanai. We'll slip you out and in the back ways."

"Thank you," I breathed. The thought of the media sticking microphones in my face was more than I could deal with right then. I was longing for a bed. "You'll let Frank know I'll be at the room?"

He nodded and motioned to a uniformed officer in the corner of the room. We went down the service elevator and to the basement where an unmarked police car was waiting for us. I nodded off before we were barely a block away. The cop had to shake me awake when we stopped in the basement of the Lanai. I felt like a zombie as we made it blessedly back to Frank's room without encountering anyone but a few guests who gave me curious looks. I must have looked like death warmed over. Talk about bags. I bet I could trip on them.

"You're famous, I guess, huh?" the officer asked.

"Why do you say that?"

"Those people looked like they wanted your autograph."

"I thought they looked like they wanted to give me a years supply of antiwrinkle cream."

The cop just shook his head and smiled. Sweet boy.

I thanked him and let myself into our room. I threw my purse down on the couch and walked straight to my bedroom.

"You've been quite busy, haven't you, Miss Cooley?"

I paused in the doorway and hoped I was hallucinating. That sure sounded like slick Cyrano or Ranocy or whatever his real name was. I looked over my shoulder. He was sitting in the chair with a gun pointed at my heart.

I survived Conner only to be killed by a porn freak. That pissed me off something fierce. "What do you want?"

"Ballsy aren't we." Cyrano smiled without any humor. I tried not to show the chill that slipped down my spine.

"Considering I could kill you by moving my finger a millimeter."

"I'm low on sleep, it makes me cranky."

"My employees cheating me makes me cranky," Cyrano snapped.

Since I had turned down the opportunity to work for him, I raised my eyebrows, crossed my arms over my chest and waited.

"Tell me what my boy Stan has done. The news is sadly misinformed. They are saying he got caught in a card scam, that Conner was in it with him. They're stupid. There's no card scam."

"Not that I know of anyway," I said.

"Then why have they arrested Conner? Why are they calling Stan a criminal mastermind? Gopher is more like it," he scoffed.

"He's dead, Cyrano," I said, watching him carefully, wondering how the news crews had left that part out.

"I know that, you stupid woman, I shot him."

Oh. Well, then.

"I want to know why they *were* after him."

"Lots of reasons," I began slowly, watching his finger as his hand began to tremble slightly from the effort of holding up the gun. "Do you want to rest your hand on your leg or something?"

He waved the gun at me. "Go on!"

"Stan was running a smuggling operation using Fresh Foods trucks—"

"I know that, he was running the operation for me. Porn videos on computer disks."

I recoiled. "You know about the snuff films?"

"No! No! No! He was the one all this time!" he shouted, his face red. He narrowed his eyes. "I knew Stan was double crossing me. Listen to me, he was nothing but a low level porn dealer when he worked at the Hold 'Em table at my casino. "Your casino?" I blurted.

The Galaxy is mine, he confirmed. A money maker mostly, but in this case, if provided me the perfect opportunity to obtain my heart's desire—an ambitious nobody to use. Stan had the buyers, I knew the suppliers down in Mexico. He used the trucks from Fresh Foods to bring in the videos and sell them. In return, I would sponsor him in his quest to be a Hold 'Em champion. I held up my end of the bargain, and he even sicced the cops on me when they came sniffing around about the snuff films. Cheating sicko murderer."

Cyrano had become so distracted by his fury at Stan that the gun had gone off center from me. I tried to distract him further. "Well, that's not all. They were also smuggling prescription drugs into Mexico—the same method, reversed."

His face went purple. "They were cheating me there too!"

Cyrano paused and narrowed his eyes. "Was Conner in on this?"

"Apparently so," I said, pleased to see the gun had drifted so far to the left I couldn't see down the barrel anymore. Whew.

"I'll kill him," Cyrano hissed. "He was paid to keep the force from sniffing around the sales. He was paid to protect the DVD shipments. And instead he was becoming his own entrepeneur."

Cyrano looked at me with a sudden shocking realization. "Is Conner talking to police?"

I shrugged. No way was I telling him Conner lawyered up. That would give Cyrano time to find someone behind bars to kill him, and the whole operation could go unpunished. "I don't know, Cyrano, Conner sure knows how to work the system. I guess he could pin it all on Stan, but I'm guessing if Conner goes down, everyone goes down with him. You will be the big boss, he was just taking orders from you and Stan. Conner just strikes me as that type. And you do have the history with the cops as being a porn dealer. You're the one who told me about that."

"I'm going to have to go to prison." Cyrano suddenly looked lost. "I can't go to prison!"

"Bee!" I heard Frank yell on the other side of the door.

It all happened at once—the gunshot, the glass shatter-ing, another gunshot, and two bodies hurling through the room, one out the window.

I don't think I moved. Except for my heart, which pounded a thousand beats in that one second.

Frank stood at the shattered window, looking down. Cyrano was gone. Spinning around and meeting my gaze, he rushed at me and gathered me in his arms, squeezing me so tightly I could barely breathe. We could heard sirens floating up the twenty five stories.

I heard Ben's voice, still gravelly, from the doorway. "Damn, did someone just jump out the freaking window?"

"Are you okay?" Frank demanded of me. He put his hand under my chin and tipped my face up, kissing the tip of my nose. "Did he hurt you?"

Ben wandered to the window and looked down. He made a face. "Ick. What a way to go."

"Why'd he do it, Bee?"

"He didn't want to go to jail." I recapped what Cyrano had told me.

Someone began to pound on the door. "Police, open up."

Ben opened the door for the cops, one of whom recog-nized us and called Patterson on his two way. Frank's phone started to ring. He looked at the caller ID and handed it to me. I looked at the readout and handed it to Ben.

"Hello?" Ben said curiously, then rolled his eyes at me. "Hi, Ma. Yeah, I'm fine."

Frank grabbed me in another hug and kissed the top of my head. As the cops began surveying the room for any ev-idence, Frank tipped my chin up again and kissed me on the lips. It was the best yet. The best ever. Better than the best. The whole room went away. I couldn't hear anything but our hearts beating. I couldn't feel anything but his lips on mine and my toes curling and my body temperature ris-ing and his fingers sending little shocks through to every erogenous zone and . . .

"Who was on TV, again?" Pause. "What do you mean Bee Bee *won*?" Ben shouted.

Frank and I reluctantly parted. The cops paused to stare at Ben.

Ben rolled his eyes and circled his finger in the air around his right ear like she'd gone bonkers. "I didn't hear you right, Ma. I thought you said BeeBee, your daughter Belinda Cooley, won the Lanai Pro-Am Hold 'Em tournament. That can't be, because she doesn't even know how to play poker. She wasn't even registered to play."

He held his hands in the air in question. Frank and I nodded. His mouth dropped open and he hung up on Mom.

"What do you mean? You stole my seat? You won the Big Kahuna?"

I shrugged. "I stole your seat. I won the Big Kahuna."

"But, how?"

"Let's just say she's a quick study." Frank put in, throwing me a proud grin. "And a bit lucky."

"Very lucky." I smiled back at him.

Ben shook his head in a combination of pride and disgust I'd seen many times before from a twin who was competitive but loyal. He liked to see his sister win, but not at something he should have.

"Wait 'til I beat the pants off you in the next tournament. You'll really be shaking your head," I threatened teasingly.

"Since you won the big money you can treat for the poker cruise I was eyeballing," Ben said. "Some big names are playing for big bucks."

"I'll fit right in then." I winked at Frank.

Ben snorted then turned to Frank. "How about you, Frank, I think she owes you something for teaching her to play Hold 'Em. What about cards on the high seas?"

"We can't assume Frank can get off work as you or I can. What is your work again, Frank?"

Frank opened his mouth.

"Besides security." I put in.

Frank shut his mouth.

I looked at Ben who just shrugged. The testosterone was banding together. Patterson walked in just then and said, "I swear I can't leave you people alone for five minutes. Haven't you had enough death and destruction for one day?"

"We've had enough for a lifetime," Frank said, turning to me and pulling me to him again. "Sign me up for the poker cruise. It's time for a real vacation."

Bee's Buzz

Texas Hold 'Em Tips
from the Recently Clueless

Listen, how many books out there brag about tips on Texas Hold 'Em from experts? You could get old and gray reading all the advice from the poker pros on the Net—only about ten percent of which makes any sense to someone who's never played poker before. Ask yourself, how many of these guys (and yes, most of them are guys) really remember when they didn't know the difference between a spade and a club?

See? That's where I come in. I remember being there. Let's face it, people, winning the pot in your neighbor's Friday night game is a long way from raking in millions at the World Series of Poker. A long, long way. And even though I DID manage to beat out the pros at my tournament, I'm far from expert. It's going to be a while before I play in the big time again, since I'll be honing my skills in between bouts of keeping my lousy brother out of trouble.

It wasn't so long ago—okay, really just days ago—that I was a total poker novice, barely learning to crawl. All the what-the-hell-does-that-mean's are painfully fresh in my

mind. So I'm going to cull from my recently mastered basics and my surprising inherent skills and let you all in on a
few poker secrets.

If you're as clueless as I recently was, consider these
tips from one of your own. If you already know your way
around the table, good for you. But I can guarantee there
are some points in my list that you won't see in any poker
tip site or read in any "Win at Hold 'Em" book out
there . . . Read and learn.

1. *Know the math, but master the psychology: Dress the part. Ladies,
   if you have good legs, wear short skirts; if you have breasts at all,
   wear a miracle bra and plunging neckline. (Caveat: If you are a
   man with breasts, don't follow this advice.)*

2. *Calm down, feminists. If you learn to play like a woman, you'll
   win more than most average men. Trust me on this one. It's the
   only way to play your way to the top. And I like it on top, don't
   you?*

3. *Men, that goes for you too: If you have broad shoulders, wear a
   nice blazer; if you have big biceps, bust out that muscle tee! But
   don't ever unbutton more than the top two buttons of your shirt, or
   you'll put yourself at an automatic disadvantage. Some people
   dislike the sight of a hairy chest so much, it'll be enough to motivate them to take uncharacteristic risks, act like a Maniac and
   bump you out of the game just to clear the aesthetics of the table.
   (See #7.)*

4. *Wear mirrored shades most of the time, but take them off or let
   players see around them at certain times—like after you just
   strategically folded. You want them to think they are getting some
   secret insight into your psyche, but what you'll really be doing is
   misleading them.*

5. *Focus only on the table. This is one of the major reasons why men
   are statistically more successful at poker than women. We are
   good at multitasking. Men are good at compartmentalizing. Girls,
   you need to ignore everything outside the table, and multitask*

within the compartment, (i.e. the table) to beat men at their game. If you have a reason to fold, use the time to study your opponents for "tells" instead of finding other ways to occupy your active mind, like trying to figure out if the woman at the next table is wearing Manolos or Jimmy Choos.

6. Play games at a full table as much as you can in the beginning. A full table will allow you more opportunities to read people, more chances for better cards, more time to place your bets and longer play outside the blinds. And, of course, better odds of finding a date. (But only after you've drained his pockets. You can afford to pay for dinner.)

7. Get caught bluffing a couple of times between winning hands—it will make your important bluff all the more effective. (And don't forget, it's impossible to bluff a "calling station," a player who calls all bets without thinking.)

8. Play based on your long term goals instead of hand by hand. Remember that guy you always wanted in high school? Be as methodical, patient and determined as you were then to get Mr. Perfect, now at the poker table! The rewards are worth it. And you'll hang onto the money longer than you hung on to that teenage studmuffin . . .

9. When a player bets on The River (the last community card), it means she—okay, possibly he—thinks she has the best hand. Be careful, she probably does!

10. Avoid calling raises too often on The Turn (the fourth community card) to protect yourself from overinvesting in the pot.

11. Don't be seduced by an ace in your pocket. George Strait says everybody needs an ace in the hole, but trust me, ace/7 is not a gift from the dealer. Resist your impulse to bet big early.

12. Last but not least, trust your intuition and be unpredictable. (See #7, again.)

See you next time.